## The Blonde Phantom

*in the same series*
Arsène Lupin vs. Sherlock Holmes: The Hollow Needle
(*adapted from Maurice Leblanc
by Jean-Marc & Randy Lofficier*)

*forthcoming*
Arsène Lupin vs. Sherlock Holmes: The Stage Play
(*adapted from Victor Darlay & Henry de Gorsse
by Frank J. Morlock*)

*also by Jean-Marc & Randy Lofficier*
Doc Ardan: City of Gold and Lepers
(*adapted from Guy d'Armen*)
Doctor Omega
(*adapted from Arnould Galopin*)
The Phantom of the Opera
(*adapted from Gaston Leroux*)
Robonocchio
Shadowmen: Heroes and Villains of French Pulp Fiction
*(non-fiction)*
Shadowmen 2: Heroes and Villains of French Comics
*(non-fiction)*

# Arsène Lupin vs. Sherlock Holmes
# The Blonde Phantom

by
Maurice Leblanc

adapted in English by
Jean-Marc & Randy Lofficier

A Black Coat Press Book

**Acknowledgements:** We are indebted to David McDonnell for proofreading the typescript.

Arsène Lupin created by Maurice Leblanc.
Sherlock Holmes created by Sir Arthur Conan Doyle.

Visit our website at www.blackcoatpress.com

# Table of Contents

# The Blonde Phantom

## *Ticket No. 514 -23*

On December 8, 1903, Monsieur Gerbois, Professor of Mathematics at the Lycée of Versailles, was rummaging through the pieces at an antique dealer's shop when he came across a small mahogany desk that took his fancy because of its many drawers.

"This is just what I need for Suzanne's birthday," he thought.

Professor Gerbois was always looking for ways to please his daughter, but his funds were limited, so he haggled over the price until finally agreeing to the sum of 65 francs.

As he was writing down his address so the desk could be delivered, a well-dressed young man, who had also been browsing around the store, caught sight of it

"How much for this?" he asked the owner.

"It's sold," replied the man.

"I see. To this gentleman?"

The Professor nodded, feeling surprisingly pleased that someone else also wanted the desk, thereby making his purchase more desirable. He saluted the young gentleman and left the store in a good mood.

He had not taken ten steps outside before the young man caught up with him.

"I beg your pardon, sir," he said, very politely, holding his hat in his hand. "Please excuse my indiscretion, but may I ask you if you went into that store looking specifically for that desk?"

"Well, since you ask, no. I was looking for an inexpensive set of scales for my experiments."

"Then, would I be correct in assuming that you're not particularly attached to it?"

Even though the stranger remained polite, the Professor, whose many years spent teaching unruly children had done nothing to soften his character, began to feel mildly irritated by his insistence.

"You would be wrong. I quite like it," he replied, gruffly.

"Because it's old?"

"Because it's convenient."

"In that case, perhaps you wouldn't mind trading it for another desk, just as convenient, but in better shape?"

"Yes I would. This one is in excellent shape. I see no reason to trade it."

"But..."

By this time, Professor Gerbois was extremely annoyed at the stranger's obstinacy.

"I won't discuss it further. I must ask you to drop the subject, sir."

But the young man stepped directly in front of him.

"If it's a question of price... I don't know how much you paid for it, but I'd be willing to offer you double."

"No, thank you."

"Three times."

"Enough!" exclaimed the Professor angrily. "That desk belongs to me and it's not for sale. Do you understand?"

The young gentleman stared at the Professor with a look that he never forgot, then turned on his heel and, without a word, walked away.

An hour later, the desk was delivered to the Professor's small house on the road to Viroflay. He called for his daughter.

"This is for you, Suzanne, that is, if you like it."

Suzanne was a young, beautiful girl, outgoing and easily pleased. She threw her arms around her father's neck and kissed him as enthusiastically as if he had just bought her jewels fit for a queen.

That evening, she and her maid, Hortense, carried the desk up to her room. She cleaned out the drawers and neatly stored in them all her papers, stationery, correspondence, collection of postcards and a few love letters from her distant cousin, Philippe.

The next day, Professor Gerbois left for the Lycée at 7:30 a.m. As she always did, Suzanne went to meet him at 11 a.m. It was a great pleasure to him to see her graceful, smiling figure waiting on the sidewalk opposite the school's entrance.

They walked home together.

"How do you like your new desk?" asked the Professor.

"It's lovely, Papa! Hortense and I have polished all its brass handles; they shine like gold now."

"So, you're happy with it?"

"Oh yes! I don't know how I've managed all this time without it."

They walked through their front garden and entered the house.

"I'd love to see what you've done with it. Then we can have lunch."

"Of course! You'll be so pleased."

She went up the stairs first, but when she arrived at the door of her room, she uttered a cry of dismay.

"What's the matter?" exclaimed Professor Gerbois, following his daughter into her room.

*The desk was gone.*

What later astonished the Investigating Magistrate who came to look at the crime scene, was the remarkable simplicity of the burglary. While Suzanne was out and Hortense at the market, a delivery man, wearing the same uniform as the man who had delivered the desk, had stopped at the house and, in plain sight of the neighbors, rung the bell twice. The neighbors, having seen the desk delivered the previous day and not knowing that the maid was out, naturally assumed that the Gerbois were sending it back when they saw the delivery man cart it out of the house undisturbed.

Another fact was recorded: nothing else had been stolen, not a cabinet had been broken into, not so much as a trinket had been displaced inside the house. Even Suzanne's purse, which she had carelessly left on top of the desk, was found on her nightstand, with not a single franc removed from it. The object of the burglary was, therefore, obvious. But that only made it harder to understand. Why would a burglar run so great a risk to steal so trivial a booty as a used mahogany desk?

The only clue that the Professor could supply was the incident at the antique dealer's.

"I had the definite impression from the start that that young man was very irritated by my refusal to part with the desk. Frankly, I even felt that the last look he directed towards me was almost a threat..."

The Police thought the whole thing rather vague. They questioned the antique store owner, but he knew nothing of either of the two gentlemen. As for the desk itself, he had purchased it at an estate auction for 40 francs and thought he had done rather well out of it. Further inquiries failed to turn up anything more substantial.

But the Professor remained utterly convinced that, somehow, he had just suffered a major loss. He had begun to firmly believe that a fortune must have been concealed in a secret drawer in the desk. That was why the mysterious young man, who obviously knew of its existence, had first tried to buy the desk back from him and, failing to do so, had stolen it.

"But, Papa, what would we have done with a fortune?" Suzanne kept repeating. "We have everything we need."

"It could have been your dowry," said her angry father. "You could have made a finer match!"

Suzanne, who loved only her cousin Philippe, who did not have a penny to his name, then became depressed as well. Thus, life in the little Gerbois house in Versailles continued less happily and good-naturedly than before, with both residents now living in the shadow of their regrets and disappointments.

Two months passed and the entire affair would have been forgotten had not a series of remarkable events, some good, others bad, combined to push it back into the limelight.

On February 1, at 5:30 p.m., Professor Gerbois, who had just gotten home with the evening paper, sat down, put on his spectacles and began to read. Since he was not interested in politics, he turned to page two, where an article immediately grabbed his attention:

### THIRD DRAWING OF THE NATIONAL LOTTERY!
*No. 514-23 Wins One Million Francs!*

The paper dropped from the Professor's hands. The walls swam in front of his eyes and his heart felt as if it had stopped beating. No. 514-23 was the number of the ticket he had bought, on the spur of the moment, to indulge one of his friends (for he didn't believe in luck himself)–and now it had won one million francs!

He quickly took out his notebook to check if his memory was correct–and it was. No. 514-23 was the number he had jotted down inside.

All he had to do was find the ticket.

He rushed to his study to get the stationery box in which he kept bills, checks, etc. and where he knew he had deposited the precious ticket. But as he stepped into the study, he stopped short and staggered back, his heart again missing a beat. The stationery box, which he kept on the mantelpiece, wasn't there. With a sinking feeling, he suddenly realized that, in fact, it hadn't been there for weeks. He used to distractedly look at it while correcting his students' papers

"Suzanne! Suzanne!" he shouted.

The young girl had just come in from the garden; hurriedly she ran up the stairs to her father.

"Suzanne... the box of stationery," the Professor stammered.

"Which one?"

"The one I bought at the Louvre... It used to be on the mantelpiece..."

"Don't you remember, Papa? We put it away together..."

"When?"

"That evening... You know, the day before..."

"Where? Please, don't tell me that it was... No, it's more than I could bear..."

"...Yes, it was in the desk..."

"The desk that was stolen?"

"Yes, Papa."

"In the desk that was stolen!"

He repeated the words in a low whisper, awestruck, almost terrified.

"It contained a million, Suzanne," he said, lower still, taking her hand, in his.

"Oh, Papa, why didn't you tell me?" she murmured innocently.

"A million," he repeated listlessly. "It was the winning ticket in the National Lottery."

The enormity of the disaster crushed them. For a long time, they remained silent, neither of them having the strength to speak.

"But, Papa, won't they pay the money anyway?" Suzanne finally asked.

"Why would they? With what evidence?"

"Do they need evidence?"

"Of course!"

"And you don't have any?"

"I would, but..."

"But?"

"It was in the stationery box."

"In the box that was in the desk that was stolen?"

"Yes. And now the other man, the thief, will get our money!"

"It can't be true, Papa! That's so unfair! Surely, you can ask them not to pay him?"

"I don't know, my darling, I just don't know... That man is very clever. He might find a way... He's so resourceful. Remember how he stole the desk in the first place..."

Suddenly, the Professor's energy returned. He sprang up and stamped his foot on the floor.

"That's it!" he exclaimed. "He won't get our money after all! How could he? Smart as he is, he can't do anything either. If he shows up to collect the winnings, they'll arrest him and lock him up! Ah ha! We'll see who gets the final word!"

"What are you planning to do, Papa?"

"I'm going to fight for our rights to the bitter end, my darling! And mark my words, we'll wind up winning! That million belongs to us by rights and we'll get it, come what may!"

A few minutes later, the Professor dispatched the following telegram to the Administrator of the National Lottery:

*AM LAWFUL OWNER WINNING TICKET NO. 514-23. WILL CONTEST BY ANY AVAILABLE LEGAL MEANS PAYMENT TO ANY OTHER PERSON. SIGNED: PROF. GERBOIS.*

At almost the same time, the Lottery received another telegram:

*AM HOLDER OF WINNING TICKET NO. 514-23. SIGNED: ARSÈNE LUPIN.*

Whenever I sit down to record one of the many adventures that comprise the extraordinary life of my friend Arsène Lupin, I feel a sense of embarrassment, because it always seems to me that even the smallest of his exploits are already familiar to my readers. In fact, there has hardly been any deed performed by our "national thief," as he is sometimes called, which has not been reported on at length in the newspapers, studied from every angle and talked about with an abundance of detail usually reserved for tales of far more heroic actions.

Is there, then, anyone who hasn't heard of the strange case of *The Blonde Phantom*, with its curious occurrences reported under mysterious-sounding headlines such as *No. 514-23 Is Missing, Bloody Murder At Avenue Henri-Martin* and *The Mystery Of The Blue Diamond*? Has anyone forgotten the remarkable intervention of Sherlock Holmes, the prodigious English detective? What passions the quasi-public struggle between those two great men aroused! And finally, what pandemonium reigned along the boulevards of Paris on the day the newsboys were able to shout: *Arsène Lupin Arrested At Last*!

My only excuse for writing this account is that I can offer something new, something that the public doesn't already know. I can provide the key to the mystery!

There is always a certain amount of mystery that remains after each of Lupin's adventures. I am able to dispel that. I may occasionally reprint previously published articles that have been read many times before, I may reproduce excerpts of old interviews, but I organize and rearrange them. I check their accuracy and I do my own research. Most importantly of all, I put my reconstructed version of the facts to the ultimate test of truth: that of Arsène Lupin himself! For my collaborator in this vast enterprise is none other than Lupin, whose kindness to me has been ample and inexhaustible. On this occasion, I am also much obliged to the generosity of the ineffable Doctor John H. Watson, Sherlock Holmes' trusted friend and confidant.

I am sure that my readers remember the tremendous mirth that greeted the publication in the press of those two telegrams. The name of Arsène Lupin alone was a guarantee of originality, a promise of much amusement for the peanut gallery which, in this case, was nearly the whole of Europe.

The National Lottery launched an immediate inquiry, which revealed that Ticket No. 514-23 had been sold by the Versailles branch to a Captain Bressy, an Artillery Officer. But, Bressy had died suddenly after a fall from his horse. According to his fellow officers, he had sold the ticket to a friend shortly before his untimely demise.

"I am that friend," declared Professor Gerbois.

"Prove it," the National Lottery told him.

"That should be easy. At least 20 people will tell you that I was good friends with Captain Bressy. We used to meet for drinks at the café on the Place d'Armes every week. One day, he was feeling financially pinched, so he offered to sell me his ticket. To help him out, I bought it for 20 francs."

"Do you have any witnesses to the transaction?"

"Well, no, but..."

"Do you have any other way of verifying your claim?"

"Yes! He wrote me a letter thanking me for the purchase."

"That would do. Where's that letter?"

"With the ticket! In the desk that was stolen!"

"..."

The letter did exist. In fact, to add insult to injury, a copy of it was sent to the newspapers by Arsène Lupin who claimed that it had been addressed to him! A brief article in *L'Echo de France*–a paper which often acts as if it was Lupin's unofficial press organ and in which some say he owns a majority stake–further stated that the original was being deposited with Maître Detinan (esquire), whom Lupin had retained to be his counsel in this matter.

Much hilarity ensued: Arsène Lupin was now being represented by counsel! Arsène Lupin had hired a respectable member of the Paris Bar to represent him in a common civil case!

The reporters rushed to interview Maître Detinan. The attorney was an influential deputy of the radical left, a man known for his integrity and keen mind. He was the type of man who could be quite pragmatic one moment, yet ready to engage in complicated legal games in the next.

Maître Detinan told the press that he was exceedingly sorry, but so far, he had not had the pleasure of meeting his famous client. Lupin had communicated with him only in writing. He had been greatly flattered at having been selected and was determined to defend his client's rights to the best of his abilities. He opened his brief and, without hesitation, showed the Captain's letter to the reporters. It did establish the sale of the ticket, but only mentioned its buyer's name in the preamble, which was simply addressed to "*My dear friend*."

" '*My dear friend*' is me," stated Lupin in his instructions. "The best proof is that I have the letter."

The journalists went to call on Professor Gerbois to hear his side of things. The hapless Professor had nothing to add.

" '*My dear friend*' is *me*," he complained. "Lupin stole the letter with the ticket."

"Let him prove it," replied Lupin.

"How can I? He stole the desk!" exclaimed Gerbois.

"Let him prove it," retorted Lupin once again.

Such delightful entertainment to the public was, therefore, provided by this bizarre battle of *communiqués* between the two self-proclaimed owners of Ticket No. 514-23. The press's constant back and forth only served to highlight the contrast between the cool irony of Arsène Lupin and the frenzied desperation of Professor Gerbois.

The papers reveled in the misery of his lamentations. He told the full extent of his misfortune in a moving and candid way.

"I'm not doing this for myself, gentlemen of the press," he said. "It's for my daughter, Suzanne. It's her dowry that this rascal has stolen. A million francs! Ten times a hundred thousand francs! Taken from a child! I always knew that that desk contained a treasure!"

He was told, quite sensibly, that his adversary, when he (allegedly) stole the desk, knew nothing of the existence of the lottery ticket inside, and even if he had, how could he have foreseen that that same ticket would win the grand prize weeks later? But the Professor remained unconvinced.

"Of course, he knew!" he moaned. "If he didn't, why would he have gone to so much trouble to steal that wretched desk?"

"We don't know that yet, but it can't have been to get hold of a scrap of paper which, at that time, was only worth 20 francs."

"We're talking about Lupin! He knew! He knows everything! One million francs! Wait until he steals that much from you, then come and tell me he didn't know!"

This conversation could have continued for some time, to the relish of its readers. But 12 days later, Professor Gerbois received a letter from Arsène Lupin, marked *"Private and Personal."*

He read it with considerable concern.

*Monsieur le Professeur:*
*The public is now laughing at our expense. Don't you think that the time has come to behave more reasonably? I, for one, wish to resolve this matter speedily and to our mutual satisfaction.*

*The facts are simple: I hold a ticket which I cannot cash; you, on the other hand, wish to cash a ticket which you do not hold. Therefore, neither of us can do anything without the other.*

*You, of course, are not willing to surrender your rights to the ticket, and neither am I.*

*So what are we to do?*

*I see only one way out of our quandary: let us divide the proceeds of the ticket equally. 500,000 francs for you, 500,000 francs for me. Is that not fair? Would this judgment of Solomon not satisfy the sense of fair play which moves us both?*

*I offer this as an equitable solution, but in exchange I want an immediate answer. This is a non-negotiable offer. You have three days in which to decide. On Friday morning, if you agree, please place a classified ad in L'Echo de France, addressed to Mister A.L. stating your unreserved acceptance of my offer in whatever discreet terms you choose. In that event, you will at once recover possession of the ticket, on the under-*

*standing that, after you have cashed it, you will hand me
500,000 francs in a way which I will specify later.*

*Should you refuse, I have taken steps to ensure the same
result, except that, in that case, you will suffer some not incon-
siderable consequences. And I will be forced to withhold an
additional 25,000 francs to cover my additional expenses.*

*I remain, Monsieur le Professeur, most respectfully
yours,*

*Arsène Lupin*

Professor Gerbois, exasperated by the whole business,
was then guilty of a most colossal blunder: he showed others
this letter and allowed it to be copied. His indignation also
drove him to behave in an extremely foolish manner.

"Nothing! He'll get nothing!" he shouted at the assembled reporters. "Why should I share what already belongs to
me? Never! He can tear the ticket up, as far as I'm concerned!"

"Still, 500,000 francs is better than nothing."

"That's not the point! It's a question of establishing my
rights in the Courts."

"You want to sue Arsène Lupin? That would be a joke."

"Not him, the National Lottery! It's up to them to give
me my million francs."

"Yes. Once you hand in the ticket, or at least the proof
that you bought it."

"The proof exists, since Arsène Lupin admits that he
stole my desk."

"Do you think that Arsène Lupin's word will be enough
to convince the Court?"

"It doesn't matter. I'm doing it."

The crowd cheered. Bets started flying back and forth:
some that Arsène Lupin would bring Professor Gerbois to his
knees, others that he would do no more than threaten. But everyone felt concerned, knowing that the two adversaries were
unevenly matched. One was a fierce predator, the other his
terrified prey.

That Friday's issue of *L'Echo de France* was snatched up and the Classifieds on page 5 were eagerly scrutinized. Not a single line was addressed to *Mister A.L.* Professor Gerbois had responded to Arsène Lupin's threats with silence. It was a declaration of war.

That evening, the papers reported that Mademoiselle Gerbois had been kidnapped.

One of the most amusing things in that which we could call the "Arsène Lupin Show" is the totally ridiculous role always played by the Police. This time too, they were in totally above their heads. He spoke, wrote, warned, ordered, threatened, carried out his plans as if the Head of the Sûreté, its detectives, the Police Commissioners, no law enforcement officers of any kind, existed in his world. They did not seem to impede him in the least.

And yet, they tried! As soon as there was any indication that Arsène Lupin was involved, from the highest echelons to the lowest ranks, everyone caught fire, boiled, steamed with rage. He was *the* enemy, and the enemy gets to you, provokes you, despises you–or worse, ignores you. What could they do against such an enemy?

At 10:50 a.m., Suzanne had left the Gerbois house. At 11:05 a.m., when her father had come out of the Lycée, he had not seen her waiting for him on the sidewalk at her usual place. Thus, the kidnapping had taken place during the 20-minute walk that took Suzanne from her home to the Lycée, or at least near it.

Two neighbors confirmed that they passed her about 300 feet from the house. A woman saw a young girl who fit Suzanne's description walking along the boulevard. And after that? After that, no one knew.

The Police searched everywhere, questioned all the employees at the railway stations and the harbors. No one had noticed anything that day that could have been in any way connected to the kidnapping of a young woman. However, at Ville-d'Avray, a grocer said that he had sold some gas to a motorcar that had come from Paris. A driver sat in the front and a blonde woman was inside–a very pretty blonde, the witness added. An hour later, the car had returned from Versailles. Several other vehicles had forced it to slow down, which had allowed the grocer to notice that, sitting next to the blonde woman whom he had previously seen, was a second woman, who was completely covered up in shawls and veils. There could not be any doubt that it had been Suzanne Gerbois.

That meant that the kidnapping had to have taken place in the middle of the day, on a busy road, right in the center of town!

How? And where? Not a single cry had been heard, not a suspicious thing had been seen.

The grocer gave the description of the car as being a dark-blue, 24 horse-power Peugeot limousine. Just in case, the notorious Madame Walthour, manager of the *Grand-Garage*, who was known to rent cars to facilitate elopements, was questioned. She stated that, on the previous Friday morning, she had rented a blue Peugeot limousine to a blonde woman for the day. She had not seen her since.

"What about the driver?"

"He was a fellow named Ernest, hired the night before on the basis of excellent recommendations."

"Is he here?"

"No. He returned the car and hasn't been back."

"Can we track him down?"

"Certainly, through the people who recommended him. Here are their names."

The references were contacted. None of them knew this Ernest.

So, every trail that seemed to lead the investigators out of the shadows, instead only ended in further mystery.

Professor Gerbois did not have the strength to carry on a fight which, for him, had turned into a disaster. Inconsolable after his daughter's disappearance, struck by remorse, he gave up.

A Classified, noted and commented on by everyone who was following the matter, appeared in *L'Echo de France*, confirming his total and abject surrender, with no further conditions.

It was a total victory for Arsène Lupin. The war was over and it had lasted only four days.

Two days later, Professor Gerbois crossed the courtyard of the National Lottery. After he had been introduced to the Director, he handed him Ticket No. 514-23. The Director bolted up.

"Ah-ha! You have it? So *he* gave it back?"

"It was lost. Now, it isn't," answered the Professor sharply.

"But you said that... There were questions of..."

"Nothing more than lies and gossip."

"Still, we'll need some kind of documentation to support..."

"Would a letter from the Captain who sold me the ticket suffice?"

"Of course!"

"Then, here it is."

"It seems all right... Would you mind leaving these with me? We'll need two weeks for verification. I'll let you know when you can come and collect your winnings. Until then, Professor, I think it's in your best interest to say nothing to the Press so that this entire business can be concluded with absolute discretion."

"That's precisely my intention."

Neither Professor Gerbois nor the Director said a word of their meeting to anyone, but sometimes, even with the best of intentions, secrets do leak out. Thus, the public learned that Arsène Lupin had boldly returned Ticket No. 514-23 to Professor Gerbois. The news was greeted with stupefied admiration. Certainly, a man who played a card as valuable as the precious ticket on the table was a master of the game. Of course, he had played it knowing full well that he still held another, equally valuable, card–Suzanne Gerbois. But what if the young girl escaped? Or if someone managed to free her?

The Police knew that this was their enemy's weak point and redoubled their efforts. Arsène Lupin, disarmed, neutralized by his own actions, trapped in the web of his own schemes, would not touch a franc of the coveted million... And then, as far the public was concerned, the joke would be on him!

But first, they had to find Suzanne–and, so far, no one knew where she was, nor had she managed to escape on her own!

So, when points were handed out by the score-keepers in the Press, it was decided that Arsène Lupin had won the first round. But the toughest part was yet to come. Mademoiselle Gerbois was in his hands and he had no intention of releasing her until he had his 500,000 francs. How and where would the exchange take place? For it to take place, there had to be a rendezvous. What would prevent Professor Gerbois from notifying the Police and, with their assistance, recovering his daughter while holding on to all the money?

The Professor was cornered and interviewed again. Beaten, wanting only to be left alone, he was uncooperative.

"I've got nothing to say," he said. "I'm waiting."

"What about Mademoiselle Gerbois?"

"The search for her continues."

"Has Arsène Lupin contacted you?"

"No."

"Do you swear?"

"No."

"Then, he has! What were his instructions?"

"I've got nothing to say."

They plagued Maître Detinan next. He was just as dismissive.

"Monsieur Lupin is my client," he responded with the utmost gravity. "Certainly, you understand that I am bound to keep everything he tells me in absolute confidence."

All of these mysteries irritated the Press. It was clear that some kind of shadowy plan was being organized. Arsène Lupin was tightening his net. Meanwhile, the Police had arranged to place Professor Gerbois under night and day surveillance. It was clear there were only three possible outcomes: Lupin's arrest, Lupin's triumph or a pitiful, ridiculous, last minute surrender by all the parties concerned.

Yet, public curiosity could only be partially satisfied at the time as many details of what took place remained hidden. It is here, in these pages, that, for the first time, the whole truth shall be revealed.

On Tuesday, March 12, Professor Gerbois received a notice from the National Lottery in a plain, brown envelope.

On Thursday, at 1 p.m., he took the train from Versailles to Paris. At 2 p.m. exactly, a thousand 1,000-francs notes were handed over to him at the headquarters of the National Lottery.

As he ruffled them with trembling hands–wasn't this money Suzanne's ransom, after all?–two men sat in a stopped automobile not far from the entrance. One of them had greying hair and an energetic demeanor that oddly contrasted with the slightly rumpled everyday clothes that he wore. He was Chief Inspector Ganimard, Lupin's old, implacable enemy. Ganimard spoke to the dark-haired, burly man sitting next to him, who was Sergeant Folenfant.

"It won't take long now," said the Chief Inspector. "I'd bet that we'll see our man in less than five minutes. Is everything ready?"

"Absolutely, Chief."

"How many men do we have?"

"Eight. Plus two on bicycles."

"And I count as three! That's enough, but not too many. Gerbois can't be allowed out of our sight, or it's all over. He'll meet up with Lupin at the rendezvous they've obviously arranged, he'll exchange the half-million for his daughter and the game is lost."

"Why didn't he trust us? It would've been so simple. That way, he'd have gotten to keep the whole million."

"Maybe so, but he's afraid. He thinks that if he tries to double-cross *that one*, he'll lose his daughter."

"*That one*?"

"*Him*."

Ganimard said the word in a somber, almost fearful, tone, as if he was speaking of some supernatural being whose grip he already felt.

"It's still pretty odd," remarked Folenfant shrewdly, "that we're forced to protect that fellow from himself."

"With *him*, the whole world is always topsy-turvy," sighed Ganimard.

A minute passed.

"Chief! Look!" the Sergeant said.

Professor Gerbois was coming out of the building. At the end of the Rue des Capucines, he turned left onto the Boulevard. He walked slowly past the shops, looking distractedly at their displays.

"Our customer's too calm," said Ganimard. "A man walking around with a million francs in his pocket shouldn't be that calm."

"What can he do?"

"Oh, nothing, obviously... I'm just suspicious. Lupin is always Lupin."

Just then, the Professor walked over to a newsstand, picked out several newspapers, got some change, opened one of the papers and holding it out in front of him, began walking while reading. Suddenly, he leapt into a car that was parked next to the sidewalk. The engine was already running. It took off quickly, going around the Place de la Madeleine and disappearing.

"Blast it!" shouted Ganimard. "Another of *his* tricks!"

He took off at a run, as did all his other men stationed around the Church of the Madeleine.

Then, he broke into laughter. Just at the entrance of the Boulevard Malesherbes, the car had stopped because of an engine breakdown and the Professor was stepping out of it.

"Hurry up, Folenfant! Question the driver! Maybe it's Ernest."

Folenfant took care of the driver. But his name was Gaston and he was only an employee of the car-rental company which owned the vehicle. Ten minutes earlier, a gentleman had hired him and told him to wait near the newsstand, with the motor running, until the other, older gentleman arrived.

"The older gentleman, what address did he give you?" asked Folenfant.

"No address. Just Boulevard Malesherbes, Avenue de Messine. Double tip. That was it."

Meanwhile, without wasting a minute, Professor Gerbois had jumped into the first taxi that had come by.

"Driver, to the Metro! The Concorde station!"

The Professor left the Metro at Palais-Royal, ran towards another car and, this time, was driven to the Place de la Bourse. This was followed by another trip in the Metro and then, at the Avenue de Villiers, yet another taxi ride.

"Driver! No. 25, Rue Clapeyron," said the Professor.

No. 25, Rue Clapeyron, is separated from the Boulevard des Batignolles by a house on the corner. Professor Gerbois went inside, walked up to the first floor and rang the bell. A gentleman opened the door.

"Is this the home of Maître Detinan?"

"At your service. You must be Professor Gerbois."

"I am."

"I was waiting for you, Professor. Please come in."

When Professor Gerbois walked into the lawyer's office, the clock was striking three.

"This is the time he gave me," he said. "Isn't *he* here?"

"Not yet."

The Professor sat, wiped his forehead, looked at his watch as if he wasn't sure of the time. "Is he coming?" he anxiously asked.

"You're asking me a question, Monsieur, on the one subject for which I, myself, am most eager to have an answer," the lawyer replied. "I've never felt this anxious in my life. At any rate, if *he* does come, *he*'ll be taking a grave risk. This building has been under Police surveillance for two weeks. They don't trust me."

"Nor me. At least, I'm certain that I was able to lose the men who were following me."

"Well, then…"

"It won't be my fault," shouted the Professor. "And no one can blame me. What did I promise? To obey *his* orders. Well, I've blindly obeyed *his* orders. I got the money at the hour specified by *him*, and I've come to your office the way *he* told me. I was responsible for the misfortune that befell my daughter and I kept my word faithfully. Now it's up to *him* to keep his."

Then, he added in the same, anxious voice, "He'll bring my daughter back, won't he?"

"I hope so."

"Have you seen her?"

"Me? Absolutely not! He simply sent me a letter asking me to receive the two of you, to send my servants away for three hours and not to allow anyone else into my apartment between your arrival and his departure. If I didn't agree with his request, I was to let him know with two lines printed in *L'Echo de France*. But I was delighted to be of service to Arsène Lupin and I agreed to all of his conditions."

"Alas, how will this all end?" sighed the Professor.

He pulled the banknotes from his pocket and laid them on the table, making two piles of equal size. Then, he said nothing else. From time to time, he listened carefully… Had someone knocked?

As the minutes passed, his anxiety grew. Even Maître Detinan felt an almost painful concern. At one point, the lawyer lost his *sang-froid*. He stood up suddenly.

"He's not going to show up," he said. "And why should he? It would be insanity! Of course, he trusts us; we're honest men who wouldn't betray him. But the danger doesn't lie just here..."

"Please let him come, my God, please! I'd give all of this just to have my Suzanne back," whimpered the Professor, feeling devastated, his two hands grasping the bank notes.

"Half of it will do just fine, Professor Gerbois."

A young, elegantly dressed man stood in the doorway. Professor Gerbois immediately recognized him as the person who had accosted him outside the antiques shop in Versailles. He ran towards him.

"Suzanne! Where is my daughter?"

Arsène Lupin carefully closed the door.

"My dear Maître," he said to the lawyer, while carefully removing his gloves, "I don't know how to thank you for the kindness you've shown in agreeing to defend my rights. I'll never forget it."

"You didn't ring the bell and I didn't hear the door..." Maître Detinan murmured.

"Bells and doors are things that should work without being noticed, wouldn't you agree? But now I'm here, and that's the only important thing."

"My daughter! Suzanne! What have you done with her?" repeated the Professor.

"My dear Professor," said Lupin, "you're so impatient! Control yourself for just a little longer and your lovely daughter will soon be in your arms again."

He walked around the room.

"Professor Gerbois, I congratulate you on the cleverness you showed this afternoon," he said in a rather patronizing tone. "If the first car had not had that ridiculous breakdown, we would have simply met at the Place de l'Etoile and spared

27

Maître Detinan the inconvenience of this visit... Well, what's done is done."

He then looked at the two piles of bank notes. "Ah! Perfect!" he exclaimed. "The million is there. Let's not waste any time. With your permission?"

"But," objected the lawyer, going to stand in front of the table, "Mademoiselle Gerbois isn't here yet."

"So?"

"So, isn't her presence indispensable?"

"I see! Arsène Lupin doesn't inspire all that much trust after all, does he? He'll take his share of the loot and not return the hostage, eh? Ah, my dear Maître, I am so misunderstood! Just because destiny has led me to perform a few actions that were a little, shall we say, unconventional, my good faith becomes immediately suspect, doesn't it? But I am a man of scruples and refinement! Besides, my dear Maître, if you feel so concerned about my morality, open the window and yell. There are at least a dozen policemen in the street."

"You think so?"

Arsène Lupin lifted the curtain.

"I believe that, despite his best efforts, Professor Gerbois was unable to lose Ganimard... What did I say? There he is, our brave Chief Inspector!"

"Is that true?" cried the Professor. "But I swear that..."

"...That you didn't betray me? I don't doubt you, but those boys from the Sûreté are cunning. Look, there's Folenfant! And Gréaume! And Dieuzy! All my old pals are here!"

Maître Detinan looked at him with surprise. He was so calm! He laughed joyfully, as if he was amused by some child's game and not in actual danger.

More than the presence of the Police, this lack of concern reassured the lawyer. He moved away from the table where the banknotes were laid out.

Arsène Lupin picked up each of the piles of notes in turn and carefully took 25 notes from each and handed those 50 notes to Maître Detinan.

"Your fee, Maître, from Professor Gerbois and from Arsène Lupin. We owe you that, at least."

"You don't owe me a thing," answered the lawyer.

"What? With all the trouble that we caused you?"

"What about all the pleasure I've taken in giving myself this trouble?"

"So, my dear Maître, you're saying that you don't want to accept anything from Arsène Lupin?" he sighed. "That's what it means to have a bad reputation."

He held the 50,000 francs out to the Professor.

"Professor Gerbois, in honor of our pleasant reunion, please allow me to give this to you. It will be my wedding gift to Mademoiselle Gerbois."

The Professor readily took the notes.

"But my daughter isn't getting married," he protested.

"She won't if you refuse to give your consent. But she's eager to get married."

"What do you know about it?"

"I know that pretty young ladies often have dreams of romance without their fathers' knowledge or permission. Luckily, there are good fairies named Arsène Lupin who discover the secrets of these charming young things in the bottom drawers of their desks."

"Did you discover anything else?" asked Maître Detinan. "I must admit that I'm quite curious to learn why this piece of furniture was the object of so much attention."

"Historical curiosity, my dear Maître. Even though, contrary to what the Professor might think, there was no other treasure inside that desk, except for his lottery ticket. And I didn't know about that at the time. I had been looking for that desk for a long time. I knew it was made of yew and mahogany and was decorated with leaves of acanthus. It had been found in a small, discreet house in Boulogne where Marie Walewska lived. [1] On one of the drawers is the inscription:

---

[1] One of the great loves of Napoléon's life, Marie Walewska (1789-1817) was a beautiful Polish countess who met the Em-

'*Dédié à Napoléon 1er, Empereur des Français, par son très fidèle serviteur, Mancion.*' [2] Below that, carved with the point of a knife, it says : '*A toi, Marie.*' [3]

"Later, Napoléon had it copied for Empress Josephine. The desk that is so often admired at Malmaison [4] is, in fact, nothing but an imperfect copy of the one which is now part of my personal collection."

"Alas! If I'd known that at the shop, I would have quickly agreed to your demand," the Professor sighed.

"And you would have had the advantage of keeping lottery Ticket No. 514-23 all to yourself!" Arsène Lupin laughed.

"And you wouldn't have been driven to kidnap my daughter, who must be in terrible shock from it all."

"All?"

"The kidnapping…"

"But, my dear Professor, you've made a mistake. Mademoiselle Gerbois wasn't kidnapped."

---

peror when he occupied Warsaw in 1807. Together, they had a child, Alexandre, in 1810. Of all of Napoléon's female companions, she was the only one to visit him during his exile on Elba.

[2] *Dedicated to Napoleon 1ˢᵗ, Emperor of France, by his most loyal servant, Mancion.*

[3] *For you, Marie.*

[4] Nowadays, it is actually kept in storage. *(Note from the Author).* The Château of Malmaison was bought by Josephine de Beauharnais in 1799 and while Napoléon lived and campaigned elsewhere, it was her favored home. After they married, it became his home and the seat of French government. When Josephine was divorced from the Emperor in 1809, Napoléon moved out. The former Empress then spent the years until her death in 1814 improving the Château, including the creation of a famous rose garden. Today, Malmaison is still a museum with fine examples of Napoleonic art, personal items of Bonaparte and Josephine, as well as historical furniture and items of clothing.

"My daughter wasn't kidnapped?"

"Absolutely not! Kidnapping implies violence. No, it was of her own free will that she served as a hostage."

"Of her own free will?" repeated the Professor, sounding confused.

"And almost at her own request. How could an intelligent young woman like Mademoiselle Gerbois, harboring a secret passion deep within her soul, refuse the opportunity to acquire a dowry! I assure you, it was easy to convince her that it was the only way to overcome your objections."

Maître Detinan was enormously amused.

"I would imagine the most difficult part was to get her to listen to you," he remarked. "I don't see how Mademoiselle Gerbois could have allowed you near her."

"Oh, but she didn't! I never even had the honor of meeting her. It was a lady of my acquaintance who agreed to undertake the negotiations."

"The blonde woman in the motorcar, I imagine," interrupted the lawyer.

"Exactly. Everything was agreed to at their first meeting near the Lycée. Since then, Mademoiselle Gerbois and her new friend have visited Belgium and Holland in a manner most enjoyable and instructive for a young woman. She'll explain the rest to you herself..."

Someone rang at the vestibule door: three short rings followed by two, single, longer rings.

"That's her," said Lupin. "My dear Maître, if you would be so kind..."

The lawyer hurried to comply.

Two young women entered. One of them threw herself into Professor Gerbois' arms. The other went to stand near Lupin. She was tall and shapely with a pale complexion; her hair was a glistening blonde worn in two loosely wrapped loops on either side of her face. Dressed in black, with no adornment other than a necklace of jade beads, she made an impression of perfect, refined elegance.

31

Arsène Lupin said a few words to her, then turned to Mademoiselle Gerbois.

"I ask your pardon, Mademoiselle, for all these tribulations, but hope that you haven't been too unhappy..."

"Unhappy? I would have been extremely happy if it hadn't been for my poor father."

"Then, everything turned out all right. Hug him again and take advantage of the occasion–for it's perfect–to talk about your cousin."

"My cousin? What do you mean? I'm afraid that I don't understand you."

"Of course you understand me. Your cousin Philippe. That fine young man whose letters you kept so carefully."

Suzanne blushed, lost her composure and, finally, following Lupin's advice. She threw herself into her father's arms.

Lupin watched the two of them tenderly.

"One is really rewarded for doing good! What a touching sight. Happy father! Happy daughter! And all this happiness is due to Lupin! These people will thank me later. My name will be passed on to their grandchildren. Ah, family, family!"

He walked over to the window.

"Is good old Ganimard still there? He just loves being part of this kind of delightful display. But no, he's gone. No one, not him, not the others... Damn! The situation's become serious... I wouldn't be surprised if they were already inside the building... Maybe even at the concierge's door... Or in the staircase!"

Professor Gerbois made an involuntary movement. Now that his daughter was back, he felt returned to reality. The arrest of his adversary meant another half-million for him. Instinctively, he took a step forward... As if by accident, Lupin suddenly stood right in front of him.

"Where are you going, Professor? Were you going to protect me from the Police? That's just too kind of you! But don't bother. Besides, I swear they'll be inconvenienced far more than I will."

He continued, while reflecting aloud. "Honestly, what do they really know? That you're here, perhaps that Mademoiselle Gerbois is here as well, since they probably saw her arriving with an unknown woman. But me? They have no idea. How could I have gotten inside a house that they searched this morning from basement to attic? No, in all probability, they're waiting to grab me on the run... Poor things! Unless they guess that the unknown woman was sent by me and think that she was meant to carry out the exchange... At any rate, they'll wait to get her when she leaves..."

A loud thump stopped him.

With a sudden gesture, Lupin stopped the Professor.

"Stop, Professor," he ordered in a dry, authoritative tone. "Think of your daughter and be reasonable, or else... As for you, Maître Detinan, I have your word."

The Professor stood still as a statue. The lawyer did the same.

Without the least sign of haste, Lupin took his hat. He brushed off a bit of dust with the edge of his sleeve.

"My dear Maître, if you should ever need me... My fondest regards, Mademoiselle Suzanne, and give my best to Monsieur Philippe."

He pulled a heavy gold watch from his pocket.

"Professor, it's now 3:42 p.m. I give you permission to leave this room at 3:46 p.m. and not a minute before, do you understand?"

"But," Maître Detinan could not help but interject, "they'll force their way in."

"Have you forgotten the law, my dear Maître? Ganimard would never dare to violate the home of a French citizen, and a lawyer to boot. We'd have enough time for an excellent hand of bridge, if we felt like it. Please, forgive me. You all seem to rather emotional, and I don't want to distress you any further..."

He placed his watch on the table, opened the door of the salon and addressed the blonde woman.

"Are you ready, my dear?"

He passed in front of her, made a last, respectful bow to Mademoiselle Gerbois, then left, closing the door behind them.

They heard him say in the entryway, in a loud voice:

"Good day, Ganimard, how are you? Please give my fondest respects to Madame Ganimard. One of these days, I must invite her to lunch. Farewell, old friend."

Then, they heard the sounds of wood being violently battered, several repeated thuds, followed by voices on the landing.

"3:45 p.m.," whined Professor Gerbois.

A few seconds later, he resolutely walked towards the entry. Lupin and his blonde companion were no longer there.

"Father! You mustn't! Wait!" cried out Suzanne.

"Wait? Are you mad? The machinations of that criminal… And what about my half-million?"

He opened the door.

Ganimard ran inside.

"That woman… Where is she? And where is Lupin?"

"He was here… He is here… He must be here!" replied Professor Gerbois.

"Then we've got him! The building's surrounded."

"What about the service staircase?" Maître Detinan said.

"The service staircase exits in the courtyard, and there's only one way out: the main door. Ten of my men are guarding it," said the Chief Inspector.

"But since he didn't enter by the main door, he certainly won't leave through it," said the lawyer.

"Then, how will he get out?" retorted Ganimard. "By flying out of here?"

The policeman pushed aside a curtain. Behind it was a long corridor leading to the kitchen. Ganimard ran down it and noticed that the door to the service stairs was closed and clearly locked.

From the window, he called to one of his officers.

"Nobody?"

"Nobody!"

"Then, they have to still be in the apartment!" he shouted. "They must be hiding in one of the rooms! It's completely impossible for them to have escaped. Ah, Lupin, you've gotten me in the past, but this time it's sweet revenge!"

At 7 p.m., Monsieur Dudouis, the Head of the Sûreté, astonished not to have heard any news about Lupin's putative arrest, turned up at the Rue Claperyon. He questioned the officers who were guarding the building, then went up to Maître Detinan's apartment, where he was led to the bedroom. There, Monsieur Dudouis saw a man or, more exactly, two legs flailing around on the rug, while the torso to which they belonged was firmly ensconced in the depths of the fireplace.

"Hello!…Hello!" bellowed a muffled voice.

And a more distant voice, which came from above, responded: "Hello!… Hello!"

"So, Ganimard, I see you're including the chimney in your sweep!" exclaimed Monsieur Dudouis, laughing.

The Chief Inspector extricated himself from the fireplace. His face blackened, his clothes covered in soot, his eyes feverish, he was unrecognizable.

"I'm looking for *him*," he groaned.

"Who?"

"Arsène Lupin… Arsène Lupin and his lady friend."

"Oh, them! But do you really think that they're hiding in the chimney flue?"

Ganimard stood up and grabbed his superior's sleeve with five soot-covered fingers.

"Where else can they be, Monsieur?" he said furiously. "They've got to be somewhere. They're human beings like you and me, flesh and blood. Human beings don't vanish in a puff of smoke!"

"No, but they seem to have gone, nevertheless."

"How? How? The building's surrounded! I've even got men on the roof."

"What about next door?"

"No door connects the two buildings."

"The apartments on the other floors?"

"I questioned all the tenants myself. They didn't see or hear anyone."

"Are you sure you spoke to all of them?"

"All of them. The concierge confirmed it. Besides, just to be sure, I stationed a man in every apartment in the building."

"We've got to take him!"

"That's what I say, Monsieur, that's what I say. We have to and we will, because the two of them have got to be here. They can't *not* be. Rest assured, if it's not tonight, it will be tomorrow. I'll sleep here if need be!"

In fact, Ganimard did sleep there that night, and the next night, and the following night as well. And, after three full days and three full nights had passed, the Chief Inspector had not found the untouchable Lupin, nor his equally untouchable companion, the "Blonde Phantom," as she was jokingly dubbed by the press. More, he had not even found the least little clue that would have allowed him to formulate the least little hypothesis on how they had escaped.

And that was why his opinion of the very first hour had also not changed in the least.

"If there are no clues pointing to their escape, it means they're still here!" he kept saying.

However, it was possible that, deep down inside himself, Ganimard was less sure. Perhaps he just did not want to admit it. But, no, a thousand times no! A man and a woman could not vanish like evil spirits in fairy tales. So, without losing faith, he continued to search and investigate as if he had any hopes of finding Arsène Lupin and the Blonde Phantom, hidden inside some secret hideout, in the very stones of the walls themselves.

# The Blue Diamond

On the evening of March 27, at No. 134 Avenue Henri-Martin, in the mansion willed to him six months earlier by his brother, the old general, Baron d'Hautrec, Ambassador to Berlin during the Second Empire, slept deeply in a comfortable armchair. His companion read to him while Sister Augusta made his bed and prepared the fire.

Sister Augusta's Mother Superior had requested that, that night, exceptionally, she return to the convent. At 11 p.m., the nun made sure that the Baron's companion knew she was leaving.

"Mademoiselle Antoinette, I've finished my work and I'm going."

"Thank you, Sister."

"And remember that the cook is also off tonight, so you're alone here, except for the valet."

"Don't worry about the Baron, Sister. I'll be sleeping in the room next to his, as we discussed, and I'll leave my door open."

The Sister left and, a few minutes later, Charles, the valet, came to see what was required of him.

The Baron had awakened and answered himself: "The same as usual, Charles: check to make sure that the electric bell is working in your room, and if you should hear it, run to fetch the doctor immediately."

"No need to worry, General."

"I'm not well, not well at all. So, Mademoiselle Antoinette, where were we with our reading?"

"Doesn't Monsieur le Baron wish to go to bed?"

"No, no, of course not. I go to bed quite late and I don't need anyone to help me."

Twenty minutes later, the old man was once again sleeping and Antoinette tiptoed away.

At the same time, Charles was carefully closing all the shutters on the ground floor, as he did every night.

In the kitchen, he bolted the door to the garden and in the vestibule, he also put on the security chain. Then, he climbed up to his third-floor attic room and went to sleep.

Close to an hour later, he suddenly leapt from his bed. The bell had rung. It rang for a long time, perhaps seven or eight seconds, and in a long, uninterrupted manner.

"I'd bet it's just the Baron feeling agitated," Charles said to himself, once he'd recovered from the surprise.

He pulled on his clothes and hurriedly ran down the stairs, stopping in front of the old man's door and, out of habit, knocking. No one answered. He went inside.

"Strange," he murmured, "No lights... Why the Devil are they out?"

In a low voice, he called out, "Mademoiselle Antoinette?"

There was no answer.

"Are you there, Mademoiselle? What's going on? Is Monsieur le Baron ill?"

The silence continued to surround him, a heavy silence that began to worry him. He took two steps forward and walked into a chair, which he realized was overturned. Then, his hand felt other objects lying on the floor: an end table and a screen. Increasingly concerned, he moved back towards the wall and, carefully, felt along it, searching for the light switch. At last, he found it and turned it on.

Lying in the center of the room, between the table and the mirrored armoire, was the body of his master, Baron d'Hautrec.

"What! How could this happen?" he moaned.

He didn't know what to do. Without moving, he let his eyes wander around the room, taking in the disorder: fallen chairs, a large, crystal candelabra broken into a thousand shards, the clock lying on the marble floor in the entry way, all signs that pointed to a horrible and savage fight. Not far from the Baron's body, the silver handle of a letter opener glinted in the light. Its blade was dripping with blood. Hanging over the edge of the mattress was a handkerchief covered in red stains.

Suddenly, Charles cried out in terror. With a supreme effort, the Baron's body had straightened, then again collapsed... It shuddered two or three times, then was still.

The valet bent over it. Blood was pouring out of a small wound in the neck and fell onto the carpet, where it showed darkly. His master's face wore an expression of absolute terror.

"They killed him," he wept. "They killed him."

He shuddered at the thought of another probable crime: wasn't the Baron's companion sleeping in the next room? Wouldn't the murderer have killed her as well?

He pushed open the door: the room was empty! He decided that Mademoiselle Antoinette must have been kidnapped, or else she'd gone out before the crime had occurred.

He returned to the bedroom and noticed that the desk had not been broken into.

Also, he saw that, on the table where the Baron placed his belongings each night, were a ring of keys, a wallet and a handful of gold coins. Charles picked up the wallet and looked inside. It contained a wad of banknotes. He counted them: 13 100-francs bills.

In an uncontrollable impulse, mechanically, without even thinking about what he was doing, he took them and put them inside his jacket. Then, he ran down the steps, turned the lock, unbolted the chain, closed the door after him and fled through the garden.

Charles was an honest man. He had barely closed the gate when, revived by the cool breeze and light rain on his face, he stopped. The full horror of what had happened suddenly struck him with a shock.

A cab was passing. He hailed the driver.

"Driver, go to the police station and bring an Inspector back... Hurry! There's been a murder!"

The driver whipped his horse. But, when Charles tried to re-enter the house, he found that he could not. He had closed the main gate and it could only be opened from inside.

It was pointless to ring the bell, since there was no one else inside the mansion.

So, he walked along the gardens that bordered the Boulevard, looking at the neatly trimmed, verdant shrubs. An hour passed before he was finally able to tell the Inspector about the crime and hand him the 13 banknotes.

During this time, a locksmith had been called. With a great deal of difficulty, the man was eventually able to force open the gate and the front door. The Inspector went inside and, after a quick glance around, said to the servant:

"I thought you told me that the room was a shambles?"

He turned and saw Charles looking as if he was frozen to the floor, hypnotized. All the furniture had been returned to their proper places! The end table stood between the two windows, the chairs were upright, the clock stood on the mantelpiece. The debris of the candelabra had disappeared.

"The body...? Monsieur le Baron...?" he asked in a shocked tone.

"Indeed," replied the Inspector. "What happened to the victim?"

He walked over to the bed. He pulled back a sheet to find the General Baron d'Hautrec, one-time French Ambassador to Berlin, in full dress uniform, decorated with the Legion of Honor. His face was peaceful. His eyes were closed.

"Someone's been here," whimpered the valet.

"How?"

"I don't know, but someone came in here while I was gone. Look, there was a thin, silver knife on the floor there... And over there, there was a bloody handkerchief... Now, there's nothing. It's all been cleared away."

"By who?"

"By the murderer!"

"But we found all the doors locked."

"Then he was still inside the house."

40

"If so, he'd still have to be here, since you never moved from outside the gate."

The servant thought a bit. "That's true," he slowly said. "I never walked away from the gate... Still..."

"Look. Who's the last person who you saw with the Baron?"

"Mademoiselle Antoinette. His companion."

"And where is she?"

"Her bed wasn't slept in, so I think she took advantage of Sister Augusta not being here to slip away herself. I wouldn't really be surprised. She's young and pretty..."

"But how would she have gotten out?"

"Through the door."

"But you locked it and put on the chain!"

"Much later! She must've already gone out."

"And the crime took place after she left?"

"Of course."

The house was searched from top to bottom, from the attic to the basement, but the murderer had fled. How? When? No one knew. Had he had an accomplice who had decided it was best to return and get rid of any compromising evidence? These were the questions for which the police sought answers.

At 7 a.m., the coroner arrived. At 8 a.m., Monsieur Dudouis, the Head of the Sûreté, appeared. Then it was the turn of the State Prosecutor and the Investigating Magistrate. The house was bursting with police officers, inspectors, journalists, the Baron d'Hautrec's own nephew and other family members.

They searched, they studied the position of the body as Charles had described it. As soon as she arrived, they interrogated Sister Augusta. Not a single thing was discovered. Indeed, Sister Augusta was astonished to learn that Antoinette Bréhat had disappeared. She had only hired the young woman 12 days earlier, based on her excellent references, and refused to believe that she would have abandoned her patient to go Heaven knows where in the middle of the night.

"Besides," insisted the Investigating Magistrate, "if that had been the case, she would have returned by now. So, we're back to this question: what has become of her?"

"I think she was kidnapped by the murderer," said Charles.

It was a plausible hypothesis and seemed to fit in with the available information.

"Kidnapped? Perhaps. I suppose it's not entirely impossible," declared the Head of the Sûreté.

"It's not only totally impossible," said a voice, "but it contradicts all of the evidence and facts of this investigation!"

The voice was rough, the tone brusque and no one was surprised to see that it came from Chief Inspector Ganimard. He was the only one who would ever be excused for expressing himself in such a presumptuous manner.

"Ha! So, you're here, Ganimard?" said Monsieur Dudouis. "I didn't see you come in."

"I've been here for two hours, Monsieur."

"So you're now interested in something other than Ticket No. 514-23, the Rue Clapeyron case, the Blonde Phantom and Arsène Lupin?"

"Ha! Ha!" laughed the Chief Inspector. "I wouldn't swear that Lupin is not involved in this case either. But, until further notice, I'm putting aside the lottery ticket business and concentrating on things here."

Ganimard wasn't one of those high caliber policemen who are studied and make a name for themselves in the annals of police history. He lacked the flashes of genius that set aside the Dupins, Lecoqs and Holmeses. But he had decent skills of observation, discernment and even a touch of intuition. His strength was his ability to work with total focus. Nothing, except perhaps his obsession with Arsène Lupin, constrained him, nor influenced him. In any event, he gave his all that morning and the Investigating Magistrate could not, in any way, reproach his efforts.

"First," Ganimard began, "I'd like you to clarify one thing, Charles: were all the objects that were displaced when you first came into the room back in their usual places when you returned?"

"Exactly."

"So, it's obvious that they could have been replaced only by someone who knew where they should go."

Everyone was struck by this fact.

"Another question," continued Ganimard. "You were woken up by the bell. In your opinion, who rang it?"

"Monsieur the Baron, of course!"

"I see. But when would he have done it?"

"After the fight, when he was dying."

"Impossible, since you found him lying unconscious at least four yards away from the call button."

"Then, he must have rung it during the fight."

"Again, impossible, since you said that the ringing was regular, uninterrupted and lasted seven or eight seconds. Do you think that his attacker would have given him the chance to do that?"

"Then it must have been before the attack."

"Still impossible, since you've told us that only about three minutes separated the moment you heard the bell and when you entered the bedroom. If the Baron had rung before, it would have meant that the fight, the murder and the escape all took place in under three minutes. So, I repeat, that's impossible."

"But," said the Investigating Magistrate, "someone rang the bell. If it wasn't the Baron, who was it then?"

"The murderer."

"Why?"

"I don't know that yet. But the fact that he rang the bell means that he knew it rang in the room of one of the servants. Who would know that, except for someone from the household?"

The noose of suspicion was tightening. With a few quick, neat, logical statements, Ganimard had framed the problem on the most logical terms. His reasoning was perfectly clear and, therefore, it was natural for the Investigating Magistrate to conclude.

"So, to put it bluntly, you suspect Antoinette Bréhat?" he asked.

"I don't suspect her at all," responded Ganimard. "I accuse her."

"Do you accuse her of being an accomplice?"

"I accuse her of having killed Baron d'Hautrec."

"What! What proof do you have?"

"These strands of hair that I found in the victim's right hand, forced into the flesh by the pressure of his nails."

He held out the hairs, which were a sparkling blonde, bright as threads of gold.

"Those are definitely Mademoiselle Antoinette's," Charles murmured. "You can't mistake them." Then he added, "There's something else... The knife, which was missing when we came back into the room... I think it was hers. She used it to cut open the pages of her books."

There was a long, pained silence, as if the crime was even more horrible because it was committed by a woman.

"Let's agree for now that the Baron was killed by Antoinette Bréhat," the Investigating Magistrate finally said. "We need to understand how she managed to escape after the crime, then get back inside after Charles left, only to escape yet again before the Inspector arrived. Do you have any ideas about that, Chief Inspector?"

"None."

"Are you sure?"

Ganimard seemed embarrassed. Finally, with a visible effort he said, "All that I can say is that this case seems to have a number of characteristics in common with that of Ticket No. 514-23. Again, someone seems to display the ability to simply vanish. Antoinette Bréhat appears and disappears from this house just as mysteriously as Arsène Lupin was able to appear inside the apartment of Maître Detinan, then disappear with the Blonde Phantom..."

"So, what does it mean?"

"It means that I can't help but wonder about two, bizarre coincidences: one, Antoinette Bréhat was hired by Sister Augusta just 12 days ago, which was the day after the Blonde Phantom slipped through our fingers. Two, the Blonde Phantom's hair is exactly the same, unmistakable shade of golden blonde that I found in our victim's hand."

"You don't mean to say that... Antoinette Bréhat..."

"...Is none other than the Blonde Phantom, yes."

"And you believe, therefore, that Arsène Lupin was behind both cases?"

"Yes, I do."

There was a peel of laughter. It was the Head of the Sûreté, unable to control himself.

"Lupin! Always Lupin! Lupin is responsible for every crime in Paris! Lupin is everywhere!"

"He's where he needs to be," thundered the irritated Ganimard.

"Precisely. Even Lupin needs a reason to be somewhere," replied Monsieur Dudouis. "In this case, there doesn't seem to be one. The desk wasn't broken into, the wallet wasn't stolen. There were even some gold coins left on the table."

"Maybe so," said Ganimard. "But what about the diamond?"

"What diamond?"

"The Blue Diamond! The famous diamond that was once part of the Royal Crown of France, that was given by the Duke of A*** to Léonide L*** and, at his death, was purchased by Baron d'Hautrec, in memory of the beautiful actress whom he had passionately loved. It's something that an old Parisian like me will never forget."

"Clearly," said the Investigating Magistrate, "if the Blue Diamond is really missing, that would explain it. Where do we look?"

"On the Baron's own finger," answered Charles. "He never took it off of his left hand."

"I looked at his hand," Ganimard said, as he walked over to the body. "As you can all see, there's nothing on it but a simple gold band."

"Look inside his palm," suggested the valet.

Ganimard opened the constricted fingers. The ring's setting was indeed turned inside, and in the center of the Baron's hand was the splendid Blue Diamond.

"Damn!" muttered Ganimard, absolutely flabbergasted. "I don't get it."

"So," snickered Monsieur Dudouis, "I hope you've given up your suspicions about poor old Lupin."

Ganimard took a few minutes to think, then answered in a harsh tone. "The more confused I am, the more I suspect Lupin!" he barked.

Such were the discoveries made by the Police the day after the bizarre crime. Vague, incoherent findings that were neither confirmed, nor clarified by further searches. Antoinette Bréhat's comings and goings remained as inexplicable as ever, just like those of the Blonde Phantom. No one truly knew the real identity of the mysterious woman with the golden hair who had killed Baron d'Hautrec, yet had not removed from his finger the fabulous Blue Diamond that had once adorned the Royal Crown of France.

Indeed, the curiosity that the Blonde Phanton inspired (if that is who she was?) gave the events the allure of a major crime that captured the public's attention.

The Baron's heirs could not help but benefit from such notoriety. They organized an exhibition at the mansion on Avenue Henri-Martin, showing off the furniture and decorations that were to be sold at auction. The furniture was modern and not of a particularly fine quality. The decorations had little artistic value. But in the center of the room, watched over by two police officers, stood a pedestal covered in garnet-colored velvet. On it, a glass dome protected the sparkling Blue Diamond.

And it was an enormous, magnificent diamond of incomparable clarity. The blue was that undefined shade that clear water takes on when it reflects the sky, the color that one sees in truly sparkling white linen. The public admired it, were in ecstasy over it... They also shivered in fear at the sight of the victim's bedchamber, the place where the body had lain, the parquet floor that was now naked after the removal of the bloodstained carpets and, especially, at the solid stone walls through which the criminal had mysteriously passed. They assured themselves that the marble fireplace couldn't move, that the moldings around the mirror hid no hinges that would allow it to pivot. They imagined gaping holes, tunnel entrances, secret passages to the sewers or the catacombs...

The sale of the Blue Diamond was held at the Hotel Drouot. The crowd sweltered and auction fever ran rampant.

Everyone who was anyone in Paris was there–those who bought as well as those who only wanted others to think that they could buy: stockbrokers, artistes, ladies from all walks of life, etc. There were two cabinet Ministers, an Italian tenor, an exiled King who, in order to buttress his deteriorating credit, allowed himself the luxury of bidding, in a very loud voice, all the way to 100,000 francs. 100,000 francs! He could safely bid them, knowing that he risked nothing. The Italian tenor risked 150,000 francs, a well-known French socialite 175,000 francs.

At 200,000 francs, however, the amateurs gave up. At 250,000 francs, there were only two serious bidders left: Herschmann, the famous financier and gold mine king, and the Comtesse de Crozon, a fabulously wealthy American lady who possessed a renowned collection of diamonds and precious stones.

"260,000 francs... 270,000 francs... 275,000 francs... 280,000 francs," announced the auctioneer, looking questioningly at each of the two competitors. "280,000 for Madame la Comtesse... No other bids?"

"300,000 francs," said Herschmann.

There was silence. All eyes turned to the Comtesse de Crozon. She stood smiling, but with a paleness that indicated her stress. She leaned heavily on the back of the chair in front of her. In truth, she knew, as did all everyone else in the room, that the outcome of the duel was certain. Logically, inevitably, it had to favor the financier, whose wishes were backed by a half-billion francs fortune. However, bravely, she responded: "305,000 francs."

More silence. Now, everyone turned to the gold mine king, awaiting his inevitable bid. It would clearly come, strong, brutal, definitive.

But it didn't come. Herschmann remained impassive, his eyes fixed on a paper which he crumpled in his right hand, while the other held the pieces of a torn envelope.

"305,000 francs," repeated the auctioneer. "Once... Twice... There's still time... No more bids? Are you sure?"

Herschmann didn't move. A final silence, then the hammer fell.

"400,000 francs," shouted Herschmann, jumping up as if the sound of the hammer had snatched him from his previous torpor.

But he was too late. The results were final.

Everyone rushed to talk to the financier. What had happened? Why hadn't he spoken sooner?

He started to laugh. "What happened?" he said. "My goodness, I have no idea. I was distracted for a minute."

"Is that possible?"

"Of course. It was a letter I was just handed."

"And that letter was enough to...?"

"To upset me, yes. For a moment."

Ganimard was there. He had watched the sale of the ring. He approached one of the waiters.

"Are you the one who handed Monsieur Herschmann a letter?" he asked.

"Yes."

"Who gave it to you?"

"A lady."

"Where is she?"

"Where is she? Let me see... Over there, Monsieur. That lady wearing a dark veil."

"The one who's leaving?"

"Yes."

Ganimard rushed for the door and saw the woman going down the stairs. He ran. A large group of people stopped him before he could get out the door. Once outside, he no longer saw her.

He returned to the hall, approached Herschmann, introduced himself and asked him about the letter. Herschmann handed it to him. Written hastily in pencil by a hand that the financier didn't recognize, were the words: *"The Blue Diamond brings bad luck. Remember Baron d'Hautrec."*

The Affair of the Blue Diamond was not over yet. Already made infamous by the murder of Baron d'Hautrec and the incident at Hotel Drouot, it gained even more celebrity six months later when, during the following summer, the precious jewel was stolen from Comtesse de Crozon, who had made such an effort to acquire it.

Since I am now at liberty to do so, I would like to throw some light on this intriguing case, and all of the poignant and dramatic events that gripped the public's attention at the time.

On the evening of August 10, the guests of Monsieur and Madame de Crozon were gathered in the salon of their magnificent chateau overlooking the bay of the Somme. It was a musical evening. The Comtesse sat down at the piano and placed her jewels, among which was Baron d'Hautrec's ring, on a small piece of furniture near the instrument.

After an hour, the Comte, his two cousins, the d'Andelles and Madame de Réal, a close friend of the Comtesse, all retired, leaving the Comtesse herself alone with Monsieur Bleichen, the Austrian Consul and his wife.

They spoke for a while, then the Comtesse put out the large lamp on the table in the salon. At the same time, Monsieur Bleichen put out the two lamps on the piano. This left a moment of total darkness, then the Austrian lit a candle and the three made their way to their rooms. But, the Comtesse had barely walked in the door when she remembered her jewels and asked her maid to go get them. The latter returned and placed them on the mantelpiece without her mistress giving them a second glance. The next morning, Madame de Crozon realized that a ring was missing: the ring that contained the Blue Diamond.

She told her husband. They immediately decided that, since the chambermaid was clearly above suspicion, the guilty party could be none other than Monsieur Bleichen.

The Comte alerted the Police Commissioner of Amiens, who opened a discrete investigation and organized a discreet, permanent surveillance of the Austrian Consul, so that there was no way he could either sell the ring or send it to anyone else.

Police officers surrounded the chateau day and night.

Two weeks passed without any new incidents. Monsieur Bleichen then announced his departure. That day, a complaint was filed against him. The Police officially stepped in and ordered the Consul's luggage to be searched. In a small bag, the key of which he constantly kept on his person, they found a bottle of soap powder. Hidden inside was the ring!

Madame Bleichen fainted. Her husband was arrested.

The accused defended himself by saying that the ring had been hidden there by Monsieur de Crozon himself as an act of revenge.

"The Comte is a brutal man, who makes his wife miserable," declared the Austrian. "I had a long discussion with her, in which I strongly advised her to seek a divorce. The Comte became aware of that conversation and avenged himself by taking the ring and, as I was preparing to leave, slipping it into my toiletries."

The Comte and Comtesse continued to press charges. Their explanation of the events was just as plausible as that of the Consul; it was now up to the public to decide whom they believed. No new facts weighed in on the scales of justice. A month of discussion, conjecture and investigation didn't bring a single solid answer.

Annoyed by all the commotion, incapable of bringing convincing proof of the guilt of Monsieur Bleichen, whom they felt justified in accusing, Monsieur and Madame de Crozon demanded that Paris send an officer of the Sûrete who would surely be capable of unraveling the strings of that complicated affair. Paris sent Ganimard.

For four days, the Chief Inspector poked around the chateau, walked around the grounds, had long conversations with the maid, the chauffeur, the gardeners, the employees at the nearby post office, visited the rooms that had been occupied by the Bleichens, the d'Andelle cousins and Madame de Réal. Then, one morning, he simply disappeared without saying a word to his hosts.

A week later, they received the following telegram:

*"PLEASE COME TO THE JAPANESE TEA ROOM, RUE BOISSY-D'ANGLAS, TOMORROW, FRIDAY, AT 5 P.M. GANIMARD."*

At exactly 5 p.m. on Friday, the de Crozons' car stopped in front of No. 9 Rue Boissy-d'Anglas. Without a word of explanation, Ganimard, who had been waiting for them on the sidewalk, led them to the first floor of the Japanese Tea Room.

There, in one of the rooms, the Chief Inspector introduced them to the two people who were already present.

"Monsieur Gerbois, Professor at the Lycée of Versailles, from whom, you may remember, Arsène Lupin stole half-a-million. And Monsieur Léonce d'Hautrec, nephew and heir to Baron d'Hautrec."

The four people sat down. A few minutes later, a fifth person arrived. It was the Head of the Sûreté.

Monsieur Dudouis was not in a good mood. He nodded to the assembly.

"What's going on here, Ganimard?" he asked. "I was handed your telephone message at the Prefecture. Is it something serious?"

"Very serious, Monsieur. In less than an hour, the events I've been investigating will find their denouement right here. Your presence was, therefore, indispensable."

"As well as that of Folenfant and Dieuzy, I suppose, since I saw them downstairs, standing guard near the door?"

"Yes, Monsieur."

"So, what is it? An arrest? Go on, Ganimard, we're all listening."

Ganimard hesitated a few seconds, then, with the clear intention of shocking his audience, began to speak.

"First, I want you all to know that Monsieur Bleichen had nothing to do with the theft of the ring."

"Oh ho! That's quite a statement–and one with serious consequences."

"Is this...revelation... the only fruit of your efforts?" asked the Comte.

"No, Monsieur. I also discovered, almost by accident, that, the day after the theft, three of your guests decided to drive to the neighboring village of Crécy. While two of them visited the famous battlefield, the third quickly went to the local post office and mailed a small, string-tied box, properly stamped, with a declared value of 100 francs."

"There's nothing out of the ordinary in that," Monsieur de Crozon objected.

"Perhaps so, but it will seem less ordinary to you when you learn that this person, instead of giving their true name, sent the package under the false identity of Rousseau, and that the recipient, a Monsieur Beloux in Paris, moved the very evening of the day he received the box–or should I say the ring."

"Was it one of my d'Andelle cousins?"

"Not one of those gentlemen."

"Then it was Madame de Réal?"

"Yes."

"You're accusing my friend, Madame de Réal?" the Comtesse cried, stupefied.

"A simple question, Madame," answered Ganimard. "Was Madame de Réal present during the auction of the Blue Diamond?"

"Yes, but she was not sitting next to me. We came separately."

"Did she encourage you to buy the ring?"

The Comtesse thought back.

"Yes. In fact, I think that she was the one who mentioned it first..."

"I note your answer, Madame. It clearly establishes that it was Madame de Réal who first mentioned the ring to you and encouraged you to purchase it."

"Even so... My friend is incapable of..."

"Please forgive me, Madame, but isn't it true that Madame de Réal is only a casual acquaintance, not a close friend as was written in the press, a fact which seems to have put her above suspicion? According to my investigations, you've only known her since this past winter. Now, I'll do my best to prove to you that everything she's told you about herself, her past and her relations, is absolutely false, and further, that Madame Blanche de Réal never existed before meeting you, and as of now, no longer exists."

"So what?"

"So what?" asked Ganimard.

"Yes. So what? This entire affair is very strange indeed, but what does it have to do with the Blue Diamond? If it's true that Madame de Réal stole the ring, which, mind you, is not yet proven, why did she then hide it in the Monsieur Bleichen's soap powder? For Heaven's sake! If someone goes to all that trouble to spirit away the Blue Diamond, they're going to keep it. What do you have to say to that?"

"Me? Nothing. But Madame de Réal will answer."

"So, she does exist!"

"She exists and, then again, she doesn't. Three days ago, while reading the local newspaper, I saw a news item at the top of the list mentioning social visitors to Trouville. It said: '*Hotel Beaurivage–Madame de Réal*, etc.' Now you understand why, that same night, I was in there interviewing the Manager of the Beaurivage! According to his description, and certain other clues that I was able to gather, this Madame de Réal was indeed the person I sought. Unfortunately, she'd already left the hotel. But she given her address in Paris as No. 3 Rue du Colisée. Two days ago, I went there and learned, without surprise, that there was no Madame de Réal there, but a Madame Réal, no 'de,' who lived on the second floor. She is a diamond merchant who travels frequently. She was returning from one of her trips that night. Yesterday, I rang her and, using a fake name, I introduced myself as the agent of wealthy foreigners with the means to buy some extremely valuable stones. She's supposed to meet me here, today."

"What! You're waiting for her?"

"At 5:30."

"Are you sure that…?"

"That she is the same Madame de Réal from the chateau de Crozon? I have irrefutable proof. But… listen! That's Folenfant's signal!"

Indeed, a whistle had blown. Ganimard hurriedly got up.

"There's not a moment to lose! Monsieur and Madame de Crozon, please go into the room next door. You too, Monsieur d'Hautrec and Professor Gerbois. Leave the door open and, at the first sign of trouble, you'll be able to intervene. Monsieur Dudouis, please stay here, if you don't mind."

"What if she isn't alone?" asked the Head of the Sûreté.

"She will be. This is a new restaurant and the owner is a friend of mine. He won't let anyone come up but the Blonde Phantom."

"The Blonde Phantom? What are you saying?"

"Yes, Monsieur! The Blonde Phantom herself–our friend Arsène Lupin's accomplice. I have absolute proof of it, but I want her standing there, in front of you and the victims of her crimes."

He looked out the window.

"She's coming. She's inside... She can't get away now... Folenfant and Dieuzy are guarding the door. The Blonde Phantom is ours, gentlemen!"

Almost at once, a woman stood in the doorway. She was tall, slim with a pale face and hair that was of a brilliant gold.

Ganimard was overwhelmed by such powerful emotions that he could only remain silent, unable to utter the least word. There she was, in front of him, totally at his mercy! What a victory against Arsène Lupin! And what a revenge! Yet, at the same time, this victory seemed too easy. He wondered if the Blonde Phantom wasn't once again going to slip through his fingers thanks to one of the miracles that Lupin always seemed able to pull off.

But she just stood there, surprised by the silence, looking around, barely hiding her concern.

"She's going to leave! She'll vanish!" thought Ganimard, horrified by the notion.

Quickly, he stepped between the woman and the door. She turned, trying to leave.

"Please don't," said the Chief Inspector. "Why would you want to leave?"

"Really, Monsieur, I don't understand your behavior... Let me..."

"There's no reason for you to leave now, Madame. Indeed, there are more compelling reasons for you to stay."

"I don't understand..."

"You will. In the meantime, you'll stay here."

She grew pale, sank down into a chair and whimpered: "What do you want from me?"

Ganimard had won. He had caught the Blonde Phantom! Proud of himself, he said: "Let me introduce you to the friend of whom I spoke. The one interested in purchasing rare jewels, especially diamonds. Were you able to get the one that you promised me?"

"No, no... I don't know... I don't remember..."

"Of course, you do. Think harder. A woman you know was going to give a colored diamond... 'Something like the Blue Diamond,' I said to you, laughing. 'Precisely,' you replied. 'I may be able to get my hands on that very item.' Do you remember now?"

She remained silent. A small purse that she had been holding fell to the floor. She hurriedly picked it up and clutched it tightly. Her fingers trembled.

"I see that you don't trust us at all, Madame Réal," said Ganimard, "so I'll set an example by showing you what information I possess."

From his wallet, the Chief Inspector produced a sheet of paper. He carefully unfolded it, revealing a lock of hair.

"These are hairs belonging to Antoinette Bréhat, pulled out by Baron d'Hautrec just before he died. I showed them to Mademoiselle Gerbois, who positively identified them as being the same color as the hair of the so-called 'Blonde Phantom.' In fact, they're the same color as your own hair... exactly the same color."

Madame Réal looked at him blankly, as if she really could not understand what the words he spoke meant.

"Also, here are two flacons of perfume, without labels of course, and empty," Ganimard continued. "But, they still retain the odor of what they contained. Mademoiselle Gerbois was able, this very morning, to recognize the perfume of the blonde woman who was her traveling companion for two weeks. Now, one of these flacons came from the room that Madame de Réal occupied in the Chateau de Crozon; the other came from your room at the Hotel Beaurivage..."

"What are you saying? The Blonde Phantom... The Chateau de Crozon..."

Without responding, the Chief Inspector laid four more sheets of paper out on the table.

"Finally," he said, "here are four documents, one with a sample of Antoinette Bréhat's handwriting, one from the woman who wrote to Baron Herschmann at the time of the sale of the Blue Diamond, one from Madame de Réal when she stayed at Crozon and the fourth from you, Madame. It's your name and address, given to the porter at the Hotel Beaurivage in Trouville. Now, if you compare the four samples, you'll see that they're identical."

"You're mad, Monsieur! Mad! What is this supposed to mean?"

"It means, Madame," cried Ganimard loudly, "that the Blonde Phantom, Arsène Lupin's accomplice, is none other than you!"

He pushed open the door of the neighboring room, grabbed hold of Professor Gerbois and dragged him in front of Madame Réal.

"Professor, do you recognize the woman who kidnapped your daughter and whom you saw at Maître Detinan's office?"

"No."

Everyone present felt as if they had received a shock. Ganimard hesitated.

"No? How is that possible? Look at her carefully..."

"I have... Madame is blonde, like the Blonde Phantom, pale like her as well, but otherwise they don't look a thing alike."

"I don't believe it... Such a mistake is unthinkable... Monsieur d'Hautrec, do you recognize Antoinette Bréhat?"

"I saw Antoinette Bréhat at my uncle's home and this isn't her."

"And Madame isn't Madame de Réal either," confirmed the Comte de Crozon.

That was the final straw. Ganimard was numb and stood silent, head bent, eyes staring. All of his theories were shattered, tumbling to the ground like a house of cards.

Monsieur Dudouis stood up.

"Please excuse us, Madame. There seems to have been a regrettable mix-up that I hope you will be able to forgive. But what I don't understand is why you've been so troubled since you've set foot in this room."

"Good Heavens, Monsieur, I was afraid. I've got more than 100,000 francs of jewels in my bag, and your colleague's behavior was not the most reassuring..."

"I see. And your frequent travels?"

"My business requires them."

Monsieur Dudouis had no further questions. He turned towards his subordinate.

"You've handled yourself deplorably, Ganimard. And you treated Madame here with extraordinary discourtesy. I want to see you in my office upon your return to explain yourself!"

Having said his piece, the Head of the Sûreté was ready to leave when something extremely unexpected happened. Madame Réal approached the Chief Inspector.

"Did I understand that you are Monsieur Ganimard?" she asked. "I'm not mistaken?"

"No. I am Ganimard."

"Then this letter that I received this morning must be for you. You can read the address yourself: '*M. Justin Ganimard, in care of Madame Réal.*' I thought it was a joke, since I didn't know you, but clearly this mysterious correspondent knew of our rendezvous."

With a flash of sudden intuition, Ganimard wanted nothing more than to grab the letter and tear it into pieces. However, with Monsieur Dudouis standing there, he didn't dare. Instead, he read it aloud in a strangled voice:

*Once upon a time, there was a Blonde Phantom, a Lupin and a Ganimard. Now, the evil Ganimard wanted to hurt the beautiful Blonde Phantom and the good Lupin didn't want him to succeed. So, the good Lupin, wishing for the Blonde Phantom to become a close confidante of the Comtesse de Crozon, had her take the name of Madame de Réal, which is that–well almost–of an honest merchant with golden hair and a pale complexion. And, the good Lupin said to himself, "If ever the evil Ganimard is on the trail of the Blonde Phantom, how useful it will be for me to be able to send him after an honest merchant instead!"*

*It was a wise precaution that bore fruit. A small note sent to the newspaper read by the evil Ganimard, a flacon of scent purposefully left by the real Blonde Phantom at the Hotel Beaurivage, the name and address of Madame Réal written in the hotel register by the same Blonde Phantom, and the game was afoot.*

*What do you think of it so far, Ganimard? I wanted to tell you the whole tale, knowing that, with your fabled sense of humor, you would be the first to laugh out loud. It's rather delicious, isn't it? I must admit that I've found the whole affair to be quite amusing.*

*So, thank you, my dear friend, and please, remember me to the ever-charming Monsieur Dudouis.*

Arsène Lupin

"He knows everything!" moaned Ganimard, who did not feel the least bit like laughing. "He knows things that I never told anyone! How could he know that I would ask you to come, Monsieur? How could he have known about my discovery of the first flacon? How could he know?"

He trembled and pulled at his hair, in the grips of the deepest despair.

Monsieur Dudouis took pity on him.

"Come now, Ganimard, don't feel bad. We'll try to do better the next time."

Then, the Head of the Sûreté left, accompanied by Madame Réal.

Ten minutes passed. Ganimard read and re-read Lupin's letter. In a corner, Monsieur and Madame de Crozon, Monsieur d'Hautrec and Professor Gerbois spoke together animatedly. Finally, the Comte approached the policeman.

"The result of all this, Chief Inspector," he said, "is that we're no better off than we were before."

"With all due respect, that is not so, Monsieur le Comte! My investigation has established that the Blonde Phantom was the undisputed perpetrator of all three crimes, and that Lupin was behind her. That's enormous progress."

"And yet, completely useless. In fact, things are even more complicated now. The Blonde Phantom killed to steal a Blue Diamond that she didn't take. She took it only to pin the blame on someone else."

"I don't have all the answers yet, but I will."

"Perhaps, but maybe someone else might…"

"What are you trying to say?"

The Comte hesitated, but the Comtesse interrupted him.

"There is another man, the only man other than yourself as far as I know, capable of fighting Lupin–and even defeating him. Monsieur Ganimard, would you object if we asked for the assistance of Sherlock Holmes?"

Ganimard was taken aback.

"Of course not… only… I don't really understand…"

"All of these mysteries are insupportable. I want them all cleared up. Professor Gerbois and Monsieur d'Hautrec feel the same way and we've all agreed to ask the famous English detective to help us."

"I understand, Madame," said the Chief Inspector with a sense of duty that was commendable. "You think Old Ganimard no longer has the strength to go one on one against Arsène Lupin, don't you? And you believe that Mister Holmes will succeed where I've failed? Well, I hope so, because I have the greatest admiration for him… However, I don't think he will…"

"You think Sherlock Holmes will fail, too?"

"Yes, I do. In a duel between Mister Holmes and Lupin, I think fate favors Lupin. The Englishman will be defeated."

"Can we count on you nevertheless?"

"Completely, Madame. I will offer my assistance unreservedly."

"Do you know Mister Holmes' address?"

"Of course. 221B Baker Street."

That very evening, Monsieur and Madame de Crozon dropped their complaint against Consul Bleichen and a joint telegram was sent to Sherlock Holmes.

## *Enter Sherlock Holmes*

"What will the gentlemen have?"

"Anything you please," replied Arsène Lupin, in the voice of a man who has little interest in food, "but no meat, nor wine."

The waiter walked away, with a scornful air.

"Do you mean that you're still a vegetarian?" I exclaimed.

"Yes, more than ever," said Lupin.

"From taste? Conviction? Force of habit?"

"For health reasons."

"And you never make exceptions?"

"I have to, when I dine out in society, in order to not attract attention. But I don't like it."

We were dining together, in a small restaurant located near the Gare du Nord, where Lupin had invited me to join him. He occasionally sends me a telegram in the morning inviting me for dinner in some corner or other of Paris. He is usually at his most loquacious during these meetings, enjoying life to the fullest, unaffected and in good spirits. He always has some surprising tale to tell me, an unexpected remembrance or the story of one of his latest adventures, which I have not heard before.

That evening, Lupin was, if anything, even more exuberant than ever. He laughed and chatted with remarkable ease, displaying that singular sense of irony which is all his own, light and spontaneous, devoid of any bitterness. It was a pleasure to see him like that and I could not help expressing my satisfaction.

"Yes," he said, "I do have days when everything seems wonderful, when life itself is so full of delights that I feel I'll never have enough time to taste them all. And yet, goodness knows that I live each day to the fullest!"

"Perhaps too much so?"

"No, Leblanc. My store of energy is truly endless, take my word for it! I can use it, squander it even, as much as I please, throw my weight around, display my power as outrageously as I wish, and still barely tap it! Every ounce of strength I use only gives me greater, renewed vigor. Life is beautiful! Life is generous! I only need to wish to become, I don't know, a politician, a captain of industry, a minister even, and I know I could. But the idea would never occur to me. I am, and always shall remain, Arsène Lupin! I've searched throughout History in vain to find a figure with a destiny comparable to mine, a fuller, more intense life... Napoleon perhaps? But only when he was nearing the end of his reign, when all of Europe marshaled their forces and tried to crush him, when each battle meant life or death and might have been his last..."

Was he serious? Was he joking? His voice had grown more heated and passionate.

"It's all about taking risks, you see, Leblanc," he continued. "The thrill of danger! Its constant pressure! I breathe it as you breathe the air around you. I love to feel it lurking behind me, lying in wait, whispering, threatening, coming ever closer... And in the midst of that storm, to force myself to remain calm, to not flinch... Because if I do, I'm lost! There are no other experience in the world that can compare to it, except, perhaps, that of a motorcar racing driver, but his race lasts only a few hours, while mine takes up my entire life!"

"How lyrical! But tell me honestly: is there no other reason to feel such excitement today?"

"You're quite a shrewd psychologist," he smiled. "Yes, there is something else."

He poured himself a glass of water and drank it down.

"Have you read *Le Temps* today?"

"I confess I haven't."

"Sherlock Holmes was to have crossed the Channel this afternoon and arrived at 6 p.m."

"Really? Why has he come?"

"He's making his little trip at the expense of the Crozons, Professor Gerbois and Baron d'Hautrec's nephew. They met him at the Gare du Nord and from there, they all went to see Ganimard. The six of them are in conference right now."

Despite the enormous curiosity which he inspired in me, I would never have dreamt of questioning Arsène Lupin about his private life, at least not before he brought it up himself. It was a matter of discretion on my part, which I never transgressed. In any event, his name, at that time, had not yet been publicly connected with the Affair of the Blue Diamond. I therefore waited patiently for his explanations.

"*Le Temps* has also published an interview with the excellent Ganimard," he continued, "in which our national sleuth credits a certain 'Blonde Phantom,' said to be my friend, for the murder of Baron d'Hautrec, and the subsequent attempt to steal the ring from the Crozons. Of course, he accuses me of being the mastermind behind those crimes."

I was slightly shaken. Could it be true? Could a lifetime of stealing have inescapably driven this man to commit murder? I looked at him. He seemed so calm; his eyes met mine with such candor!

I looked at his hands: they were fine and delicate, a model's hands, not the hands of a murderer but the hands of an artist.

"Ganimard is mad," I muttered.

"No, no," he protested. "Ganimard is clever, shrewd even!"

"Shrewd?"

"Yes, shrewd. That interview, for instance, was a masterstroke. First, he managed to alert me to the coming of his British rival so as to make Holmes' task more difficult. Secondly, he specified the exact point to which he has carried his own investigation so that the Englishman cannot take credit for it–not that he would. All's fair in love and war."

"That may well be, but now you've got two foes to fight–and what foes!"

"Oh, please, one hardly counts!"

"But the other?"

"Holmes? Ah, yes, I admit that one is a worthy adversary. But that's why I love it and why I'm in such high spirits. To begin with, it's rather flattering that they think they need the help of the Greatest Detective in the world to untangle my web and capture me. Then, think of the joy that a scrapper like me must feel at the prospect of a full-blown battle with Sherlock Holmes! At last, I'll have to exert myself to the fullest, for I know the fellow: he won't miss an opportunity."

"He's good."

"Very good. As a detective, I don't think he has any peers, anywhere, or ever had. Still, I've got one advantage over him, which is that he is forced to take the offensive, while I only need to remain on the defensive. Mine is the easier game to play. Besides..." He gave an almost imperceptible smile before completing his sentence. "Besides, I know his methods but he doesn't know mine. And I have a few tricks in store for him that will make him think twice before he challenges me on my own turf again..."

He tapped the table lightly with his delicate fingers and spoke in short, punchy sentences with an air of mischievous delight.

"Arsène Lupin versus Sherlock Holmes! France versus England! Revenge for Trafalgar and Waterloo at last! He doesn't know that I'm waiting for him and that I've been preparing for..."

He stopped abruptly, seized with a fit of coughing, and buried his face in his napkin like someone who swallowed wrong.

"What is it?" I asked. "A crumb? Drink some water."

"No, it's not that," he gasped.

"What is it then?"

"I need some air."

"Shall I open a window?"

"No. I must go. Quick, hand me my hat and coat, I must be off!"

"But why? Is it something I did?"

"No, not at all... Do you see those two men who just walked in? Especially the taller of the two? Well, I want you to stay on my left as we walk out of here so that he can't see me."

"The one who's about to sit behind you?"

"Yes, that one. I don't want him to... Personal reasons. I'll tell you outside."

"But who is he?"

"Sherlock Holmes."

He made a prodigious effort to regain control of himself, almost as if he now felt ashamed of his brief moment of panic. He put down his napkin, took a slow drink of water and, after at last having calmed down, said with a smile:

"It's funny, isn't it? I'm not normally so easily flustered, but you must admit, this totally unexpected encounter..."

"What are you afraid of? No one can recognize you under all your disguises. Every time I see you, even I feel as if I were meeting someone new."

"*He* will recognize me," said Lupin. "*He* only saw me once, but I felt that he saw me for life.[5] What he saw was not my outside appearance, which I can indeed alter at will, but my very essence... Besides, I wasn't prepared... What a strange coincidence... In this little restaurant..."

"Well," I asked, "are we leaving?"

"No, we're not."

"We're not? What do you mean?"

"I feel the best thing to do, under the circumstances, is to come clean and to trust him."

"You can't be serious!"

"Oh, but I am... Besides, it would be useful to find out what he knows... And I can't stand it anymore! I feel his gaze boring into my neck, my shoulders... trying to remember... to recollect..."

---

[5] In *Sherlock Holmes Arrives Too Late*, included in Volume 1, *The Hollow Needle*.

He thought for a minute. I noticed a light, mischievous smile play on his lips. Then, on a whim, obeying his impulsive nature rather than the necessities of the situation, he spun around on his chair to face his foes.

"What an incredible stroke of luck!" he said merrily, with a small tip of the head. "If it's not my good friend, Mister Sherlock Holmes! Please allow me to introduce Monsieur Leblanc…"

For a brief second, the Englishman was taken aback. Then, he started to make a move, as if he was about to throw himself upon Lupin, but my friend shook his head and put his hand lightly on the Detective's arm.

"That would be a mistake. Besides, it would lack fair play–and would be totally useless."

Holmes looked around him, as if to see if Lupin had any accomplices, or possibly looking for assistance.

"That won't work either," said Lupin, reading his mind. "Also, are you quite sure you have the legal authority to arrest a harmless-looking French citizen? Come on, Mister Holmes, be a good sport!"

For myself, I thought that being a good sport, considering the opportunity that was being presented, would not be especially tempting. Still, it must have appealed to the Detective, for he half-rose from his chair and introduced his companion.

"This is Doctor Watson, my friend and collaborator. Watson, this is Monsieur Arsène Lupin."

The good Doctor's stupefaction almost made us laugh. His eyes and mouth opened wide. His expansive, square-jawed face gleamed like a well-polished apple. His bristly, thick hair and mustache stood up like so many hardy blades of grass.

"Watson, you don't seem able to conceal your stupefaction at one of the most natural incidents in the world," jeered Holmes, with an undisguised note of sarcasm in his voice.

"But… aren't you going to arrest him?" stammered Watson.

"Don't you see that Monsieur Lupin is standing between the door and myself, barely ten feet away. He would be outside before I could lift a finger."

"Don't let that stop you," said Lupin.

He walked around the table and sat down so that the Englishman was now between him and the door, thus placing himself at his enemy's mercy.

Watson looked at Holmes, uncertain at his reaction to such an act of bravado, but the Detective's face remained inscrutable. After a moment, he called out:

"*Garçon*!"

The waiter rushed over.

"Two whiskey and sodas and two beers," he ordered.

Peace had been made... at least, for the moment. Soon after, the four of us, seated calmly around a single table, were chatting quietly.

Sherlock Holmes is a man... of the sort one might actually meet in daily life, as hard it seems to believe, such is his reputation. He is tall, over six feet, and lean, clean-shaven and about 50 years of age. He looks much like a keen banker or accountant who might have spent his life poring over ledgers. Nothing would distinguish him from any other ordinary, respectable Londoner, not even his hawkish nose–nothing, except his incredibly keen, bright and penetrating eyes.

And then, of course, he *is* Sherlock Holmes! A phenomenon capable of miracles of intuition, observation, insight and ingenuity. It is as if nature had amused herself by taking the two most extraordinary detectives in the history of man, Auguste Dupin and Monsieur Lecoq, then combined them into one single, formidable human being, even greater and more incredible than his two predecessors. When one reads of the exploits of such a man, ably narrated by the good Doctor Watson, one is hard-pressed to believe that they are the feats of a real man, and not those of a prodigious construct of the human imagination, made up by some fantastic writer, such as the great Sir Arthur Conan Doyle.

When Lupin asked him how long he planned to stay in Paris, Holmes immediately brought the conversation back to the topic at hand.

"That depends on you, Monsieur Lupin."

"If that's the case," replied my friend, laughing, "then I'd urge you to take the midnight ferry."

"Tonight is rather too soon. But I hope that in a week, ten days…"

"Are you in that much of a hurry?"

"I'm a very busy man. There's the robbery at the Anglo-Chinese Bank, the kidnapping of Lady Eccleston… Tell me, Monsieur Lupin, do you think that a week will do?"

"Amply, if you confine yourself to the two cases connected with the Blue Diamond. It's also the time I need to take certain precautions, in the event that, by solving those two mysteries, you manage to get your hands on information that could endanger my personal safety."

"I confess that, in that next week to ten days, I do expect to get my hands on such information," said the Englishman.

"And then, you will have me arrested on the eleventh?"

"No, the tenth, at the very latest."

Lupin reflected, shaking his head.

"It will be difficult. Very difficult," he said.

"Difficult, yes, but possible, and therefore inevitable."

"Quite inevitable," confirmed Watson, as if he saw in his mind the long chain of events that would ineluctably lead to his friend's eventual triumph.

"Watson, who knows what he is talking about, can confirm that I'm not prone to fits of overly enthusiastic predictions," said Holmes, smiling. "Of course, I don't have all the facts yet," he continued, seriously. "The cases are a good many months old. I haven't had the opportunity to search for the type of clues on which I usually rely…"

"Mud stains, cigarette ashes," explained Watson.

"…But I do have the results of Chief Inspector Ganimard's remarkably detailed investigation, all the newspaper articles written on the subject, all the evidence gathered so far, and therefore I've already been able to reach some preliminary conclusions…"

"Based on logical deductions and analysis," added Watson, rather pretentiously.

"Would it be indiscreet," asked Lupin, in the deferential tone he used when talking to the Detective, "to ask what those preliminary conclusions might be?"

It was really most exciting to see those two men sitting face to face, with their elbows on the table, discussing the momentous issues of their impending confrontation calmly and reasonably, as if they'd been talking about the weather. The whole scene was also full of the sort of irony that they both thoroughly appreciated and enjoyed, and practiced as experts. Doctor Watson was in seventh heaven.

Holmes slowly filled his pipe and lit it.

"I think that this case is, in fact, far less complicated than it would appear to be at first glance," he said.

"Far less indeed," echoed the good Doctor.

"I say 'this case' because, in my opinion, there is only one case. The death of Baron d'Hautrec, the story of the Blue Diamond and, let's not forget, the matter of Ticket No. 514-23, are only various facets of a single mystery that one might call the Affair of the Blonde Phantom. The only thing left to do, I believe, is to discover the link which connects these three chapters of the same story. Chief Inspector Ganimard, who tends to be a bit overdramatic at times, thinks that that link is the ability to appear and disappear at will while remaining invisible. Needless to say, I do not believe in such supernatural explanations…"

"Indeed. And so?"

"And so," Holmes continued in a deliberately slow and methodical tone, "my own opinion is that the common characteristic shared by all three incidents has been your deliberate and manifest intention to have them take place on a stage which you had preselected. That aspect of the case has not yet been investigated. Yet, I think it is the most important element in the case. It is more than a simple plan on your part, it is a necessity, a *sine qua non* condition of its success."

"Could you elaborate on that?"

"Of course. For example, from the very beginning of your battle with Professor Gerbois, isn't it perfectly *obvious* that Maître Detinan's office was the inevitable location selected by you in which the final confrontation had to take place? There obviously was no better place, to the extent that you felt safe enough to set what one might almost call a public rendezvous there with the Blonde Phantom..."

"And Mademoiselle Gerbois," added Watson.

"Now, let us discuss the matter of the Blue Diamond. Did you try to steal it at any time during all the years that Baron d'Hautrec had it in his possession? No. But suddenly, a mere six months after the Baron moved into his brother's house, the so-called Antoinette Brehat appeared upon the scene and a first attempt was made... However, you failed to secure the Blue Diamond and a public auction took place with great publicity at the Hotel Drouot. Was it a fair auction? Was the wealthiest bidder guaranteed to get the Diamond? Not at all! Just as Monsieur Herschmann was about to make the final bid, the Blonde Phantom sent him a threatening letter and the Diamond went to the Comtesse de Crozon, who, as it turned out, had also been influenced by said lady. Was the Diamond then going to vanish? No. Why? Because you lacked the means to succeed. So, an interval ensued. But as soon as the Comte and the Comtesse moved to their country estate–obviously, what you were hoping and waiting for–the ring disappeared..."

"Only to reappear in Consul Bleichen's bottle of soap powder," remarked Lupin.

"Come, come! I wasn't born yesterday, Monsieur Lupin," said Holmes, striking the table with his fist. "You can take in the press, the Crozons, and even an old fox like Ganimard with tricks like that, but not Sherlock Holmes."

"Meaning?"

"Meaning…" Here, the Detective took his time, as if he wished to savor the effect of his next revelation. "Meaning that the Blue Diamond found in Herr Bleichen's soap powder was obviously a fake. You have the real Blue Diamond, Monsieur Lupin."

Arsène Lupin remained silent for a while. Then, with his eyes fixed on the Englishman, he said very simply:

"You are a great man, sir."

"Isn't he?" said Watson, basking in the reflected rays of homage.

"Yes, he is," said Lupin. "Everything now becomes clear; the truth is revealed for all to see. Not one of the Magistrates, not one of the special reporters who have investigated this case, not even Ganimard, have come half close to the truth. This is a marvel of insight and logic."

"Elementary deductions," said Holmes, nevertheless flattered by the compliments paid to him by so great an expert. "It only required a little thought."

"It only required the *ability* to marshal one's thoughts, but so few people know how! But now that you have redefined and narrowed our battleground, what remains to be done?"

"The only thing left for me to do is to discover why you chose those three specific locations: Maître Detinan's office, No. 25 Rue Clapeyron, the d'Hautrec house, No. 134 Avenue Henri-Martin and the Crozons' chateau. That is the key to the entire mystery. The rest is all smoke and mirrors, wouldn't you agree?"

"I do indeed."

"In that case, Monsieur Lupin, am I not justified in saying that my business here won't take me more than ten days?"

"Yes, in ten days, you will have learned the whole truth."

"And have you arrested."

"No."

"No?"

"For me to be actually arrested, there would have to be a conjunction of such extraordinary circumstances, a series of such amazing reversals of fortune, that I cannot admit the possibility."

"What neither circumstances nor fortune may bring about, Monsieur Lupin, another man's will and persistence might."

"Only if the will and persistence of that man are not confronted by an immovable obstacle, Mister Holmes."

"There is no such thing as a truly immovable obstacle, Monsieur Lupin."

The look that the two men exchanged was calm, without fear or provocation, yet full of steely, inflexible resolve. It was the ringing clash of two swords touching before the start of the duel. It was clear and frank.

"Good!" exclaimed Lupin, rubbing his hands. "Finally, a foe worthy of my mettle. And not just any kind of foe, but the great Sherlock Holmes himself! We shall have some sport!"

"Aren't you concerned?" asked Watson.

"Truthfully, a little, Doctor Watson," said Lupin, rising. "And the best proof is that I now intend to accelerate my own plans for retreat because I don't want to run the risk of being caught unprepared by your associate. Ten days, we said, Mister Holmes?"

"Ten days, Monsieur Lupin. This is Sunday. It will all be over by Wednesday week."

"And I'll be under lock and key?"

"Without the slightest doubt."

"Good Lord! And only a few minutes ago, I was congratulating myself on my peaceful life. No major troubles, a good, steady business, barely any interference from the Police and the comforting notion of the universal approval of my fellow citizens... Well, it looks like all that may soon be over. That's life, I suppose. After sunshine comes rain. No more time for laughing, now. I'll say my good-byes..."

"Don't dilly-dally," said Watson, full of concern for a man whom Holmes so clearly respected. "Don't waste any time."

"I don't intend to, Doctor Watson, except to tell you how pleased I've been to make your acquaintance. Mister Holmes is lucky indeed to have such an invaluable collaborator."

Courteous salutations were exchanged, as if we stood upon a battlefield, between these two foes who bore no hatred towards each other but whom destiny had forced into a fight to the finish. Then, Lupin grabbed my arm and dragged me outside.

"What do you say to that, my dear Leblanc? There's a dinner that will be worth recounting in your memoirs of me."

He closed the door of the restaurant and we took a few steps outside.

"Do you smoke?" he suddenly asked.

"No, but you don't either, if I recall..."

"Quite."

Yet, he took out a cigarette, lit it with a wax match, which he waved a couple of times before throwing it away, Then, he put out the cigarette and got rid of that, too. He ran across the street and met with two men who had emerged from the shadows, as if summoned by a signal–the cigarette, undoubtedly. He spoke with them for a few minutes on the opposite sidewalk, then returned to me.

"I beg your pardon, but I'm going to have my work cut out for me with that damned Englishman. But I swear he hasn't bested me yet! I'll show him a trick of two he doesn't expect. Good-bye, Leblanc. The good Doctor Watson is right, I mustn't waste any time."

He quickly walked away.

Thus ended that strange evening, or at least that part of the evening which I witnessed myself. Many other incidents occurred during the hours that followed, and I am grateful to Doctor Watson for having shared with me the notes he took of what ensued after our departure, thus enabling me to reconstruct what happened accurately and in detail.

Just as Arsène Lupin was leaving me, Sherlock Holmes took out his watch and rose from his chair.

"Twenty to nine. At 9 p.m., we're supposed to meet the Comte and the Comtesse de Crozon at the railway station."

"Let's go then," said Watson, finishing his drink.

They walked outside.

"Don't turn your head, Watson," said Holmes. "We may be followed. If so, let's act as if we don't care either way... Tell me, why do you think Lupin was in that restaurant?"

"To have dinner, I suppose?"

"Yes, Watson. The longer we work together, the more pleased I am by your progress."

Watson blushed with pride in the dark.

"Yes, he went out to have dinner and was as surprised as I was by our chance encounter. But then, most likely, he wanted to know what my intentions were, and especially if I plan to visit the Crozons, as Ganimard so selflessly mentioned in his interview. I shall leave, therefore, since that is what he expects me to do, but in reality, I shall not."

"I don't understand."

"Here is what I want you do to, old friend. Go down this street, hail a cab, no two, three cabs. Send them to different addresses, I don't care where. Then come back here, fetch the bags we left in the cloakroom and take another cab to the Elysée Palace."

"And after I get there?"

"Ask for a room, go to bed and sleep soundly until I return."

Watson, proud of the important task delegated to him, went off. Holmes continued to the Gare du Nord, bought a ticket and stepped onto the express train to Amiens. He quickly found the Comte and Comtesse de Crozon who had been waiting for him.

He merely bowed to them, lit a second pipe and stood calmly in the corridor, smoking it.

Ten minutes later, after the train had left the station, he walked into the compartment and sat down beside the Comtesse.

"Do you have the ring, Madame?" he asked.

"Yes."

"Could I please look at it?"

The Detective took the ring and examined it closely.

"Just as I thought: it's fake."

"Fake?"

"Yes. The result of a new process which consists in subjecting diamond dust to enormous heat until it melts and then can be reshaped into a single diamond."

"But my diamond is real!"

"Yours, yes. But this is not yours."

"Where is mine, then?"

"In Lupin's hands."

"And this one?"

"This one was exchanged with it and slipped into Herr Bleichen's soap powder, where you found it."

"So it *is* a fake!"

"Absolutely."

Bewildered and upset, the Comtesse said nothing while her husband, just as incredulous, turned the stone over and over in his hands.

"But that doesn't make any sense," Madame de Crozon finally stammered. "Why didn't Lupin simply take the Diamond? And how did he get it?"

"That's what I intend to find out."

"At the chateau?"

"No. I'll get off at Creil and return to Paris. That's where the battle between Lupin and myself must take place. It's better if he thinks that I'm out of town. That will give me an advantage…"

"But?…"

"Why should you care where I am, Madame? Our main objective now must be to recover the Blue Diamond, musn't it?"

"Well, yes."

"Then, set your mind at rest. Earlier this evening, I committed myself to succeed in a far greater task. You have my word that I will return the real diamond to you."

The train slowed down. Sherlock Holmes pocketed the fake diamond and opened the carriage door.

"You're getting off on the wrong side of the train," exclaimed the Comte.

"This way, if Lupin is having me followed, he'll lose my trail. Good-bye Madame, Monsieur."

The Detective ignored the complaints of a railway employee and proceeded to the stationmaster's office. There, he purchased a new ticket and, 50 minutes later, he jumped into another train which got him back to Paris just before midnight.

He ran across the station, walked into the Buffet and exited through the service door. Once outside, he hailed a cab.

"Rue Clapeyron," he told the driver.

After making sure that he had not been followed, Holmes had the driver stop at the end of the street. He made a careful examination of Maître Detinan's house and the two adjacent buildings. He carefully paced off certain distances and took measurements which he jotted down in his notebook.

"Avenue Henri-Martin," he then instructed the driver as he got back into the cab.

Holmes dismissed the carriage at the corner of the Avenue and the Rue de la Pompe. He walked along the sidewalk to No. 154 and went through the same procedure of taking measurements of the Baron's house and its two neighboring buildings. He concentrated especially on the lengths of their respective facades and the depths of their small front gardens.

The Avenue was deserted and very dark under its four rows of trees, amongst which an occasional gaslight vainly struggled to dispel the thickening gloom. One of those lamps threw a pale light upon a section of the front wall and Holmes saw a sign that said "To Let" hanging on the railings. He also took notice of the neglected garden and the great, empty windows that marked the house as being uninhabited.

"That's right," thought Holmes, "there's been no new tenant since the Baron's death... I wonder if I can get inside and have a discreet look around..."

The idea had no sooner occurred to him than he began to search for a way to execute it. But it was not an easy task. The railings were too tall to be easily climbed. From his pocket, the Detective took a small electric lantern and a skeleton key which he always carried with him. To his surprise, he found that one of the gates had not been separately secured with a chain and a deadbolt and he was easily able to pick its lock. He slipped into the garden, careful not to close the gate behind him. He had not gone three steps when he stopped. A glimmer of light had moved across one of the windows on the second floor.

The light moved across a second window, then a third. Holmes could only see a shadow behind it, silhouetted against the walls. Then, the light went from the second floor to the first. There, it wandered for a while from room to room.

"Who on Earth can be walking about in Baron d' Hautrec's house in the middle of the night?" thought Holmes, immensely curious.

The only way to find out was to go in himself. The Detective did not hesitate and stepped forward. But his intended target must have caught sight of him when he crossed into the pool of light cast by the gaslamp outside and made his way to the steps, for the glimmer of light suddenly vanished. Holmes peered into the darkness but did not see it again.

The Detective tried the door at the top of the steps. It was open. Hearing no sounds, he softly turned the handle and ventured inside. There was only silence and darkness. He felt for the banister and went up one floor.

Upon reaching the landing, he entered one of the rooms and went to the window which shone brightly against the dark surroundings. From there, he distinctly saw the silhouette of a man trying to get away, slipping amongst the hedges that lined the wall separating the two gardens. The prowler had undoubtedly caught sight of the Detective and gone down by another staircase.

"Damn," said Holmes. "He's getting away!"

The Englishman rushed downstairs and leapt into the garden, planning to cut off the other man's retreat. But once there, he saw no one. It took him a few seconds to finally distinguish the darker shape of the man hiding among the shrubs.

The Detective paused to reflect. Why had the prowler not tried to run away when he could? Why was he still here, still spying on him?

*In any case*, thought Holmes, *it can't be Lupin. He would be far more clever. It must be one of his men.*

Long minutes passed. The Detective stood still, his eyes fixed upon the other man. But as he was not moving, and the Englishman was not the type to stand and do nothing, he checked his gun, loosened his knife in its sheath and walked straight up to the enemy with the daring and audacity that made him so formidable a foe.

Suddenly, Holmes heard an unmistakable sound. The prowler had just cocked his own gun. Immediately, the Detective rushed into the hedge and fell upon the other man, who had no time to flee. There was a violent and desperate struggle. Holmes became aware that his enemy was trying to draw his knife. But stimulated by the thought of an impending victory in his battle against Arsène Lupin, the Detective felt his strength well up. He threw his adversary to the ground and bore upon him with all his weight, pinning him down. With one hand, he clutched at the prowler's throat while with the other, he grabbed his electric lantern. He pushed the button to throw a light upon his prisoner's face.

"Watson!" he exclaimed in horror.

"Holmes!" gasped a hollow, strangled voice.

They remained that way for a while staring at each other, without exchanging a word, bewildered and stupefied. In the distance, they heard the sound of a car horn. A little wind gently rustled through the leaves. Holmes did not stir, his hands still gripping his friend's throat.

Suddenly, the Detective let go. Filled with frustration and concern, he grabbed Watson by the shoulders and shook him frenetically.

"What the Devil were you doing here? Answer me, Watson! Did I ask you to come here and spy on me?"

"Spy on you?" groaned Watson. "But I didn't know it was you, Holmes."

"Then what? What are you doing here? You were supposed to wait for me at the Elysée Palace."

"I did!"

"You were supposed to be in bed, asleep."

"I was."

"Obviously not, since you're here now!"

"It was your letter…"

"What letter?"

"The letter from you that a bellhop brought me at the hotel."

"A letter from me? What are you talking about?"

"I assure you…"

"Where is it? Show it to me."

Watson produced a sheet of paper and, by the light of his lantern, Holmes read in amazement:

*Watson, get up and go at once to Avenue Henri-Martin. The d'Hautrec house is empty. Take a good look around, draw a map of the premises and go back to bed.*

*Holmes*

"I was busy measuring the rooms," said Watson, "when I saw a shadow in the garden. I decided to…"

"…catch the man to whom it belonged," continued Holmes, helping his friend to get up and leading him away. "An excellent idea, except that in this case, I was that man. Next time you get a letter from me, Watson, first make sure that it's not a forgery."

80

"Are you saying that you didn't write that letter?" said Watson, who was beginning to see the truth.

"I'm afraid I did not."

"Who did then?"

"Arsène Lupin."

"But why did he do that?"

"I don't know, and that's what concerns me. Why the Devil should he go to the trouble of getting you here in the middle of the night? If it were me, I would understand, but you... I can't see why he..."

"I'm anxious to get back to the hotel."

"So am I."

They reached the gate. Watson, who was in front, took hold of one of the bars and pulled it.

"Holmes... Did you shut it behind you?"

"Certainly not. I left it slightly ajar."

"And yet it's shut."

Holmes pulled in turn, but to no avail. He then took a closer look at the lock.

"Damn it all! It's locked!" he swore.

He shook the gate with all his strength, then realizing the uselessness of his efforts, let his arms fall to his side, discouraged.

"Now I understand," he said with a tinge of bitterness. "It's all *his* doing. He foresaw that I would get off the train and return to Paris, and laid out a trap for me here in case I should start my investigation tonight. And he was kind enough to arrange for you to come here to keep me company. All this to make me lose a day, and probably to teach me to mind my own business..."

"Do you mean to say that we're Lupin's prisoners?"

"Yes, we are. Sherlock Holmes and Doctor Watson, prisoners of Arsène Lupin! Ha! The adventure begins beautifully! But no, I refuse to surrender to..."

Suddenly, Watson grabbed his friend.

"Look!" he said. "Up there! There's a light!"

Indeed, a light had just appeared at one of the first floor windows.

Holmes and Watson rushed back into the building and ran to the first floor, each taking a different staircase. They reached the door of the lit room at the same time. A candle was burning in the middle of the floor. Next to it was a picnic basket from which protruded a bottle of wine, a roasted chicken and half a loaf of bread.

Holmes bust out laughing.

"Splendid! Now he provides our dinner! This is an enchanted palace, a regular fairyland! Don't make that face, Watson. This is all rather amusing."

"You think so?" said Watson, dolefully.

"Yes," replied Holmes, whose gaiety seemed somewhat forced. "I don't think I've ever seen anything quite so comical in my life. What a prankster Lupin is! He tricked us, but he did it in such a gentlemanly fashion. I wouldn't trade this basket for all the dinners in Mayfair. Watson, old friend, you disappoint me. Aren't you the kind of man who can bear such minor disappointments with fortitude? What have we really to complain about? We could both be lying dead, here, our throats slashed by murderous daggers, and instead, we're being wined and dined. Come now! Look upon the bright side…"

Holmes managed to restore Watson's morale and the two men proceeded to eat the chicken and drink the wine so kindly provided by Arsène Lupin. Later, however, after the candle had gone out and they had to lay on the floor to sleep, with the wall their only pillow, the Detective reflected on the painful and humiliating side of the situation, and found it bitter to swallow. Their sleep was restless and dispirited.

In the morning, when Watson woke up, aching in every bone and shivering with cold, he saw that Holmes was already on his knees, examining each inch of the room with a magnifying glass. He was paying particularly close attention to some figures drawn on the floor with chalk and was copying them down in his notebook.

Followed by Watson, who took great interest in watching his friend at work, the Detective inspected each room in turn, finding similar chalk marks in two of the others. He also noted two circular marks on two oak panels, an arrow on a door and four, small figures on four steps of the staircase.

"The figures are correct, aren't they" asked Watson after an hour.

"I don't know yet," replied Holmes, whose good humor had returned. "But I will after I discover their meaning."

"Oh, that," said Watson. "They represent the number of slates in the parquet floor."

"Really?"

"Yes. The two circles indicate that the panels sound hollow, and the arrows point to the direction of the dinner lift."

"How do you know all this?" asked Holmes, torn between genuine admiration and skepticism. "I'm almost embarrassed by your perspicacity."

"No need to be," said Watson, delighted by his friend's approval. "I drew these marks myself last night. I strive to follow your methods whenever I can, you know."

I would guess that, at that very moment, Watson was in greater danger of coming to harm than at any other time during the entire case, as the Detective must surely have felt the desire to wring his neck. But Holmes mastered himself, smiled–or at least, tried to–and complimented his friend.

"Well done, Watson. That's excellent work. Very useful. Have you applied your powers of observation upon any other parts of this house? You might as well tell me now."

"No, that's all I had time to do."

"Too bad. It was a promising start. Well then, as things are, there's nothing left for us to do but leave."

"Leave? But how?"

"The way people usually do. Through the gate, old friend."

"But it's locked."

"Someone will unlock it for us."

"Who?"

"Anyone. Those two policemen walking down the avenue, for example. Let's call them."

"But…"

"But what?"

"It will be embarrassing, Holmes. What will people say when they learn that we spent the night as prisoners of Arsène Lupin?"

"I would imagine they'll have a good laugh," replied Holmes, gritting his teeth. "But we can't go on living here, can we?"

"And there's nothing else to do?"

"No."

"Still, the man who brought the food basket did not come in or leave through the garden. There must be a secret exit somewhere. Why don't we look for it instead of calling on the French Police for help?"

"You are correct, except for the fact that the same French Police have been looking in vain for that very same secret passage for the past six months. I, myself, while you were asleep, examined the house from top to bottom and found nothing. My dear Watson, Lupin is not the kind of game we're accustomed to hunt: he leaves nothing behind him, not a single clue…"

Sherlock Holmes and Watson were let out of the property at 11 a.m. by the Police and were taken to the nearest station. There, the local Commissioner, after some perfunctory questioning, let them go with the most embarrassing display of commiseration.

"I cannot apologize enough for your misadventure, gentlemen. You certainly have a very poor opinion of French hospitality. What a horrible night you must have spent! That wretch Lupin really ought to have shown you more consideration…"

They took a cab back to the Elysée Palace, where Watson asked for a key to his room.

"But, Monsieur, you checked out this morning," said the clerk.

"I did? When?"

"A friend of yours gave us a note…"

"What friend? What note?"

"This note," said the clerk, handing Watson a sheet of paper. "See, your business card is still attached to it."

Watson took the note and looked at it. It was certainly one of his cards, and the handwriting was uncannily like his.

"Good Heavens!" he muttered. "Another clever bit of forgery." Then, he added, anxiously: "What about our luggage?"

"Your friend took it with him."

"And you let him do it?"

"But, Monsieur, your note said…"

"I see."

The two Englishmen went out and wandered down the Champs-Elysées, slowly and silently. A beautiful autumn Sun shone upon the Avenue. The air was filled with a soft breeze.

At the Rond-Point, Holmes stopped to light his pipe, then resumed his walk.

"I don't understand you, Holmes," exclaimed Watson. "Lupin toys with us like a cat with a mouse and you say nothing, you do nothing!"

The Detective stopped.

"I'm thinking," he said. "I'm thinking about your business card, Watson."

"What about it?"

"Here is a man who anticipated a possible confrontation with us, and in order to prepare for it, managed to get his hands on samples of our business cards and handwriting. Ask yourself what degree of precaution, determination and organization all this represents."

"I see."

"Yes, Watson, to fight such a formidable enemy, so well prepared, so well armed, and to have a chance to defeat him, it takes… Well, it takes a man like myself. And even then," he added, laughing, "one can't say that our first engagement was crowned with success, was it?"

At 6 p.m., the evening edition of *L'Echo de France* published the following article:

*This morning, Police Commissioner Thenard of the 16th Arrondissement released Mister Sherlock Holmes and Dr. John Watson who had been confined by order of Arsène Lupin in the late Baron d'Hautrec's residence, where they spent a pleasant evening.*

*They were subsequently relieved of their luggage and have filed a complaint against Lupin.*

*Arsène Lupin declared that he was satisfied with teaching them a little lesson, and earnestly begged the two Englishmen to not force him to take more drastic measures.*

"Pah!" said Holmes, crumpling up the newspaper. "These are schoolboy tricks. That's the only fault I find with Lupin. He's too childish, too fond of playing to the crowd... Still a street urchin at heart..."

"So, Holmes, no change of heart?"

"No, Watson," replied the Detective in a voice shaking with carefully suppressed rage. "I won't let him make me angry. It won't work, because *I am completely certain that I shall have the last word!*"

## *The Light at the End of the Tunnel*

However unaffected by adverse circumstances a man's character may be–and Sherlock Holmes did not allow himself to be moved by reversals of fortune–there are nevertheless times when even such as he feel the need to marshall their forces before again rushing into battle.

"Today, I shall take a break," said Holmes.

"What about me?" asked Watson.

"You, old friend, must go and buy us fresh clothes to replace our wardrobe. Meanwhile, I shall rest."

"Yes, you rest, Holmes. I'll keep watch."

Watson uttered these words with all the importance of a sentry standing guard at an outpost, exposed to the worst dangers imaginable. He puffed out his chest and stiffened his sinews. With a sharp eye, he glanced around the small hotel bedroom where the two Englishmen had taken up residence.

"That's right, keep watch, Watson. Meanwhile, I'll draw up a new battle plan, better suited to the foe we're facing. You see, old friend, I'm afraid I underestimated Lupin. I must start afresh."

"But we've only got nine days left."

"That's five days more than I'll need."

The Detective spent the day in deep concentration, smoking in his room. The next morning, however, he was full of renewed energy.

"I'm ready now, Watson! Let's go! Take your best pair of shoes. We'll be doing some walking."

"I'm glad to hear it," said the Doctor, full of enthusiasm. "I've been on pins and needles!"

That morning, Holmes conducted three long interviews: first, with Maître Detinan, whose apartment he inspected thoroughly; then, with Suzanne Gerbois, whom he had telegraphed to come meet him and whom he questioned about the Blonde Phantom; and finally, with Sister Augusta, who had returned to the Convent of the Visitandines since the murder of Baron d'Hautrec.

During each interview, Watson kept watch outside.

"Are you satisfied?" he asked after each visit.

"Very satisfied," replied Holmes.

"I'm glad to hear it. I know we're on the right track."

They did a great deal of walking. They visited the two houses on either side of Baron d'Hautrec's mansion on the Avenue Henri-Martin, then they returned to Rue Clapeyron.

"It's obvious that there have to be secret passages between all these houses," Holmes said, while examining the front of No. 25. "But what I can't figure out…"

For the first time ever, deep in his heart, Watson began to doubt his friend's infallibility.

"With that Devil of a Frenchman," exclaimed Holmes, as if he had heard his friend's unspoken thoughts, "one has nothing to work with! Not a single clue! Instead of deriving the truth from precise facts, I must intuit first and verify afterwards if it is supported by the evidence."

"But about those secret passages?…"

"What about them? Even if I discovered their secret, if I knew how Lupin entered Maître Detinan's office, or how the Blonde Phantom left Baron d'Hautrec's house after the murder, would I be more advanced? Would that give me a weapon against Lupin?"

"I should think so, yes."

Watson had barely finished speaking when he jumped back with a cry. Something had come crashing down near their feet. It was a sandbag, which might have seriously injured them if it had landed upon their heads.

Holmes looked up: some men were working on a scaffolding hooked over the balcony of the fifth floor.

"We've been lucky," he said. "That bag missed us by barely a few feet. I hate to think what…"

Suddenly, he stopped, rushed into the house, ran up the stairs, rang the bell of the apartment on the fifth floor and burst into the place, much to the alarm of the butler who had opened the door. The Detective went out on the balcony. There was no one there.

"Where are the workmen who were here a moment ago?" he asked the butler.

"They've just left."

"How?"

"Down the service stairs."

Holmes leaned over the balcony. He saw two men leaving the building, riding away on their bicycles.

"Have they been working here long?"

"No. Only since this morning. They were new."

Holmes rejoined Watson in the street.

They went home feeling rather depressed. Their second day ended in silent gloom.

The next day, Holmes followed the same pattern. They retraced their steps, then sat on a bench on the Avenue Henri-Martin. Watson became so thoroughly bored by this endless watch over the same three houses that he finally broke the silence.

"What are you hoping for, Holmes? To see Lupin come out of one of them?"

"No."

"To catch sight of the Blonde Phantom?"

"Not that either."

"Then what?"

"I'm hoping for some small thing to happen, some tiny, little clue that will be like the light at the end of the tunnel."

"And if nothing of the sort happens?"

"It will. It must."

But the only incident that shattered the monotony of their morning watch turned out to be unpleasant.

A gentleman was riding along the bridal path that paralleled the Avenue. His horse suddenly swerved, striking the bench upon which the two Englishmen were sitting and smashing into Holmes' shoulder.

"Hey! Be careful!" exclaimed the Detective. "Your horse almost dislocated my shoulder!"

The rider was still struggling with his mount. Suddenly, Holmes drew his gun and took aim. But Watson immediately seized his arm.

"Holmes! What are you doing? You might kill that gentleman!"

"Let go, Watson! Let go!"

While they wrestled, the horseman regained control of his horse and galloped away.

"I don't understand! You could have hurt than man" said Watson, with a reproachful look.

"That man, you confounded fool, was one of Lupin's men!" snarled the Detective.

Watson's jaw dropped.

"I… I never thought," he stammered pitifully.

"You cost us an opportunity to further our investigation!"

"Surely not by shooting that man?"

"Not the man! His horse! The two of us could then have captured him and interrogated him. But thanks to you, he's escaped."

That afternoon, too, was morose. Holmes and Watson barely spoke to each other. At 5 p.m., as they were pacing up and down the Rue Clapeyron, while taking care to remain at a distance from the suspect houses, three young workers who were walking and singing arm-in-arm collided with them and tried to keep going without separating. Holmes, who was in a bad temper, rebuffed them. Shouts were exchanged, followed by a short scuffle. The Detective put up his fists, struck one of the louts in the chest and another in the face. The two men desisted and walked away with their companion.

"I feel much better now," said Holmes. "I was feeling a little tense…. A good bit of business…"

But then, he saw Watson leaning against the wall, looking pale.

"Watson!" he exclaimed. "What's wrong? You look sick."

His friend showed him his arm which was hanging limply by his side.

"I'm not sure," he stammered. "It's my arm…"

"Does it hurt much?"

"Yes. I think it's broken."

Despite all his efforts, Watson could not move the injured limb. Holmes felt it gently at first, then a little more roughly, and upon hearing Watson's sharp cries, agreed that his friend's diagnosis was accurate. He helped Watson lean against him and, together, they hobbled to a nearby pharmacist. There, Watson was invited to lie down and given a mild pain-killer.

The pharmacist immediately sent his assistant to fetch a doctor, who arrived promptly and confirmed that Watson's arm had indeed been broken in several places. The physician recommended a surgeon and a local hospital.

While arrangements were being made to transport the unfortunate Watson, Holmes sat by his friend's side, trying to relieve his suffering.

"You'll be all right, old friend," he said, patting Watson's hand. "Just a little patience… The doctor said that in five or six weeks, you won't know you've been hurt… Don't worry, I'll make those thugs pay for this… *Him*, especially, for I'm certain it's that wretched Lupin who sent those men! I swear to you that I shall…"

Suddenly, he stopped in mid-sentence, dropped Watson's hand and struck his forehead.

"Watson! I've got it! Could it be?…" He stood still, his eyes fixed before him, muttering short sentences. "Yes, of course, that's it! It's all clear now! It's been staring us in the face! I knew it was only a matter of time… Ah, my dear Watson, I'm going to justify the faith you've placed in me!"

And upon saying that, the Detective left his friend's bedside, rushed out into the street and ran towards No. 25.

As is the custom in France, one of the stones above the doorway, on the right, bore the name of the building's architect. It read: *"Destange, Architect. 1875."*

The same inscription appeared at No. 23.

*All very innocent,* thought the Detective. *But what about Avenue Henri-Martin?*

Holmes hailed a passing cab.

"Driver, No. 134, Avenue Henri-Martin! And hurry!"

During the drive, he urged the driver to go faster, promising him a handsome tip.

He was in agony when the cab turned the corner of the Rue de la Pompe. Had he at last caught a glimpse of the truth?

On one of Baron d'Hautrec's house's keystones, he read: *"Destange, Architect. 1874."*

And on the adjacent buildings, he similarly saw: *"Destange, Architect. 1875."*

Holmes' reaction to this exciting discovery was so great that he sank back into his seat inside the cab for a few minutes, trembling with joy. At last, the light at the end of the tunnel! He had finally picked up his enemy's trail amidst the thousand intersecting paths that crisscrossed the vast and mysterious forest that was Paris.

He had the driver drop him at a nearby Post Office and there, asked to make a telephone call to the chateau of Crozon. The Comtesse herself answered.

"Hello, is that you, Madame?"

"Mister Holmes! How are things going?"

"Supremely well, Madame. I shan't keep you long. I just need a small bit of information that you might supply..."

"Of course. What is it?"

"When was your chateau built?"

"Well, it was burnt down 30 years ago, then rebuilt..."

"I see. Would you know by whom, and when?"

"There's an inscription over the front door. It says: '*Lucien Destange, achitect. 1877.*' "

"Thank you, Madame. That's all I needed to know."

Holmes left the Post Office muttering: "Destange... Lucien Destange... I've seen that name somewhere, but where?..."

He went to a Public Library and consulted several biographical dictionaries until he found what he sought: "*Lucien Destange, born 1840, Grand Prix of Rome, Officer of the Légion d'Honneur, author of several major works on modern architecture including...*"

Holmes then returned to the pharmacy where he had left Watson and discovered that his friend had, in the meantime, been taken to the local hospital. He went there and found the unfortunate Watson lying in bed, with his arm in a splint, shivering with fever.

"My poor Watson," said the Detective. "But take heart. We're one step nearer victory. I found the clue..."

"What clue?"

"The clue that will help me unravel Lupin's web, old friend!"

"Cigarette ashes? Blood stains?" asked Watson, who was slightly delirious.

"No. I finally found the connection between the three houses, between the three crimes that involved the Blonde Phantom, the reason why those three locations were specifically chosen by Lupin."

"They were?"

"Yes, Watson, because all three houses, and the adjacent buildings were built by the same architect! It was easy to find out, and yet no one else thought about it."

"No one but you, Holmes."

"Just so! And now I understand how the same architect, by contriving similar plans, made it possible to carry out these seemingly miraculous crimes in three totally different locations."

"And no one thought of it..."

"It was high time, too, old friend. I was growing impatient. This is Day Four."

"Out of ten."

"But now I'm certain of my success." Holmes paced up and down the room, exulting in his triumph, completely absorbed by the challenge, somewhat oblivious to his friend's suffering. "When I think that those ruffians earlier might have succeeded in incapacitating me just as they did you... That would have been too terrible to contemplate..."

"Just awful," said the compassionate Watson who knew his friend too well to take umbrage at this.

"Let this be a lesson, Watson," Holmes continued. "Our greatest mistake has been to fight Lupin openly, to obligingly expose ourselves to his blows, to make it easy for him to attack us..."

"And have my arm broken."

"They might have done worse. Still, more discretion is now warranted. Alone, in broad daylight, in public, I'm condemned to fail. Working freely, in obscurity, I shall win—whatever Lupin's resources might be."

"Ganimard might be able to help you."

"I don't think so! But the day I can call him and say, 'Here is Arsène Lupin, here is his lair, and here is how to capture him,' then I shall call him, either at the Prefecture of Police or at his home on Rue Pergolèse, since he kindly gave me his number there as well—or perhaps at the Swiss Tavern on the Place du Châtelet, which he seems to often frequent! But until then, I'll act alone."

Holmes went over to the bed and put his hand on Watson's shoulder.

"Take care of yourself, old friend," he said with affection in his voice. "Your job from now on will be to keep Lupin's accomplices, who undoubtedly watch this place, busy. Make them believe that you're waiting for me to drop by to inquire after you, tell the nurses that you're expecting me, and they'll redouble their vigilance."

"I shall do my best, Holmes," Watson replied. "But I suppose... this means I shan't see you until after this wretched case is over?"

"Indeed, it does, old friend. But you understand why that must be?"

"Yes, yes… You're quite right, of course... Besides, I'm getting on as well as can be expected… Holmes, can I bother you for one last thing?"

"Of course, Watson. What is it?"

"Could you get me a glass of water? I feel parched."

"Naturally. Let me see…"

The Detective fumbled about looking for a glass, then for a jar of water. Not finding any, he left the ward in search of a nurse. He wandered around the corridors for a while, but then, suddenly, he was struck by an idea. Without thinking, he put the glass on a shelf and rushed out of the hospital. Watson, knowing his friend and not seeing him return, sighed and rang for the nurse.


"I'm here to see Monsieur Destange,"

The butler eyed the person to whom he had just opened the door of the home–a magnificent house located at the corner of the Place Malesherbes and the Rue Montchanin. He was a grey-haired, ill-shaven man wearing a long, black and rather spotty coat, which poorly hid an oddly misshapen body.

"Monsieur Destange may not be in," replied the butler with appropriate scorn. "Do you have a card?"

The stranger had no card, only a letter of introduction. The butler took it to Monsieur Destange, who read it and ordered the newcomer to be shown in.

He was ushered into a large, circular room, lined with books on all the walls, which occupied one of the wings of the house.

"Are you Mister Strickmann?" inquired Monsieur Destange.

"I am, sir."

"My personal secretary writes that he has been taken ill and has sent you to continue the cataloguing of the books in my library, which he had begun under my supervision–in particular, the German books. Have you any experience with this sort of work?"

"Yes, sir, a long experience," replied Strickmann with a discernible German accent.

The matter was soon settled and Monsieur Destange quickly set to work with his new secretary.

Sherlock Holmes was now inside his enemy's position.

To escape Lupin's constant surveillance and in order to gain entrance, without being observed, to the house that Monsieur Destange occupied with his daughter Clotilde, the Detective had been obliged to employ a variety of cunning stratagems and to win the favor and confidence of various people under a series of fake identities; in short, he had spent two of the most complex days of his prodigious life.

However, he was now in possession of the following information: Monsieur Destange, who was in failing health and in need of rest, had retired and now devoted all of his time to his hobby: collecting old architectural books. He had no other interests in life.

His daughter, Clotilde, had the reputation of being an eccentric. Like her father, she spent all her time in the house–in another wing–and rarely went out.

As Holmes wrote book title after book title under Monsieur Destange's dictation, he thought: *This isn't much, but at least, it's a step in the right direction. I'm bound to find out whether Destange is Lupin's accomplice, or his dupe. Does he see him now? Are there any plans relating to the three houses? If so, they might lead me to other houses, similarly faked, which Lupin may be reserving for his own use or that of his gang...*

The Detective was the first to acknowledge that the notion of the venerable Monsieur Destange, Officer of the Legion d'Honneur, as one of Lupin's accomplices was preposterous. Besides, how could the architect have planned for Lupin's various escapes 30 years earlier, when the Gentleman Burglar was still in his cradle?

Nevertheless, Holmes persevered because logic told him that the key to the entire case was in this house. He felt an aura of mystery surrounding him. Small, almost imperceptible signs which had impressed him from the moment he had set foot inside the Destange house, minute clues that he would have been at pains to describe precisely, but which he knew were unmistakable signals that he was nearing the truth.

Yet, on the morning of his second day, he realized he had as yet uncovered nothing of real substance. At 2 p.m., for the first time, he met Clotilde Destange when she came to fetch a book from the library. She was a woman of 30, dark-haired, with quiet and measured gestures. Her face bore the indifferent look of those who live mostly an inner life. She exchanged a few, banal words with her father and left without paying any notice to "Mister Strickmann."

The afternoon dragged on monotonously. At 5 p.m., Monsieur Destange announced that he was going out. Holmes remained alone on the circular catwalk that encircled the library, half-way between floor and ceiling. It was growing dark and the Detective was about to leave, too, when unexpectedly he heard a creaking sound. At the same time, he felt he was no longer alone in the room. Several, long minutes went by. Holmes did not dare to make a sound. Suddenly, he shuddered. A shadow had emerged from the semi-darkness, not far from him, near the balcony. How long had the mysterious figure been there? Or alternatively, where did he come from?

The man walked down a few steps and moved towards a large oak filing cabinet. In an effort to see better, Holmes got to his knees, while hiding behind the drapes that hung from the ceiling. He saw the man rummage amongst the papers with which the cabinet was crammed. What was he looking for?

Suddenly, the door opened. Clotilde Destange walked in quickly, talking to someone behind her.

"So you've changed your mind about going out, Papa?" she was saying. "In that case, I'll turn on the lights. Wait here, give me a minute…"

The man closed the filing cabinet and hid himself in the embrasure of a French window, drawing the curtains behind him. How could the young woman not see him? How could she not hear him? She calmly turned on the electric lights and stood back for her father to enter. They sat down side by side. Clotilde opened a book which she had brought with her and began to read.

"Has your secretary gone?" she said after a while.

"Er, yes... So it seems..."

"Are you still happy with him?" she asked, as if she did not know of the real secretary's illness and the arrival of "Mister Strickmann."

"Yes, very."

Monsieur Destange's head began to droop. Finally, he fell asleep in his chair.

A moment elapsed. The young woman went on reading. But presently, the curtain was moved aside and the man stepped out. He slipped along the wall towards the door, an action which made him pass behind the architect, but right in front of Clotilde. This time, Holmes was able to identify him. It was Arsène Lupin!

The Detective felt a rush of joy. His deductions were correct. He had penetrated into the very heart of the mystery! Lupin was exactly where he had expected to find him.

Clotilde Destange, however, did not stir; yet, it was impossible for her to not have noticed Lupin. The Gentleman Burglar had almost reached the door, his hand was about to grasp the handle, when suddenly a book fell to the ground. Monsieur Destange woke with a start. In a moment, Lupin stood before him, smiling, hat in hand.

"Maxime Bermond!" exclaimed the architect with joy. "My dear Maxime! What stroke of good luck brings you here?"

"The wish to see you, and Mademoiselle Destange."

"So at last, you've returned from your travels."

"I arrived yesterday."

"You will stay for dinner, of course?"

"I'm afraid I can't. Tonight, I'm dining out with some friends."

"Well, then, what about tomorrow? Clotilde, ask him to come. My dear Maxime! I was thinking of you only the other day..."

"Really?"

"Yes, I was filing some of our old papers away in that filing cabinet and I came across our last job..."

"Which one?"

"Avenue Henri-Martin's."

"Why do you keep all those old files? You should throw them into the waste basket and make yourself some room."

The three moved into a small drawing room adjacent to the library.

*Is it Lupin? Is it really* him*?* thought Holmes, suddenly seized by doubt.

Yes, all the evidence shouted that "Maxime Bermont" was indeed Lupin, and yet he was also another man, a man who did resemble Lupin in some respects, but who also was very different from him in others–a man who had his own individuality, his own features, his own looks...

Clad in formal dinner jacket, with a white tie and a tight silk shirt, Bermond talked cheerfully, telling stories that made Monsieur Destange laugh and brought a smile to his daughter's lips. And each of these smiles was like a reward Lupin sought and enjoyed. His verve and gaiety increased and, slowly, at the sound of his clear and happy voice, Clotilde's face brightened and began losing its earlier look of severity that made her seem cold and unattractive.

*She's in love with him*, thought Holmes. *That much is clear. But what about him? What is the nature of their relationship? Does she know that Maxime Bermond is none other than Arsène Lupin?*

The Englishman stayed until 7 p.m., anxiously listening to every word of the conversation. Then, taking great precautions to not be overheard, he snuck down, exited the library and left the house.

Once outside, Holmes, after checking that there was no motorcar or cab waiting, limped away along the Boulevard Malesherbes. Then, he turned down a side street, put on the overcoat which he carried over his arm, changed the shape of his hat, straightened himself up and, thus transformed, returned to the square where he waited, his eyes fixed upon the door of the Destange house.

Arsène Lupin came out almost at once and walked down the Rue de Contantinople and the Rue de Londres towards the center of Paris. Holmes followed him at a hundred yards' distance.

This was an exhilarating moment for the Detective. He sniffed the air as intently as a hunting dog on a fresh trail. It was an enormously pleasant feeling to be the one following Arsène Lupin, the uncatchable Arsène Lupin, instead of the other way around. By never letting his prey out of his sight, the Englishman felt that he was virtually keeping him on an invisible and yet unbreakable leash. And he reveled in watching, amongst the other pedestrians, the elegant figure of the man who would soon be his prisoner.

But soon, he noticed a curious phenomenon: other people seemed to be following Lupin, weaving in and out of the crowd between him and his prey. In particular, he noticed two tall men on the left sidewalk wearing bowler hats, and two others, wearing caps and smoking cigarettes, on the right.

At first, Holmes thought this might be merely a coincidence. But he observed that all four men stopped when Lupin entered a tobacconist's, then started again as he came out, all the while each remaining on their side of the Chausée d'Antin.

*Damn!* thought Holmes. *He's already being shadowed!*

The idea that others might be on the Gentleman Burglar's trail exasperated him. Who were they who might rob him not of the glory–he cared little for that!–but of the intense pleasure of single-handedly defeating the most formidable enemy he had ever encountered? Yet, there was no possibility of a mistake: all four men had that studied, nonchalant expression that is all too characteristic of people who try to remain inconspicuous while secretly following someone else.

*Could Ganimard know more than he told me?* thought the Detective. *Is he trying to embarrass me?*

The Englishman felt tempted to talk to one of the four men to find out if they were agents of the Sûreté, but as they approached the boulevards, the crowds grew denser and he became afraid of losing Lupin. He increased his pace and caught up with the Gentleman Burglar just as he was about to step into the *Restaurant Hongrois* at the corner of the Rue du Helder. The door remained open and Holmes, sitting on a bench on the other side of the street, saw Lupin sit down at a table lavishly decorated with flowers. Three men and two women, all dressed in fine evening clothes, were already there waiting for him and greeted him warmly.

Holmes then looked for the four men whom he presumed to be Sûreté agents and noticed them in a café next door, listening to Gypsy music. Strangely, they no longer seemed so much interested in Lupin as in the people surrounding them.

Suddenly, one of them took a cigarette from a case and addressed another gentleman in a coat and tall hat. The man offered him a light, but Holmes had the impression that they were talking far longer than the mere lighting of a cigarette demanded. At last, the man went out and glanced into the restaurant next door. Seeing Lupin, he walked up to him, exchanged a few words and finally sat down at a nearby table. Holmes recognized him at last: he was the horseman that had tried to injure him on Avenue Henri-Martin!

Now, the Detective understood. These men were not Ganimard's men but Lupin's! The Gentleman Burglar was not followed but escorted. These were his bodyguards, his vigilant guardians. Wherever their master was exposed to any danger, his accomplices were there, ready to warn him or to protect him. The four men and the gentleman in the tall hat were all members of Lupin's gang!

Holmes experienced a retrospective shiver, thinking that he might have given himself away. But would he ever succeed in capturing a man so well guarded? The power implied by such a praetorian-like guard, at the service of such a master, was awe-inspiring.

After a moment of reflection, the Detective wrote a few lines on a page of his notebook, tore it off and gave it and five francs to a 15-year-old boy who had just sat down on the bench.

"Here, lad. Find a cab and take this note to the Swiss Tavern on the Place du Châtelet. Give it to the lady behind the cashier's desk. Be quick as you can."

The boy took off.

A half-hour went by. The crowd had grown even more voluminous and Holmes only occasionally caught sight of Lupin and his associates.

Suddenly, someone tapped him lightly on the shoulder.

"Mister Holmes? Is that you?" a voice whispered in his ear.

"Yes, Chief Inspector, it is I," said the Englishman to Ganimard, who stood behind him. "I see that you've received my note."

"Yes, I got it. What is it?"

"*He*'s there."

"You don't mean?…"

"I do. Over there. Inside the *Restaurant Hongrois*. A little to the right. Do you see him now?"

"No."

"He's pouring some champagne to the lady on his left."

"But that's not *him*!"

"Yes, it is."

"I assure you that… And yet… I suppose it could be him… Ah, the rascal! *How like himself he is*!" muttered Ganimard candidly. "And who are the others? Accomplices?"

"Not at his table. The woman beside him is Lady Cliveden. The other is the Duchess of Cleath. Opposite him is the Spanish Ambassador to London."

Ganimard stepped forward. Holmes held him back.

"Don't be so reckless, Chief Inspector. You're alone."

"So is he."

"Not so. He has four men on the boulevard watching him. Plus one more fellow inside the restaurant."

"But I only have to grab him by the collar and shout his name and the whole restaurant will rush to lend me assistance…"

"I would rather have a few detectives."

"That would alert his men. I'm afraid we don't have any choice here, Mister Holmes…"

He was right and the Detective knew it. It was an extraordinary opportunity not to be missed. Still, the Englishman felt the need to further advise Ganimard.

"Do your best not to be recognized until the last minute."

He himself slipped behind a newsstand, never losing sight of Arsène Lupin, who was presently leaning over Lady Cliveden, smiling.

Ganimard crossed the street, his hands in his pocket, looking straight ahead. But just as he stepped onto the opposite sidewalk, there was the sound of a shrill whistle…

As the Chief Inspector stepped into the restaurant, he collided into the Maître d' who had appeared as if out of nowhere and suddenly blocked his way. The man pushed him back indignantly as he would have, in fact, repelled any intruder whose dubious attire might have disgraced the luxury of such an establishment. Ganimard staggered back. At that same moment, the man in the tall hat came out. He took the part of the policeman and a fierce argument ensued between him and the Maître d'. Both of them had grabbed Ganimard; one was pushing him forward, the other back. Finally, despite all his efforts to get through, the hapless Chief Inspector was soundly hustled out of the restaurant.

Outside, a crowd had gathered. Two policemen moved in to investigate and tried to make their way through, but encountered an inexplicable resistance. They were unable to get clear of the shoulders pushing against them or the backs blocking their way.

And suddenly, as if by magic, the way was clear. The Maître d', realizing his mistake, made the most abject apologies; the man in the tall hat left and vanished into the crowd, which dispersed and melted away. Ganimard, followed by the two policemen, went inside and rushed towards Lupin's table. But now there were only five guests! The Chief Inspector looked around. There seemed to be no other way out except through the front door.

"Where is the man who was sitting here?" he asked the five bewildered guests. "Yes, there were six of you. Where is the sixth person?"

"You mean, Monsieur Destro?"

"I mean, Arsène Lupin!"

A waiter stepped up.

"The gentleman went up to the mezzanine floor," he said.

Ganimard rushed upstairs. The mezzanine floors consisted of private dining rooms and had a separate exit to the boulevard.

"We'll never catch him," groaned the Chief Inspector. "He's too far away by now!"

In fact, Lupin was not that far away. He was only about 200 yards distant, in the Madeleine-Bastille omnibus which lumbered peacefully along behind its three horses, crossing the Place de l'Opera, going down the Boulevard des Capucines. The two tall men in bowler hats stood talking on the conductor's platform. On the top, near the stairs, an old man sat dozing.

It was Sherlock Holmes.

His head swayed from side to side along with the pace of the vehicle. *If only Watson could see me now*, he thought. *How proud he would be. As soon as I heard that whistle, I knew that Ganimard's plan was doomed. The only thing left to do, then, was to keep an eye on the back of the restaurant. But I'll say this, that Devil of a man knows how to keep one busy!*

As the omnibus reached the end of its route, Holmes leaned over. When Lupin walked past his men, he heard him whisper: "To the Etoile."

*The Etoile is the next rendezvous, then*, thought the Detective. *I shall be there. But I'd better let him go ahead in that motor cab. I'll follow his two men instead.*

The pair went off on foot and eventually made it to the Rond-Point de l'Etoile and, from there, went into No. 40, Rue Chalrgin, a small, narrow house located in an undistinguished side street. Holmes was able to hide himself in the shadow of a recess formed by the angle of the street.

One of the two windows on the ground-floor opened. A man in a bowler hat closed the shutters. But almost at once, a light went on behind them.

Ten minutes later, another man came and went into the house, soon followed by yet another man. Finally, the motor cab showed up and two people got out: Arsène Lupin and a woman wrapped in a cloak and wearing a thick veil.

*The Blonde Phantom, I presume*, thought Holmes, as the cab drove away.

The Detective waited for a moment, then went up to the house, climbed onto the window sill and, by standing on tiptoe, managed to look into the room through the interstice above the shutters.

Arsène Lupin was leaning against the mantelpiece of the fireplace and was talking in an animated fashion. The others stood around him, listening attentively. Holmes recognized the man in the tall hat, and the Maître d' from the Restaurant. As for the Blonde Phantom, she sat in a chair, her back turned towards him.

*They're holding a council*, thought the Englishman. *The night's events must have alarmed Lupin. He must be reviewing all his precautions. Ah, if I could only catch them all in one fell swoop!*

One of the men left. Holmes immediately jumped down to the ground and rushed back to hide in the recess. The man in the tall hat left next, soon followed by the Maître d'. Then, the first floor lights were turned off and someone closed the shutters. It was now dark, both upstairs and downstairs.

*Lupin and the Blonde Phantom must have remained on the ground floor*, theorized Holmes. *The men in the bowler hat live upstairs.*

Holmes waited during a good part of the night without stirring from his hide-out, fearing that Arsène Lupin might leave unnoticed during his absence. At 4 a.m., however, noticing two policemen at the end of the street, he went up to them, introduced himself, explained the situation and left them to watch the house.

Then he went to Ganimard's home, on the Rue Pergolese, and told the Chief Inspector's servant to wake up his master.

"I've got him again!" said Holmes when Ganimard showed up.

"Arsène Lupin?"

"Yes."

"If you've got him the way you got him last time, I might as well go back to bed. Still, let's go to the station..."

They went to Rue Mesnil, and from there to the residence of Police Commissioner Decointre. Having secured a force of six men, they then proceeded to the Rue Chalgrin.

"Any news?" Holmes asked the two policemen he had left watching the house.

"No, sir, none."

Dawn was beginning to break. Commissioner Decointre, having positioned his men, finally rang the bell and entered the Concierge's loge. Terrified by this intrusion, the poor woman, all trembling, said that there was no tenant on the ground-floor.

"What do you mean, no tenants?" said Ganimard.

"Well, the people from the first floor–two gentlemen called Leroux–they've furnished it and sometimes, they use it to accommodate some relatives from the country..."

"A lady and a gentleman?"

"Yes."

"Were they here last night?"

"I don't know, I was asleep... They may have... Although I don't think so, because I've got the key and they didn't ask to borrow it."

With the key, the Commissioner opened the door of the apartment, across the hallway, opposite the Concierge's loge. It contained only two rooms and they were both empty.

"Impossible!" said Holmes. "I saw them together, here, last night!"

"I dare say," the Commissioner said with heavy irony, "but they're not here now, are they?"

"Let's go to the first floor. They might be there."

"The first floor is rented by the Leroux."

"Let's ask them."

They all went upstairs and the Commissioner rang. At the second ring, a man, who was none other than one of Lupin's two bodyguards, came out, dressed in shirt sleeves and looking angry.

"What is it? What's all this ruckus? What are you waking people up for" But suddenly, he stopped and his face took an air of confusion. "Good Heavens! I must be dreaming! It's Commissioner Decointre! And Monsieur Ganimard, too! What can I do for you, gentlemen?"

Ganimard burst out laughing, soon followed by Decointre. The Chief Inspector was laughing so hard his eyes were tearing.

"So it's you, Leroux?" he spluttered out. "That's the funniest thing I've heard so far. Victor Leroux, Arsène Lupin's accomplice... Oh dear! It'll be the death of me! And where's your brother, Leroux? Is he here?"

"Yes, of course, Chief Inspector. I'll call him. Edmond! It's Monsieur Ganimard who's come to pay us a visit!"

Another man came forward. Upon seeing him, Ganimard's hilarity redoubled.

"Well, well, well! My dear Leroux, you could be in a bit of a pickle now if I wasn't here to vouch for you... Who would have thought it possible?... It's a good thing that your old friend Ganimard is around... Don't worry about a thing now, it's all a misunderstanding that will soon be cleared up..."

He then turned towards Holmes.

"Mister Holmes, let me introduce you to Monsieur Victor Leroux, Inspector of the Sûreté, one of the elite of what we call our 'iron brigade.' And this is his brother, Edmond, who works as head clerk in our Anthropometric Section."

## *Kidnapped*

Sherlock Holmes remained silent. What would be the use of protesting? Of accusing the brothers Leroux? Short of evidence, which he did not have, it would be a waste of time and no one would believe him.

Angry, fists clenched, he had but one thought: to not betray his fury and disappointment before the triumphant Ganimard. He respectfully saluted those two faithful protectors of society, the brothers Leroux, and walked downstairs.

In the hallway, he spotted a door that led to the cellar and, on the floor, next to it, found a small garnet stone.

Outside, Holmes looked up and, unsurprisingly, read close to the number of the house the inscription: "*Lucien Destange, architect, 1877.*"

The same inscription adorned No. 42.

*Again, there must be a secret passage between No. 40 and No. 42*, he thought. *Why didn't I think of that last night? I should have stayed here...*

"Did two people leave No. 40 while I was gone? He asked the two policemen who had stood guard, pointing to the neighboring house.

"Yes, sir. A man and a woman."

As Ganimard came out, Holmes took his arm and led him along.

"Chief Inspector, you've had too much fun at my expense to be upset with me for having dragged you out of bed in the middle of the night."

"I'm not upset with you in the least, Mister Holmes."

"Excellent. Then you agree with me that this charade has gone on for too long. I think it's time to wrap it all up."

"I agree."

"Today is my seventh day in Paris. I must be in London in three days…"

"I say!"

"…And I fully intend to be there. Therefore, I'm asking you to be on call on Tuesday night."

"For an expedition of the same kind?" asked Ganimard with a note of irony.

"You might say that."

"And what might we hope to achieve then?"

"Nothing less than the arrest of Arsène Lupin."

"Do you really believe that?"

"I will stake my honor on it."

Holmes took his leave and went to take a short rest in a nearby hotel. Afterwards, feeling refreshed and confident again, he returned to Rue Chalgrin. He gave two *louis* to the Concierge, learned that the house belonged to one Monsieur Harmingeat, made sure that the Leroux were gone and, lighting his way with a candle, found his way down to the cellar through the small door near which he had found the garnet stone.

At the bottom of the stairs, he picked up another of the same size and shape.

*I was right,* thought the Detective. *This is where the secret passage is… I wonder if my skeleton key will open the section of the cellar which is reserved for the ground-floor tenant… Yes, it does! Excellent… Now to take a closer look at that wine rack… Aha! Here are places where the dust has been removed… And there are footprints on the ground…*

Suddenly, Holmes heard a slight sound. Immediately, he closed the door, blew out his candle and hid behind a pile of empty crates. After a few seconds, he observed that one of the wine racks was rotating slowly on a pivot, along with the wall which supported it. He then saw the light of a lantern, followed by an arm holding said lantern, and finally a man came through the opening.

He was crouching over, as if looking for something he might have dropped. He sifted through the dust with his fingers; several times, he picked up something which he deposited in a cardboard box he carried in his other hand. Then, he attempted to erase any traces of his passage, as well as the footprints left earlier by Lupin and the Blonde Phantom.

As he was about to enter the secret passage again, Holmes jumped on him. The man fell with a hoarse cry. In less than a minute, the Detective had him stretched on the floor, his wrists and ankles bound with a thin wire.

"I'll pay you to tell me everything you know," said the Englishman. "How much do you want?"

The man said nothing but smiled with such mockery that Holmes realized he would get nowhere with bribery.

The Detective searched his captive's pockets and found a key ring filled with keys, a handkerchief and the little cardboard box that contained a dozen garnet stones similar to those Holmes had picked up.

He pondered what to do with the man. Wait until his friends came to his rescue, capture them all and deliver them to the Police? What would be the use? How would that help him capture Arsène Lupin?

He was still considering his options when he noticed that the box bore the name of a jeweler: *Monsieur Leonard, Rue de la Paix*.

Holmes decided to simply leave the man where he was. He pushed the wine rack back and locked the cellar behind him. He then left the house. At a nearby Post Office, he sent a telegram to Monsieur Destange to let him know that he could not come to work until the next day. Then, he went on to the jeweler and handed him the garnets.

"Madame sent me with these stones," he said. "They came off a piece of jewelry she bought here."

The Englishman had hit the nail on the head.

"That's right," replied Monsieur Leonard. "The lady telephoned me. She'll be here presently."

At 5 p.m., Holmes, who had been standing guard on the sidewalk, saw a woman arrive. She was wrapped in a thick veil and her whole appearance struck him as suspicious. Through the store window, he saw her place an old piece of jewelry set with garnets on the counter.

She left right away, did a few errands on foot, walked towards Clichy and down other streets with which the Detective was unfamiliar. At nightfall, he followed her, unnoticed by any Concierge, into a five-story apartment complex comprised of two separate buildings on either side of a central courtyard and therefore housing numerous tenants. She stopped at a door on the second floor and entered.

Two minutes later, Holmes decided to try his luck. He carefully tried all the keys on the key ring which he had taken from the man in the cellar of the Rue Chalgrin. The fourth key fit the lock.

Through the darkness that filled the apartment, he saw a series of rooms which were totally empty, with their doors open, like those of an unoccupied residence. But he noticed a dim light at the end of a corridor. He silently tip-toed towards it; it was a glass door, leading into a small bedroom, with a one-way mirror facing the bedroom. The Detective arrived in time to observe the veiled woman take off her dress and hat and lay them on the single chair inside the room. Then she put on a red velvet dressing gown.

She walked towards the fireplace and pushed the electric bell once, then twice. Immediately, one half of the wall to the right of the fireplace moved back and slid into a space built inside the other half.

As soon as the entrance was wide enough, the woman walked through it and disappeared, taking the lamp with her.

The working of the secret passage was simple; Holmes had no trouble following her.

He found himself in the dark, groping to find his way. His hands felt something soft. By the light of a match, he saw that he was in a closet filled with dresses and clothes hanging on coat hangers. He made his way through it and stopped before the outline of a door covered with a tapestry, or more accurately the back of a tapestry. Holmes' match had gone out but he realized he could see into the other room through the loose and worn threads of the tapestry.

The Blonde Phantom was there, in front of his very eyes, almost within his grasp.

She put out her lamp and turned on the electric lights. For the first time, Sherlock Holmes was able to see her face. He could not repress a shiver. The woman whom he had finally unmasked after so many false leads and misadventures was none other than Clotilde Destange!

Clotilde Destange, the murderess of Baron d'Hautrec, who had stolen the Blue Diamond! Clotilde Destange, Arsène Lupin's mysterious mistress! Clotile Destange–the Blonde Phantom!

*Of course,* he thought. *What an idiot I've been! Just because Lupin's mistress was blonde and Clotilde a brunette, I never thought of connecting the two. As if the Blonde Phantom could remain blonde after the Baron's murder and the theft of the Blue Diamond!*

Holmes could see part of the room: an elegant boudoir decorated with light-colored drapes and precious *objets d'art*. A mahogany settee stood on a slightly raised platform. Clotilde had sat down on it and remained still, her head between her hands. Holmes noticed that she was crying. Tears flowed down her pale cheeks, trickled on her lips and fell, a drop at a time, on her velvet gown. The source of her tears seemed inexhaustible. There was no sadder sight than the dull and quiet despair expressed by the slow, endless flow of her tears.

Suddenly, the door opened. Arsène Lupin walked in.

They looked at each other for a long time, without exchanging a word. Then, he knelt down beside her, pressed his head to her chest and embraced her with his arms. There was infinite tenderness and great mercy in that embrace. They remained still. A soft silence united them, and her tears finally stopped.

"I so wanted to make you happy," he whispered.

"But I am happy."

"No, you're crying. And your tears break my heart, Clotilde."

Almost despite herself, she allowed the sound of his soft voice to comfort her, hungry for hope and happiness. A small, sad smile appeared on her face.

"Don't be sad, Clotilde," he begged her. "You shouldn't be. You have no reason to be."

She showed him her delicate, white hands.

"As long as these hands are mine, Maxime," she said, gravely, "I shall be sad."

"But why?"

"Because they're the hands of a killer."

"Hush!" he exclaimed. "You mustn't think of that! The past is gone, it no longer matters."

He kissed her long, white hands and she looked at him with a brighter smile, as if each of his kisses was removing a portion of the blot of her hideous memories.

"You must love me, Maxime," she said. "You must because no other woman will ever love you as I do. To please you, I have done things, I am still doing things–not only obeying your orders, but also your deepest, unspoken wishes. I have done things against which all my instincts rebel, my conscience revolts, but I cannot resist you... All that I do, I do mechanically, because it is of use to you and because you wish me to do it... And I'm ready to do it again tomorrow, and always."

"Ah, Clotilde," he replied bitterly. "Why did I ever involve you in my adventurous life? I should have remained the Maxime Bermond whom you fell in love with five years ago and never shown you... the other man I am."

"I love that other man, too," she whispered. "And I regret nothing."

"Yes, you do. You regret your earlier life, your life in the public eye."

"I regret nothing when you're with me," she said, passionately. "There is no guilt, there are no crimes when I see you. What do I care if I'm miserable apart from you, if I suffer

114

and loathe all that I do for you! My love redeems it all! I accept everything… But you must love me!"

"I don't love you because I have to, Clotilde, but simply because I do."

"Are you telling me the truth?" she asked, trustingly.

"Yes. I'm as sure of my feelings as I am of yours. But my life is violent and tumultuous and I can't always give you as much time as I would like."

Immediately, she became very concerned.

"What is it? A new threat? Please, tell me!"

"Nothing too serious yet. Still…"

"What?"

"He's on my trail."

"Who?"

"Sherlock Holmes. It was he who sent Ganimard into the Restaurant Hongrois. It was he who posted two policemen outside the house on the Rue Chalgrin. Ganimard searched it this morning and Holmes was with him. And…"

"And what?"

"…And one of our men is missing. Jeanniot."

"The concierge?"

"Yes."

"I sent him to the Rue Chalgrin this morning to pick up some garnets that had fallen off my bracelet."

"He must have fallen into one of Holmes' traps."

"But how can that be? The garnets were returned to the jeweler on the Rue de la Paix?"

"Yet, Jeanniot remains missing."

"Maxime! I'm afraid!"

"No reason to be, yet. But I admit that the situation is worrisome. What does Holmes know? Where is he? His strength is his isolation. No one, nothing can betray him."

"What do you plan to do?"

"To be exceedingly cautious, Clotilde. For a while, now, I've decided to wrap up my operations here in Paris and move my headquarters to that inviolate refuge I'm the only one to know.[6] Holmes' intervention only hastens the need. When a man like him is on a trail, he is bound to follow it to its logical end. He will discover everything; it's only a matter of time. So, the move will take place the day after tomorrow, Wednesday. At noon, it will all be over. By 2 p.m., I shall myself be able to leave, after getting rid of the last traces of our activities, which is no small job. Until then..."

"Until then?"

"...We must not see each other again, Clotilde. Don't go out. I fear nothing for myself, but I fear everything where you're concerned."

"It's impossible for that Englishman to get to me."

"Don't think that. Everything is possible for Sherlock Holmes. I'm worried. Yesterday, when I was nearly caught by your father, when I was trying to remove his old ledgers, I felt a danger surrounding me. There's danger everywhere. I feel him lurking in the shadows, drawing ever closer... I feel him watching us... laying his traps around us... It's one of these intuitions that have never failed me before."

"In that case, go, Maxime!" she said. "Ignore my tears. I'll be brave. I'll wait for the danger to be over. Good-bye, my darling!"

She gave him a long kiss, and then she herself pushed him outside. Holmes heard the sound of their voices grow fainter in the distance.

Feeling emboldened by what he had just learned, Holmes carefully exited the closet, entered the boudoir, then walked down a corridor at the end of which was a flight of stairs. But just as he was going down them, he heard the sound of a conversation below. He decided to change his course and took another corridor that brought him to a different staircase. On the floor below, he was surprised to see furniture that he thought he recognized. A door stood half-open. He went through it and found himself in Monsieur Destange's circular library!

---

[6] See *Arsène Lupin vs. Sherlock Holmes: The Hollow Needle*.

"Wonderful! How clever!" Holmes whispered. "Everything falls into place. Clotilde's boudoir communicates with one of the apartments in the house located behind theirs, not on the Boulevard Malesherbes but on the Rue Montchanin, if memory serves... Brilliant! That's how the Blonde Phantom can meet her lover and slip out while maintaining the reputation of someone who never leaves her father's house. And I understand now how Lupin managed to appear yesterday evening in the library... There must be another secret passage between the library and the house on the Rue Montchanin..." He concluded: "Another faked house, very likely credited to *Destange, Architect*. Since I'm here now, I might as well take this opportunity to examine to contents of Monsieur Destange's filing cabinet and find out as much as I can about the other faked houses."

The Detective returned to the landing above and hid patiently behind some curtains. He stayed there until the evening, when the butler came to put out the lights. An hour later, the Englishman decided it was safe to proceed. Using his electric lantern, he went down to the library and stealthily opened the filing cabinet. As he suspected, it contained the old architect's plans, ledgers, estimates and accounts. At the back was a row of books, arranged in chronological order.

Holmes took out the most recent volumes, one at a time, and looked through the indices. Under the letter H, he found the name *Harmingeat*, followed by the number 63. He turned to page 63 and read:

*Harmingeat, 40 Rue Chalgrin.*

There followed a detailed statement of the renovation work done for this client, in order to install central heating in the building. In the margin, there was a note:

*See File M.B.*

"Of course!" exclaimed Holmes. "Maxime Bermond! That file will tell me everything I need to know about Lupin's whereabouts!"

But it took until dawn for the Detective to actually find *File M.B.*

It consisted of 15 pages. One was a copy of the page relating to Monsieur Harmingeat and his building on the Rue Chalgrin. Another detailed the work executed for Monsieur Vatinel, the owner of No. 25, Rue Clapeyron. A third was devoted to Baron d'Hautrec, No. 134, Avenue Henri-Martin. A fourth to the restoration of the château de Crozon. The eleven others all concerned other Parisian landlords, other Parisian houses.

Holmes carefully copied the list of names and addresses, then just as carefully returned the file to where he had found it. He then opened a window and climbed down to the deserted square, after having carefully closed the shutters behind him.

Back in his hotel room, he lit his pipe, with all the gravity he always applied to that task, then enveloped by clouds of smoke, began studying the contents of *File M.B.* and planning his next move.

At 8 a.m., the Detective sent the following telegram to Ganimard:

*I shall probably call on you at home, on the Rue Pergolese, this morning and will place in your charge a person whose capture is of the highest importance. Please, also remain at home tonight and tomorrow Wednesday until noon. Have 30 men ready at your disposal.*

Then, Holmes put on his disguise as "Mister Strickmann," went out and, on the boulevard, picked out a motorcab with a driver whose good-humored but unintelligent face appealed to him. He had him drive to the Place Malesherbes and park 50 yards away from the Destange House.

"Wait for me here," he instructed the driver. "Bundle up because it's cold and I may be over an hour. When I return, start the engine as quickly as possible and we'll drive straight to the Rue Pergolese."

As he was about to ring the bell at the Destange house, Holmes wondered briefly if it was not a mistake to secure the Blonde Phantom first, while Lupin was still at large, planning his escape? Perhaps it would have been wiser to use the list from *File M.B.* to find his lair and capture him at home?

*No*, he finally concluded. *If I capture the Blonde Phantom, Lupin will be powerless. I shall be in control of the battlefield.*

He rang the bell.

Monsieur Destange was already working in the library. They worked together for a little while. The Detective was looking for a pretext to go up to Clotilde's room, when the young woman entered, said good morning to her father, sat down in the adjacent drawing room and began to write some letters.

From where he sat, Holmes saw her as she leaned over the table and, occasionally, reflected with poised pen and a thoughtful look on her face. He waited for a while, then finally grabbed a book and addressed Monsieur Destange.

"I believe this is the book which Mademoiselle Destange asked me to give her when I found it," he said.

He walked into the drawing-room and positioned himself in front of Clotilde so that her father could not see her.

"I am Mister Strickmann, your father's new secretary," he said.

"Oh?" she said without moving. "I didn't realize my father had hired a new secretary."

"My predecessor was taken ill. But I would like to speak with you privately, Mademoiselle."

"By all means. Take a seat, Monsieur. I'm almost finished."

She added a few words to her letter, signed it, sealed it inside an envelope, pushed back her papers, grabbed the telephone, asked to speak to her dressmaker, begged her to hurry on a coat which she needed urgently and, finally, turned towards the Detective.

"I'm at your service, Monsieur. But can't our conversation take place in front of my father?"

"I'm afraid not, Mademoiselle. In fact, I beg you not to raise your voice. It would be better if Monsieur Destange did not hear us."

"Indeed? Better for whom?"

"For you, Mademoiselle."

"For me? But I would never indulge in a conversation that my father could not hear."

"Yet, you must indulge in this one."

They both stood up, Holmes no longer bothering to disguise who he really was. Their eyes met.

"Speak, Monsieur," she said.

"You must forgive me if I get certain minor details wrong," the Detective began, still standing. "But I will vouch for the general accuracy of what I am going to say..."

"Please, Monsieur, no speeches. Facts."

From the sudden change in tone, Holmes felt that Clotilde was now fully on her guard.

"Very well. Facts," he continued. "Five years ago, your father met one Maxime Bermond, who introduced himself as a young architect, or contractor... I'm not sure which. In any event, Monsieur Destange took a liking to the young man.. As his state of health made it difficult for him to continue running his business, he entrusted the execution of several jobs ordered by former clients of his to Monsieur Bermond, since they appeared to be well within the young man's capacities..."

Holmes stopped. It seemed to him that Clotilde had grown significantly paler. Yet, outwardly, she behaved with the greatest calm.

"I'm not well acquainted with my father's business, Monsieur, and I fail to see how all this should be of interest to me."

"It should, in so far as Maxime Bermond's real name was, as you well know, Arsène Lupin."

She burst out laughing.

"Maxime Bermond, Arsène Lupin? You must be joking!"

"That would hardly be appropriate, Mademoiselle. But since you obstinately refuse to understand me, I shall speak more plainly. Arsène Lupin found, in this house, not only the means to commit his crimes, but also a friend... More than a friend... An ally... An accomplice... blind and madly in love..."

She still betrayed so little emotion that Holmes was impressed by her extraordinary self-control.

"I do not know the reasons for your behavior, Monsieur," she said. "And I have no wish to know them. I will ask you, therefore, not to say another word and simply leave."

"I have no intention of forcing my company on you for any longer than necessary, Mademoiselle," said Holmes, calmly. "I shall leave this house at once. However, I shall not be alone."

"Not alone? Who will be going with you, Monsieur?"

"You, Mademoiselle."

"Me?"

"Yes. We shall go out together and you will accompany me without a word, without a protest."

What was odd about this scene was the complete calmness of its two protagonists. Rather than an implacable duel between two powerful wills, their attitudes and the tone of their voices was more indicative of a polite conversation between two persons of different opinions.

In the library, Monsieur Destange continued to examine his books with carefully controlled gestures.

Clotilde shrugged and sat down. Holmes took out his watch.

"It is now 10:30. We will leave in five minutes."

"What if I refuse?"

"I'll go to Monsieur Destange and tell him the truth."

"You wouldn't..."

"The whole truth. The false identity of Maxime Bermond and the double life of his accomplice."

"His accomplice?"

"She whom the newspapers have dubbed the Blonde Phantom."

"I see. What evidence will you give him?"

"Rue Chalgrin, I will show him the secret passage behind the wine rack in the cellar that Lupin has built, connecting No. 40 to No. 42, when he was in charge of the works there. The same passage that you and your lover took last night to escape the Police."

"And then?"

"Then I'll take your father to Maître Detinan's apartment on the Rue Clapeyron. We will descend the service stairs which you took with Lupin to escape Ganimard, and no doubt we will find a similar passage connecting that house to the one around the corner, on the Boulevard des Batignolles."

"And after that?"

"After that, I'll take your father to the chateau de Crozon. It will be child's play for him, who knows the nature of the works executed by Lupin during the castle's renovation, to discover more secret passages. At least one that enabled the Blonde Phantom to enter the Comtesse de Crozon's room at night and steal the Blue Diamond ring from the mantelpiece, then a fortnight later, to hide a fake ring inside Herr Bleichen's tube of soap powder... That last point remains rather obscure... Perhaps it was a woman's petty vengeance? I don't know and it makes no difference."

"Is that all?"

"No, it isn't," said Holmes in a voice graver yet. "Lastly, I'll take your father to No. 134, Avenue Henri-Martin, and there, we shall discuss Baron d'Hautrec's death..."

"No! No! Please!" stammered Clotilde, whose *sang-froid* had suddenly collapsed. "You can't! You mustn't! How can you? Would you dare to accuse me of...?"

"Yes, I accuse you of killing Baron d'Hautrec."

"No! That's monstrous!"

"You did kill Baron d'Hautrec, Mademoiselle. You entered his service under the name of Antoinette Bréhat, with the intention of stealing his Blue Diamond, and you ended up killing him."

Now, she broke down and was almost on the verge of tears.

"Monsieur, please! I beg you... If you know so much, you must also know that I did not murder the Baron."

"I did not say that you murdered him, Mademoiselle. I know that the Baron was subject to violent fits of insanity, which only Sister Augusta was capable of controlling. She told me so herself when I questioned her. I suppose he must have attacked you with the letter opener when he woke up in the middle of the night and caught you red-handed. A skirmish ensued and it was in the course of that struggle that you struck him in self-defense. Horrified by what you had done, you rang the bell and fled, forgetting to remove the Blue Diamond ring from the Baron's finger. Afterwards, you returned with one of Lupin's accomplices, probably a domestic in the neighboring house, and put the body back in bed, but still without daring to take the ring. That's what happened. Therefore, I repeat, you did not murder the Baron; yet, he died by your hand."

She was, in fact, holding her fine, delicate white hands clasped on her forehead. She remained like that, silent, motionless, for a long time. Then, she uncrossed her fingers and revealed her sorrow-stricken face.

"And you plan to tell all this to my father?"

"If you force me to. I also have witnesses: Mademoiselle Gerbois, who will identify the Blonde Phantom, Sister Augusta who will identify Antoinette Bréhat and the Comtesse de Crozon who will identify Madame de Real. That is what I will tell him."

"You wouldn't dare!" she exclaimed, recovering her presence of mind in the face of such immediate danger.

Holmes merely turned and took a step towards the library.

"Wait, Monsieur," she hurriedly said.

She reflected, once again fully in control of herself.

"You are Sherlock Holmes, aren't you?" she asked.

"I am."

"What do you want from me?"

"It is very simple, Mademoiselle. I am presently engaged in a contest of wills with Arsène Lupin, a contest which, of course, I shall win. In the meantime, I think that holding a hostage such as yourself could be an invaluable weapon against my enemy. Therefore, I want you to come with me. I will leave you in the hands of a friend of mine. As soon as this case is over, you shall be set free."

"Is that all?"

"Yes. I don't belong to the Police, and I have no taste for the administration of justice."

She seemed to have made up her mind; yet, she asked for a moment's delay. She closed her eyes. Holmes looked at her, calm, seemingly indifferent to the perils that threatened her.

*Does she even believe herself to be truly threatened?* he thought. *Probably not. She thinks Lupin will protect her, will save her... As long as Lupin is free, she thinks nothing can happen to her. Lupin is omnipotent, Lupin is infallible...*

"Mademoiselle," he said aloud, "I said five minutes and it's been almost half-an-hour."

"May I go to my room, Monsieur, and fetch my things?" she asked.

"If you please, Mademoiselle. I can just as well wait for you on the Rue Montchanin. I'm well acquainted with Monsieur Jeanniot, the Concierge..."

"Ah, so you know that, too?" she said with visible awe and dismay.

"I know a great many things."

"Very well. Then, I'll ring for them."

The servant brought her her hat and coat.

"It might be wise to give your father some reason to explain our departure," said Holmes. "Believable enough to explain your absence for two or three days."

"It is not necessary," she replied. "I shall be back soon enough."

Again, they exchanged defiant looks, both of them daring the other.

"You trust him so much?" asked the Detective.

"And more."

"He can do no wrong in your eyes, can he? Whatever he wishes happens. You approve of everything he does and you will do just about anything for him."

"I love him," she replied, passionately.

"And you believe that he will come to your rescue?"

She merely shrugged. She then approached Monsieur Destange.

"Papa," she said, "I'm borrowing Mister Strickmann. I've got an errand to run at the Bibliothèque Nationale."

"Ah? Will you be back for lunch?"

"Possibly... but unlikely... But you're not to worry on my account." She then turned towards Holmes and said firmly: "I am ready, Monsieur."

"Without reserve?"

"With my eyes wide open."

"If you try to run away, I'll shout and call for help. You will then be arrested and taken to jail. Don't forget that there is a warrant out for the Blonde Phantom."

"I understand. Let's go."

They left the house together, just as the Detective had predicted.

The Englishman's car was still waiting for him, parked alongside the boulevard facing in the opposite direction. They could see the driver's back and his cap. The upturned collar of his jacket protected him against the bitter wind. As they approached, Holmes heard the engine idling. He opened the door, asked Clotilde to step in, then sat down beside her.

The car started immediately and soon reached the outer boulevards: Avenue Hoche, Avenue de la Grande Armée.

Holmes sat silently, thinking out his next steps. *Ganimard is at home. I'll leave the girl with him, but I won't tell him who she really is. Otherwise he'll take her straight to jail, which would upset all my plans. Once I'm alone, I'll look at File M.B. again and will discover Lupin's lair. Tonight, tomorrow at the latest, I'll go to see Ganimard again, as planned, and deliver him Lupin and his gang...*

He rubbed his hands, glad to see that we was finally nearing his goal and happy to see that no serious obstacle stood in his path.

"You must forgive me, Mademoiselle," he said, feeling it necessary to explain his sense of triumph, which was not in keeping with his usual nature. "It was a particularly difficult battle, and my success is thus much more enjoyable."

"A legitimate success, Monsieur. You have every right to rejoice."

"Thank you, Mademoiselle." Then: "Wait! Where are we going? Didn't the man understand my directions?"

The car was now leaving Paris through the Porte de Neuilly, the direction opposite to the Rue Pergolese. Holmes lowered the window that separated the back of the cab from the driver.

"I say, driver, I told you to go Rue Pergolese..."

The man made no reply.

"I told you to go Rue Pergolese," repeated Holmes, more loudly.

"Look here, my man! Are you deaf? This isn't where I told you to go. Rue Pergolese, do you hear? Turn around at once!"

The man took no notice. Holmes began to feel alarmed. He looked at Clotilde. A wisp of a smile played on her lips.

"Why are you smiling?" he asked. "This doesn't have anything to do with..."

Suddenly, he stopped, seized by a ghastly thought. Half rising from his seat, the Detective took a better look at the driver. His shoulders were slimmer, his gestures smoother... A cold sweat broke out on his forehead, his hands clutched empty air... He now knew who was the driver was: Arsène Lupin.

"So, Mister Holmes, what do you think of our little drive through the beautiful French countryside?" inquired Lupin.

"Delightful, Monsieur Lupin," replied Holmes. "Truly delightful."

Never before in his life had the Englishman made such a supreme effort as what it cost him to utter these banal words without the least tremor in his voice, without betraying in any fashion the fury he felt inside. But then, he felt he still had one card to play, one trump in his hand. He pulled out his gun and pointed it squarely at Clotilde.

"Monsieur Lupin, I order you to turn around or I will shoot Mademoiselle Destange!"

"I'd advise you to aim at her cheek if you want to hit the temple," said the Gentleman Burglar without even turning his head.

"Don't go too fast, Maxime," said Clotilde. "The road is slippery and you know how I worry about accidents."

She was still smiling, her eyes fixed on the road.

"Stop! Stop or I'll shoot!" shouted Holmes. "I'll do it, you know."

The muzzle of his gun grazed Clotilde's hair.

"No, you won't, Mister Holmes," she said gently. "You're not the type to shoot a woman in cold blood." With her hand, she pushed his gun down. "How reckless Maxime is! We're sure to skid, at this speed..."

Holmes put the revolver back in his pocket. Then, he grabbed the door handle, ready to jump out, notwithstanding the chances of a severe injury.

"Don't do that," Clotilde said. "We have another car following us."

The Detective turned and looked through the back window. Another car was indeed following them, huge, fearsome with its red color, pointy hood and its four burly passengers, all wearing fur coats.

"I see. I'm well guarded."

Holmes then crossed his arms on his chest, with the proud defiance of one who knows how to wait for his luck to turn and is ready to seize the opportunity. He remained silent and resigned, displaying no anger or bitterness, as they crossed the Seine and went through Suresnes, Rueil and Chatou. He tried to discover how Lupin had been able to replace the Driver he himself had hired at random that morning. The man could not have been an accomplice; it was impossible. And yet Lupin had acted in time. So he must have been warned. But when, and how? Such a warning could only have been delivered after Holmes had revealed himself and threatened Clotilde, since no one knew of his plans before. But he had not left the girl's side since…

Suddenly, he was struck by a memory: Clotilde had called her dressmaker. And at once, he understood. She had guessed who he was as soon as he had asked to speak with her. She had guessed the nature of his request. And ignoring the danger, acting naturally, as if she was performing an ordinary daily chore, she had acted immediately and called Lupin, pretending to call her dressmaker, and used a series of codewords that must have been agreed on between them beforehand.

How Arsène Lupin had come, taken notice of that single car idling in front of the Destange house, and probably paid off the real driver, mattered little now. What fascinated Holmes, to the point of appeasing his fury, was remembering how calm and collected Clotilde had been. How in order to give her lover as much time to act as possible, she had feigned rebellion, then despair, and forced him to lay all his cards out on the table. True, she was a woman in love, but her resourcefulness, her cleverness had thoroughly fooled him.

What was he to do against a man assisted by such allies, a man who, by the sheer force of his personality, was able to inspire such daring and brilliance in a woman like Clotilde?

They crossed the meandering Seine again and climbed the hills of Saint-Germain. Five hundred yards after they left the town behind, Lupin stopped the cab. The other car slowed down and stopped, too. There was no one else around.

"Mister Holmes, may I trouble you to change cars?" asked Lupin. "Our is much too slow..."

"Certainly," said the Detective, all the more politely since he had no choice.

"Let me also lend you this fur coat. We'll be traveling fast and it's cold in the country. And please take these two sandwiches. There's no telling when you'll get your dinner..."

The four men had gotten out. One of them stepped closer and, as he took off his goggles, the Detective recognized the man in the tall hat.

"Take this cab back to its driver," instructed Lupin. "He's waiting in the wine bar at the corner of the Rue Legendre. Give him the other 1,000 francs I promised him. Ah, and yes, please give Mister Holmes your goggles."

The Gentleman Burglar exchanged a few words with Mademoiselle Destange, then sat behind the wheel and they took off. Holmes sat beside Lupin, and one of the men sat behind him.

When Lupin had said they would be traveling fast, he had not exaggerated. He drove at maximum speed. The horizon rushed towards them, as if attracted by a mysterious force, and vanished behind as if swallowed by the same abyss that also engulfed the trees, the houses, the plains and the forests, and all other things which they encountered on their path.

Holmes and Lupin did not exchange a word. Above their heads, the poplar leaves rustled in waves, separated by the regular spacing of the trees alongside the road. Town after town vanished before their eyes: Mantes, Vernon, Gaillon... Hill after hill, from Bon Secours to Canteleu... Then, it was Rouen, with its suburbs, its harbor, its miles of piers... They rushed though it so quickly that it was no more than a jumble of blurry streets... They flew by Duclair, Caudebec and the Pays de Caux, skimming over its hills and plains, and Lillebonne and Quilleboeuf... Finally, they found themselves on the banks of the Seine again, near its estuary, on a small, isolated pier alongside which lay a small steam-powered yacht, with fine and powerful lines and puffs of black smoke curling out of her funnel.

The car stopped. In two hours, they had traveled over a hundred miles.

A man dressed in a blue sailor jacket and wearing a cap with gold braids stepped forward.

"Well done, Captain," said Lupin. "Did you get my telegram?"

"I did."

"Is the *Hirondelle* ready?"

"It is."

"In that case, Mister Holmes…?"

The Detective looked around him. He saw a small group of people sitting outside a café and another, a little closer. He hesitated for a moment. But these might belong to Lupin's gang, and besides, he realized that, before anyone could interfere, he would be grabbed, forced on board and packed off to the bottom of the hold. Better to cooperate. He crossed the gang-plank and followed Lupin into the Captain's cabin.

It was roomy, spotlessly clean and shone brightly with its varnished wainscoting and gleaming brass.,

Lupin shut the door.

"What do you know?" he asked the Englishman without beating around the bush.

"Everything."

"What do you mean, everything? I want details."

There was none of that tone of respect or polite irony that he had earlier used when addressing the Detective. This was the imperious voice of a master of men, a man accustomed to commanding and being obeyed, a man used to seeing everyone bend before his will–even a man like Sherlock Holmes.

Their eyes met, this time as declared enemies, passionate foes.

"You've crossed my path once too many times," said Lupin, sounding irritated. "I'm tired of having to constantly avoid the traps you lay for me. I warn you, my conduct towards you now is going to depend upon the answers you give me next. What do you know?"

"Everything," repeated Holmes, coolly.

"Very well," continued Lupin, barely hiding his annoyance. "I'll tell you what you know. You know that, under the name of Maxime Bermond, I... 'fixed' 15 houses originally built by Monsieur Destange."

"I do."

"You know four of those 15 houses."

"I do."

"You have a list of the other 11."

"I do."

"You copied that list from Monsieur Destange's files last night."

"I did."

"And since you presume that, among these 11 buildings, there must inevitably be one which I use for my own ends, you have told Ganimard to search them all."

"I did not."

"Really?"

"No. I work alone. I intend to capture you by myself."

"I see. So I've got nothing to fear now since you're my prisoner..."

"You've got nothing to fear *as long as* I remain your prisoner."

"You mean, you're not going to remain my prisoner?"

"I do."

Arsène Lupin leaned over the Englishman and gently put his hand on his shoulder.

"Listen to me carefully, Mister Holmes. I'm not in the mood to argue and you, unfortunately, are in no position to cause me anymore trouble. Let's put an end to this."

"Yes, let's."

"Give me your word of honor that you won't try to escape from this boat until she reaches English waters."

"On the contrary, I give you my word of honor that I shall try to escape by every means possible," replied Holmes, undaunted.

"Damn it! Don't you realize I only have to say a word and you'll be done for? All these men obey me blindly. At my signal, they'll put a chain around your neck…"

"Chains can be broken."

"…And you'll be thrown overboard ten miles from the coast."

"I can swim."

"Well said," said Lupin, suddenly laughing. "I apologize, Mister Holmes. I was unreasonably angry. Please excuse my outburst and let's wrap things up. You will agree that I have the right to take measures to protect myself and my friends…"

"Of course, but all your measures will prove useless."

"Possibly, but you can't fault me for trying."

"It is indeed your duty."

"To work, then!"

Lupin opened the door and called in the Captain and two of the crew. The men grabbed the Detective and, after searching him, bound his legs together and tied him to the Captain's berth.

"Enough!" said Lupin. "Again, I apologize, Mister Holmes. Nothing short of obstinacy and the exceptional gravity of the danger you represent for me would force me to use such crude methods…"

The sailors withdrew.

"Captain," instructed Lupin, "one of your men must remain to wait on Mister Holmes at all times, and you yourself must keep him company as often as possible. Treat him well. He isn't a prisoner, but a guest. What is the time by your watch?"

"2:05 p.m."

Lupin looked at his own watch and at a clock hanging on the cabin wall.

"Our watches agree. How long will it take you to reach Southampton?"

"About nine hours, without hurrying."

"Make it 11. You must not land before the departure of the steamer which leaves Southampton at midnight and arrives in Le Havre at 8 a.m. the next morning. You understand, don't you, Captain? This is of the utmost importance! It would be exceedingly dangerous for all of us were this man able to return to France tonight. So you mustn't arrive at Southampton until 1 a.m."

"Understood."

"My respects, Mister Holmes. We will meet again, in this world or the next one, I'm sure."

"I shall see you tomorrow, Monsieur Lupin."

A few minutes later, Holmes heard the car drive away. At once, the engines of the *Hirondelle* began throbbing with the full power of steam. The yacht threw off her moorings.

By 3 p.m., they had barely left the Seine estuary and were about to enter the open sea. At that moment, Sherlock Holmes lay soundly asleep in the Captain's berth.

The next morning, the tenth and last day of the battle between the two rivals, *L'Echo de Paris* published the following derisive article:

*A decree of expulsion was pronounced yesterday by Arsène Lupin, Gentleman Burglar, against Mister Sherlock Holmes, the Great English Detective. Signed at noon, the decree was executed on the same day. Mister Sherlock Holmes was dropped off at Southampton at 1 a.m. this morning.*

# *The Second Arrest of Arsène Lupin* [7]

By 8 a.m. that Wednesday morning, a dozen moving vans began blocking the Rue Crevaux, between the Avenue du Bois-de-Boulogne and the Avenue Bougeaud. The neighborhood learned that Monsieur Felix Davey was vacating the apartment he occupied on the fourth floor of No. 8, while Monsieur Dubreuil, who had knocked into one the fifth floor of No. 8 and the fifth floor apartments of the two adjacent houses, was also moving. It was, of course, a pure coincidence, as the two gentlemen were not acquainted. Monsieur Dubreuil collected antique furniture and was often visited by foreign experts and collectors at all times of the day.

A detail that was noticed by the neighborhood, but which no one commented upon until much later, was that none of the 12 vans bore the name of the moving company, and none of the movers spent time loitering in the local cafés. They worked so quickly that it was all finished by 11 a.m. Nothing remained but the piles of old paper and rags that are always left behind in the corners of empty rooms.

Monsieur Felix Davey was an elegant young man, who dressed in the latest fashion. He carried a heavily-weighted cane, which seemed to indicate an unusual degree of strength. During the move, he sat quietly across the street on a bench, near the alley that intersects the Avenue du Bois across from the Rue Pergolese. Beside him sat a young woman, dressed in ordinary, middle-class clothes, reading a newspaper. Nearby, a child played with a spade in a sandbox.

Without turning his head, Monsieur Davey addressed the young woman.

"Ganimard?" he asked.

---

[7] The title is a reference to the title of the very fist *Arsène Lupin* story, "*The Arrest of Arsène Lupin.*"

"Gone since 9 this morning."

"Where?"

"To the Prefecture of Police."

"Alone?"

"Yes."

"No telegram last night?"

"None."

"They still trust you in his house?"

"Totally. I run small errands for Madame Ganimard, and she tells me everything her husband does...We spent the morning together."

"Good. Continue coming here at 11 every morning until you hear otherwise."

Monsieur Davey got up and walked to the Porte Dauphine, where he ate a frugal lunch at the Pavillon Chinois: two eggs, some vegetables and a piece of fruit. Then he returned to the Rue Crevaux.

"I'm going to take a last look upstairs," he told the Concierge, "and then I'll give you back the keys."

He ended his inspection in the room which had been his study. There, he grabbed the end of what looked like a gas pipe, unscrewed a nozzle, attached a little funnel to it and blew.

A faint whistle sounded in reply.

"Anyone there, Dubreuil?" he asked, talking into the pipe.

"No one."

"Can I come up?"

"Yes, Monsieur."

He rescrewed the pipe shut, saying as he did so:

"Where will progress stop? Our age is full of wonders that make life so much easier and enjoyable... especially when one wants life to be easy and enjoyable!"

He touched one of the marble moldings of the fireplace, causing it to pivot. The marble slab itself moved and the mirror above slid back on invisible grooves, revealing an opening with a secret staircase, built behind the chimney. It was all very clean, made of carefully-polished iron and white ceramic tiles.

He went up to the fifth floor and used a similar secret passage to enter another room through its fireplace. Dubreuil was waiting for him.

"Is everything done here?"

"Yes, we're finished."

"Nothing incriminating left behind?"

"No. It's all been cleared up."

"What about the men?"

"All gone except the three keeping watch."

"Let's go then."

One after the other, they inspected every floor all the way up to the servants' quarters under the roof. There, the three men were keeping an eye on the neighborhood, watching out of the windows.

"Anything suspicious?"

"Nothing, boss."

"Is the street empty?"

"Yes."

"I'll leave in ten minutes; you, too. In the meantime, if you notice anything at all out of the ordinary, let me know."

"Not to worry. I've got my finger on the alarm bell, boss."

"Dubreuil, you told the movers not to touch those wires?"

"Of course! It works fine."

"All right, then."

Lupin and Dubreuil returned to Felix Davey's apartment. The Gentleman Burglar carefully readjusted the marble molding behind him.

"My dear Dubreuil, I'd love to see the faces of those who'll discover all of our wonderful devices: the electric alarms, the wires, the speaking tubes, the secret staircases, the sliding floorboards, the moving walls, the invisible passages... A triumph of stagecraft!"

"And what publicity for Arsène Lupin!"

"I could have done without it, frankly. It's a pity to be forced to abandon such a wonderful installation. I'll have to start all over again fresh, using new methods, of course, for one must never repeat oneself... Damn Sherlock Holmes! It's all his doing!"

"He hasn't returned yet, has he?"

"How could he? There's only one ferry from Southampton, which leaves at midnight; from Le Havre, there's only one train, which leaves at 8 a.m. and arrives in Paris at 11:11 a.m. Once he missed the midnight ferry, and my instructions to Captain Jeanniot on the subject were clear, then he couldn't be back in France until late afternoon today at the earliest, via Newhaven and Dieppe."

"I bet he won't even bother to come back."

"You're wrong there. Sherlock Holmes will never give up. But again, this time, he will arrive too late. We'll all be gone."

"What about Mademoiselle Destange?"

"I'm to meet her in an hour."

"At home?"

"Oh, no! She won't go home for a few days, until this storm's blown over... and I'm able to fully devote my efforts to making her safe. But you must hurry, Dubreuil. It'll take a long time to ship all our loot, and your presence at the wharf is necessary."

"Are you certain we're not being watched?"

"By whom? The only man I feared was Holmes, and he isn't here."

Dubreuil went away. Felix Davey took a last walk around the apartment. He picked up a couple of torn letters. Then, noticing a piece of chalk on the floor, he took it, drew a large circle on the dark wall-paper of the dining-room and wrote the following commemorative inscription:

*Here lived Arsène Lupin, Gentleman Burglar, for five years at the beginning of the 20th century.*

He appeared to derive a great deal of amusement from his little joke, and whistled happily looking at it.

"Now that I've set the record straight for future historians, I've got to go!" he said. "Hurry up, Mister Holmes, because in three minutes, I'll have flown the coop and your humiliation will be complete... Another two minutes! I'm waiting, Mister Holmes... Only one minute to go! You're not here? You disappoint me! Very well, I unilaterally proclaim my victory and your defeat! And now I take my leave. Farewell, my Kingdom! I shall look upon you no more. Farewell, my 55 rooms in the five apartments over which I reigned! Farewell, my austere and humble abode!"

The sound of a bell cut short his mocking and lyrical speech. A short, shrill, strident bell, twice interrupted, twice resumed. It was the alarm bell.

What could it mean? Some unexpected danger? Ganimard? Surely not...

He was about to return to his study and flee, but first, he decided to check out the street. He looked out of the window. There was no one suspicious down there. Had the enemy already invaded the house? He listened intently and thought he heard a jumble of confused sounds. Now, without any hesitation, he ran back to the study. As he walked into the room, he heard the characteristic sounds of someone trying to open the door with a skeleton key.

"Curses!" he swore. "I'm running out of time. The house must be surrounded... But they can't have found out about the service stairs yet... Thanks to the passage behind that fireplace, I'll..."

He pushed the molding; it refused to move. He pushed with all his strength, to no greater result.

At the same moment, he thought he heard the front door open. A thunder of steps followed.

"Damn it!" he swore again. "I'm lost unless that confounded spring..."

His fingers clutched the molding. He bore upon it with all his weight. Obstinately, it still refused to move! By some

138

incredible bad luck–if that was what it was?–a malicious accident of fate, the spring which was working only moments ago now refused to open his only path to freedom.

He persisted, fought with, swore at the inert piece of marble which still refused to move. He was livid with rage. Could such a stupid obstacle stand in his way? He struck the marble with his fists, hammered it with furious blows, called it names...

"Why, Monsieur Lupin, is something not going according to your plan?"

Lupin turned around, terror-stricken. Sherlock Holmes stood before him!

Sherlock Holmes! Lupin looked at him, his eyes blinking as if trying to dispel some nightmarish vision. Sherlock Holmes whom he had, only the day before, packed off to England as one might get rid of a troublesome parcel. Sherlock Holmes who, now, stood before him, triumphant and free. For that impossible, miraculous event to occur despite Arsène Lupin's will, there must have been some inexplicable upset in the very laws of nature. It was the victory of all that is illogial and irrational. It just could not be. And yet, Sherlock Holmes stood before him!

The Detective displayed the same polite irony that his foe had so often used against him.

"Monsieur Lupin," he said, "from this minute onward, I shall never again give another thought to the awful night you forced me to spend in Baron d'Hautrec's house, to my friend Dr. Watson's injuries, to my kidnapping and to my humiliating sea voyage, tied down to an uncomfortable berth at your orders. This moment wipes all that out. I have forgotten all my earlier setbacks. I am rewarded, very richly rewarded."

Lupin remained silent.

"Wouldn't you agree?" asked the Englishman.

He insisted, as if demanding an acknowledgement of defeat from his foe, a sort of receipt with regards to the past.

After a moment's reflection, during which the Detective felt himself scrutinized to the very depths of his soul, Lupin spoke:

"I presume, Mister Holmes, that your question is supported by some very serious motive?"

"Extremely serious, Monsieur Lupin."

"The fact that you managed to escape from Captain Jeanniot and his men is nothing but a minor skirmish in our struggle. But the fact they you dare appear before me here, *alone* against Arsène Lupin, leads me to believe that your victory must be as complete as can be."

"Indeed. As complete as possible."

"This house?"

"Surrounded."

"The two neighboring houses?"

"Surrounded."

"The apartment above this one?"

"The *three* apartments on the fifth floor occupied by Monsieur Dubreuil are also surrounded."

"So that…?"

"So that you are caught, Monsieur Lupin. Irredeemably caught."

Lupin now experienced the same feelings that Holmes had felt during his kidnapping: the same fury, the same hopeless revolt, but also, it must be said, the same sense of fair play which compelled him to bow down before adversity. Both men were equally strong-willed; both were equally capable of accepting defeat as an occasional evil which must be faced with equanimity.

"You're right, Mister Holmes," said Lupin without reservation. "We are indeed quits."

Holmes seemed delighted by Lupin's admission. They both remained silent for a while. Then, the Gentleman Burglar appeared to regain his usual self-control and natural sense of humor.

"I'm not sorry, either," he said with forced bravado. "It was becoming boring to win every time. I only had to put out my arm to hit you in the chest every time. But now, it's your turn. *Touché*, Mister Holmes!" He now laughed with genuine good humor. "Now we shall have some fun. Lupin is caught and well trapped. How will he escape? Can he escape? What an adventure! I have to thank you for giving me such emotions, Mister Holmes! That's what I call living life to the fullest!"

He pressed his fists to his temples, as if to contain the jumble of emotions that swelled up inside him. His behavior reminded Holmes of a child stressed beyond his endurance.

"What do you want?" he suddenly and abruptly asked the Detective.

"What do you mean?"

"Ganimard is here with his men. Why doesn't he come in?"

"I asked him not to."

"And he agreed?"

"I promised to deliver you to him only on the express condition that he would explicitly follow all my instructions. Besides, he doesn't know who you are. He thinks Felix Davey is merely one of Lupin's men."

"So I'm asking you again, what do you want? Or if you prefer, why did you come here alone?"

"I wanted to talk to you first."

"Ah-ha! You wanted to talk to me…"

That fact pleased Lupin greatly. There are situations in life where words are much preferable to deeds, and this was one such situation.

"I'm sorry not to have a chair to offer you, Mister Holmes," he said graciously. "Would this half-broken crate do? Or maybe that window ledge? I wish I had a glass of beer to offer you, too… Pish!"

"Never mind all that. Let's talk."

"I'm listening."

"I shall be brief. As you know, the purpose of my visit to France wasn't your arrest. If I was forced to go after you, it was because I couldn't see any other means to accomplish my first objective…"

"Which was?"

"To recover the Blue Diamond."

"I see."

"Since the one found in Herr Bleichen's tube of soap powder was but a fake…"

"Indeed. The real gem was mailed by the Blonde Phantom. I had an exact copy made. As I had designs upon the Comtesse de Crozon's other jewels, and the Austrian Consul was already a suspect, it seemed a good idea to hide the fake diamond in his luggage in order to divert attention from the so-called Madame de Real."

"While you kept the real one."

"Of course."

"I want that diamond."

"Impossible, I'm sorry."

"I promised the Comtesse de Crozon I'd recover it and, therefore, I mean to have it."

"How do you plan to achieve that since it's in my possession?"

"I shall have it *precisely* because it's in your possession."

"Do you mean that you expect me to surrender it to you?"

"Yes."

"Willingly?"

"I'll buy it from you, if you want."

Lupin laughed.

"How British! You make it sound like a business transaction!"

"It is."

"And what would you offer me in exchange?"

"Mademoiselle Destange's freedom."

"Her freedom? I wasn't aware she'd been arrested."

"I'll give Chief Inspector Ganimard the necessary information. Deprived of your protection, she'll be arrested."

Lupin laughed again.

"I'm afraid you're offering me something you do not possess, Mister Holmes. Mademoiselle Destange is safe and has nothing to fear. I want something else."

The Englishman hesitated, obviously embarrassed. Then, he put his hand on Lupin's shoulder.

"What if I offered you..."

"My freedom?"

"Not quite, but I could... leave the room, talk with Monsieur Ganimard..."

"And leave me alone, say, to think things over?"

"Exactly."

"That would be an attractive offer if this damn mechanism was still working," said Lupin, pushing the molding with irritation.

Suddenly, they both stifled an exclamation of surprise. This time, fate had intervened and the hidden passage had sprung open! Escape was now possible. Why deal with Holmes under such circumstances?

Lupin paced back and forth as if he was considering his answer. Then, he in turn put his hand on the Englishman's shoulder.

"All things considered, Mister Holmes, I'd rather carry on my business without your assistance."

"Still..."

"Thank you, but I don't need anybody's help."

"When Ganimard has you, it'll all be over. They won't ever let you go."

"Who knows?"

"Come, now! This is madness. Every exit is being watched."

"Not quite. There's one which isn't."

"Which one?"

"*The one I plan to take.*"

"Words! Your arrest is just a question of minutes!"

143

"It isn't."

"Then...?"

"Then I'll keep the Blue Diamond."

Holmes took out his watch.

"Do reconsider. It's now ten minutes to three. At three o'clock sharp, I'll call Ganimard."

"Then, that gives us ten minutes to chat. Let's make the most of our time together, Mister Holmes. And first, to satisfy my curiosity, could you tell me how you procured my address and the name Felix Davey?"

Holmes kept a close eye on Lupin, whose good spirits always made him uneasy. But answering the Gentleman Burglar's question appealed to his professional vanity.

"I had your address from your lady friend."

"Clotilde?"

"Yes. Remember, yesterday morning, when I tried to force her to come with me, she pretended to call her dressmaker..."

"So she did."

"I understood later that there was no dressmaker and that she had called you instead. Last night, in the boat, I remembered the last two digits of the number she had dialed: 73. Since I had the list of the houses you had rigged, it was child's play for me, upon my return to Paris this morning at 11 a.m., to look through the telephone directory for the house matching a telephone number ending with 73. That's how I discovered the name of Monsieur Felix Davey. Once I knew your name and address, then I called on Monsieur Ganimard."

"Brilliant! Absolutely first-rate! Congratulations, Mister Holmes. But how did you manage to take that train in Le Havre? How did you manage to escape from the *Hirondelle*?"

"I didn't."

"I don't understand."

"You gave strict orders to Captain Jeanniot to not reach Southampton until 1 a.m. In fact, they landed at midnight, just in time for me to grab the last ferry to Le Havre."

"Jeanniot betrayed me? Impossible!"

"He did not betray you."

"What then…?"

"It was his watch."

"His watch?"

"Yes, I put his watch forward an hour."

"How?"

"The only way possible: by turning its stem. We were sitting together chatting and I told him about some of my most famous cases and he was so caught up that he didn't notice a thing."

"Bravo! Well done! It's a clever trick and I'll remember it. But what about the cabin clock?"

"That one was more difficult because my legs were tied. But the sailor who was watching me when the Captain went on deck kindly agreed to give the hands a push."

"One of my men? He agreed to help you…?"

"Oh, he didn't realize the consequences of what he was doing. I told him I had to catch the last train to London and… he allowed himself to be persuaded."

"In consideration of…?"

"Of a small gift… which the decent fellow, I'm sure, intends to faithfully send to you."

"What gift?"

"A mere trifle."

"Yes, but what?"

"The Blue Diamond."

"The Blue Diamond?"

"Yes, the fake one, which the Comtesse de Crozon entrusted to me…"

Lupin suddenly burst out laughing, so spontaneously and so full of gaiety that his eyes teared up.

"What a remarkable joke! My fake Blue Diamond handed back to my own man! And the Captain's watch! The hands of the clock!…"

Never before had Sherlock Holmes felt that the battle between Arsène Lupin and himself had grown so intense as at this very moment. With his prodigious intuition, he guessed that Lupin's hilarity was but a mask. Under it, the Gentleman Burglar was marshalling his own, formidable powers, readying every fiber of his being, preparing to strike.

Lupin had stealthily drawn closer to the Detective. The Englishman stepped back and put his hand in his pocket.

"It's 3 p.m., Monsieur Lupin," said Holmes.

"Already? What a pity! We were having such good fun."

"I'm still waiting for your answer."

"My answer? Goodness me! So our game's over, with my freedom as the stakes?"

"Or the Blue Diamond."

"The answer's no. Your move. Show me your cards, Mister Holmes."

"I play the king," said Holmes, firing a shot with his revolver, which he had kept hidden in his pocket.

"And here's *my hand*!" exclaimed Lupin, hurling his fist at his rival.

Holmes had fired in the air to summon Ganimard, whose intervention he had now deemed necessary. But Lupin's fist caught him full in the stomach and he turned pale and staggered back. Lupin leaped towards the secret passage. But he was too late! The door was smashed open.

"Surrender, Lupin, or else…"

Ganimard, who had doubtless been waiting nearer than Lupin thought, stood in the doorway, his revolver aimed squarely at the Gentleman Burglar. He was not alone. Ten, 20 men stood behind him, guns drawn, the type of men who would have shot him like a dog, without a second thought, at the least sign of resistance.

Lupin made a quiet gesture.

"Put your guns down. I surrender."

And he crossed his arms over his chest.

A moment of stupor followed. In the room, empty of its furniture and curtains, Lupin's words echoed ringingly.

"I surrender!"

Those words sounded incredible. Everyone expected him to vanish in a puff of smoke, or down a trapdoor, or through a sliding wall, escaping once again at the last minute from the desperate grasp of his would-be captors. But no! Instead, he surrendered, meekly, like any ordinary criminal caught red-handed!

Ganimard stepped forward. Greatly moved, with all the gravity that the circumstance demanded, he slowly brought his hand down upon his old enemy's shoulder and uttered the ritual words with infinite pleasure:

"Arsène Lupin, I'm arresting you in the name of the Law."

"Brrr!" mock-shivered Lupin. "You're trying to impress me, Ganimard. Why such a somber face? You look like you're delivering a eulogy at a friend's gravesite. Drop those funereal airs!"

"I'm arresting you."

"Yes, I heard you the first time! In the name of the Law, whose faithful servant you are. Chief Inspector Ganimard is arresting the wicked Arsène Lupin. I suppose this is a historical event. I wonder if your men grasp its full importance... And this is the second time you've done it, too! Congratulations, Ganimard, you should do well in your career!"

The Gentleman Burglar held out his wrists for the handcuffs.

They were fastened almost solemnly. The policemen, despite their usual roughness and their pent-up resentment towards Lupin, were acting with a certain amount of reserve, amazed at being able to actually touch this semi-magical being.

"Alas, poor Lupin!" he sighed. "What would your friends from the Faubourgs say if they saw you humbled like this?"

He then pulled his wrists apart in a progressive effort, mustering all of his strength. The veins of his forehead swelled. The chain dug into his flesh.

"Now!" he said.

The chain snapped and broke in two.

"Another one, my good man," he jeered. "This one's no good."

This time, they put two pairs on him.

"That's better," he approved. "You can't be too careful."

Then, he counted the detectives.

"How many of you are there? Twenty-five? Thirty? That's a lot. I can't do anything against 30. Ah, if there'd only been 15 of you!"

He had all the mannerisms of a leading actor playing the role of his life, with verve, impertinence and an overabundance of charm. Holmes watched him as only a fellow thespian could, appreciating the beauty and each nuance of Lupin's play. And for a minute, he indeed believed that the struggle might have been equal had Lupin faced only 15 men instead of 30! The Police, backed by all the formidable power of the Law, and the Gentleman Burglar, alone, unarmed and in chains–the two were equally matched.

"Well, Mister Holmes, are you satisfied with your handiwork?" said Lupin. "Thanks to you, I shall rot away on the ever-damp straw of the cells of La Santé jail. It must bother your conscience a little, no? And surely you feel some pangs of remorse?"

The Englishman shrugged, as if to say: "I gave you a chance." Lupin understood the unspoken reply.

"Never!" he exclaimed. "I'll never give you the Blue Diamond! It cost me too much to acquire it. I value it too much to surrender it lightly. When I see you again next month, I'll tell you why... Shall we meet in London? No? Would you prefer Vienna? Saint-Petersburg?"

Suddenly, he gave a start. A bell had just rung. It was not the alarm-bell, but the sound of the telephone, which had not been disconnected and which sat on the floor between the two windows.

The telephone! Who would fall into a trap laid out by cruel fate? Lupin made a furious move towards the device as if

148

he hoped to smash it and, by so doing, stop the mysterious voice which sought to speak to him. Ganimard was faster. He took the receiver from its hook and bent down.

"Hello? Hello? 648-73? Yes, that's right..."

But Holmes was even faster. With a brisk gesture, he pushed the Chief Inspector aside and grabbed the receiver. He put his handkerchief over the mouthpiece to muffle the sound of his voice.

At that moment, he exchanged a meaningful glance with Lupin. The same thought had struck both men simultaneously. In a flash, the two understood the last-minute consequences of the hypothesis that had formed in both their minds: it was the Blonde Phantom who was calling. Clotilde thought she was talking to Felix Davey, or Maxime Bermond; instead, she was about to confide in Sherlock Holmes!

"Hello, Clotilde?" said the Englishman.

A pause.

"Yes, it's Maxime," said Holmes.

At once, the drama took shape with tragic, almost-mathematical precision. Lupin, the mocking Lupin, the in-domitable Lupin, no longer sought to hide his anxiety. His face pale with fear, he strove to hear, to guess the exact nature of Holmes' conversation with Clotilde.

"Yes, it's all finished. I'm done here and I was just about to come to meet you as we arranged... Where? Why, where you are... Isn't that best?"

Holmes hesitated, seeking his words, then stopped. It was obvious that he was trying to make Clotilde reveal where she was without admitting that he, himself, had no idea where that was, which would have given the game away. Ganimard's presence hindered him, too... Lupin was praying for some miracle to suddenly cut off the diabolical cat-and-mouse conversation that was almost too much for his nerves.

"Hello? I can't hear you," Holmes continued. "Yes, it's a bad connection. I almost lost you. Can you hear me now? Good. On second thought, I think you'd better go home... No,

149

there's no danger, none at all… Holmes? He's still in England. I just had a cable from Southampton…"

The irony of those words. Holmes uttered them with a supreme sense of satisfaction.

"Go at once, my darling," he added. "I shall be with you soon."

He hung up the receiver.

"Chief Inspector," he said, "I would like to borrow three of your men."

"To arrest the Blonde Phantom, I presume?"

"Indeed."

"You know who she is? Where she is?"

"I do."

"By Jove! A fine capture! Lupin and the Blonde Phantom, on the same day! Folenfant, take two men and go with Mister Holmes!"

The Detective walked away, followed by the three policemen.

The battle was truly over. The Blonde Phantom, too, would soon be arrested by Sherlock Holmes. Thanks to his prodigious faculties, his incredible perseverance and a few lucky occurrences, the Detective triumphed while Lupin's fate was an irreparable disaster.

"Mister Holmes!"

The Englishman stopped.

"Yes, Monsieur Lupin?"

The Gentleman Burglar seemed deeply affected by this final blow. His face was wrinkled, tired-looking and somber. Still, he managed to draw himself up and recover some of his earlier energy, addressing his rival in a voice of feigned indifference.

"You must admit that fate is dead against me. Earlier, it prevented me from escaping through my secret passage and delivered me straight into your hands. Now, through this idiotic telephone, it delivers my lady into your hands as well. I surrender to its whims."

"Meaning?"

"Meaning that I'm willing to reopen negotiations if you are."

Holmes took Ganimard aside and asked his permission, in a tone that clearly entertained no refusal, to exchange a few private words with Lupin.

Then, the Detective walked up to his rival and looked him squarely in the eyes.

"What do you want?" he asked.

"Mademoiselle Destange's freedom," replied Lupin.

"You know my price."

"Yes."

"You agree to pay it?"

"I agree to all your conditions."

"But just now," exclaimed the Englishman, "you refused... for yourself..."

"It was for myself, Mister Holmes. Now, it involves a woman... a woman whom I love. We have very strict ideas about such things in France, me more than most probably."

He said this quite simply. Holmes gave him an almost imperceptible nod of the head.

"Where is the Blue Diamond?" he whispered.

"Take my cane; it's over there, leaning against the mantelpiece...Hold the knob tightly in one hand and turn the iron ferrule with the other."

Holmes did as instructed and the knob came unscrewed. Inside was a ball of putty, and inside that, the Blue Diamond.

He examined it closely. It was genuine.

"Mademoiselle Destange is free, Monsieur Lupin."

"Free in the future as well as in the present? She has nothing to fear from you?"

"From anyone."

"No matter what happens."

"No matter what happens. I have forgotten her name and her address."

"Thank you. And *au revoir*, for we shall meet again, isn't that so, Mister Holmes?"

"I have no doubt about it."

A more or less heated discussion followed between the Detective and Ganimard. It was cut short by the Englishman.

"I am very sorry, Chief Inspector, to have to disagree with you, but I don't have any more time to argue with you. I leave for London in an hour."

"But... What about the Blonde Phantom?"

"I know of no such person."

"Only a moment ago, you said..."

"I know what I said, but take it or leave it. I have already handed you Lupin. Here is the Blue Diamond, which you may have the pleasure of handing to the Comtesse de Crozon yourself. I can't see that you have any reason to complain."

"But the Blonde Phantom..."

"Find her."

He put his hat on and walked away briskly, like a gentleman who has no desire to loiter once his business is done.

"Good-bye, Mister Holmes!" shouted Lupin. "Have a pleasant journey. I'll never forget the pleasant moments we spent together. And my kind regards to Dr. Watson!"

He received no reply.

"That's what we call taking English leave," he chuckled. "Ah, those worthy Englishmen do not have the same sense of panache that characterizes us Frenchmen, eh, Ganimard? Just think of the exit I would have made had our roles been reversed? With what exquisite civility I would have disguised my triumph... Bless my soul, Ganimard, what are you doing? Executing a search warrant? But there's nothing left, my friend! Not a scrap of paper! All my archives have been moved to a place of safety."

"Who knows? One can never tell."

Lupin resigned himself. Held by two policemen, surrounded by all the rest, he patiently looked on as Ganimard thoroughly searched the apartment. However, after 20 minutes, he raised a protest.

"Come on, Ganimard," he sighed. "You'll never be finished at this rate."

"Are you in a hurry?"

"As it happens, yes! I have an important engagement."

"In jail!"

"No, about town."

"Pah! At what time?"

"At 2 p.m."

"It's past 3 p.m. now."

"Exactly, I'm going to be late and you know how much I hate that."

"Another five minutes."

"OK, but do hurry up!"

"I'll do my best."

"Your best isn't fast enough… There's nothing in that closet!"

"Not so. Here are some papers."

"Old bills."

"Tied with a ribbon?"

"A pink ribbon? Oh, Ganimard, don't look at them, I beg you!"

"Why? Are they from a woman?"

"Yes."

"A lady?"

"Yes."

"What's her name?"

"Madame Ganimard."

"Very funny! Very funny!" said the Chief Inspector, clearly not amused.

At that moment, the men returned from the other room and reported that they had not found anything. Lupin laughed.

"Of course not! I told you so! Did you expect to find a list of all my friends? My secret correspondence with the Kaiser? What you should have been looking for, Ganimard, were the solutions to all the little mysteries of this hideaway. For example, that gas pipe is a speaking tube, this wall here is hollow, that fireplace hides a secret staircase and there's a veritable tangle of bell wires. For instance, try that button…"

Ganimard did as requested.

"Did you hear anything?"

"No."

"Nor I. Yet you've just signaled to the captain of my airship to get it ready for take-off in a few minutes."

"Enough of your nonsense," said Ganimard. "Let's go!"

He took several steps, followed by his men.

Lupin, however, did not budge.

The policemen pushed him and pulled him, but in vain.

"You refuse to come with us?" asked Ganimard.

"Not at all."

"Then…"

"It all depends."

"Depends on what?"

"On where we're going."

"You're going straight to jail, where else?"

"I don't want to go to jail."

"You should have thought of that before."

"Besides, didn't I just tell you I had a pressing engagement?"

"Lupin!"

"The Blonde Phantom is waiting for me and you think I would be rude enough to keep her waiting. That wouldn't be the conduct of a gentleman!"

"Lupin, I'm warning you!" said the Chief Inspector who was beginning to lose his temper. "So far, I've treated you with excessive consideration, but there are limits to my patience. Follow me!"

"Impossible. I've got an engagement and I mean to keep it."

"For the last time?"

"Impossible."

Ganimard gestured. Two men tried to grab Lupin beneath his arms, but they dropped him at once, screaming in pain. He had stabbed them with two long needles he had hidden in his sleeves.

The other policemen, mad with rage, their hatred finally unleashed, eager to avenge their two comrades and themselves for the endless ignominies the Gentleman Burglar had visited upon them in the past, fell on him and rained a shower of blows upon his body. Hit in the temple, Lupin fell down to the ground.

"If you've injured him," growled Ganimard, "you'll answer to me."

He bent over the limp prisoner, prepared to help, but finding that Lupin was breathing normally, he told his men to take him by the shoulders and feet, while he himself grabbed his waist.

"Slowly now... Gently... Don't shake him... You brutes, you might have killed him... Well, Lupin, how do you feel?"

The Gentleman Burglar opened his eyes.

"Not great, Ganimard," he stammered. "You shouldn't have let them knock me about so much."

"Damn it! It's your own fault! Being so stubborn, so insolent," replied Ganimard with genuine distress. "Are you hurt?"

They had reached the landing.

"Please, Ganimard," moaned Lupin. "Take the elevator... Otherwise, they'll break my bones..."

"Excellent idea," agreed the Chief Inspector. "Besides, the stairs are so narrow. It would be too difficult to carry you down..."

He called up the elevator. They laid Lupin on the seat with every imaginable precaution. Ganimard finally sat down beside him.

"Go downstairs at once," he told his men. "Wait for me by the Concierge's lodge. Understood?"

He shut the door. Almost at once, the elevator shot up like a balloon. Screams of fury were heard, answered only by a long, sarcastic laugh.

"Damn!" shouted Ganimard, feeling frantically in the dark for the lever. Failing to find it, he shouted: "The fifth floor! Get to the fifth floor!"

The policemen rushed upstairs, four steps at a time. But a strange thing happened: the elevator seemed to go straight through the ceiling of the fifth floor right in front of the detectives' amazed eyes. It emerged on an upper story, just beneath the roof, where the servants' quarters were located.

Three men were waiting and opened the door. Two overpowered Ganimard who, hampered in his movements and bewildered, was hardly able to defend himself. The third man helped Lupin out.

"I told you, Ganimard," he joked. "Carried off by a hot-air balloon, and all thanks to you. Next time, you must show less compassion. And remember that Arsène Lupin doesn't let himself be bashed about by a gang of brutes without a valid reason. Good-bye…"

The elevator door was closed and the elevator, with Ganimard trussed up inside, was sent back towards the lower floors. All this happened so quickly that the Chief Inspector caught up with his men just as they arrived at the Concierge's lodge.

Without a word, they hurried across the courtyard and up the service stairs, the only means of reaching the top floor.

A long corridor lined with small, numbered doors led them to a door that had been left ajar. Beyond it was another, similar corridor, in the adjacent house, also with rows of numbered doors. At the end of that corridor was another service staircase. Ganimard rushed down, crossed another courtyard, then a hall and came out on the Rue Picot. At last, he understood: the two houses were built back to back, their fronts facing two parallel streets, about 60 yards from each other.

Ganimard went into the Concierge's lodge and identified himself.

"Have four men just gone out?"

"Yes. Two servants from the fourth and fifth floors, and two friends of theirs."

"Who lives on the fourth and fifth floors?"

"Two cousins by the names of Fauvel and Provost. They moved out this morning. Only the two servants remained. They've just left."

"What a fine arrest we could have made," said Ganimard, collapsing into a chair. "The whole gang occupied this entire block..."

Forty minutes later, two gentlemen arrived by cab at the Gare du Nord and rushed to catch the Calais Express, followed by a porter carrying their bags.

One had his arm in a sling and his face was drawn and pale. The other looked as if he was in great spirits.

"Hurry up, Watson. We mustn't miss our train! I shall never forget these ten days."

"Neither shall I!"

"What a superb battle we fought!"

"Never more magnificent."

"A few, minor setbacks now and then along the way..."

"My arm broken..."

"...But at the end, victory! Lupin arrested! The Blue Diamond recovered! What is a broken arm against such a success?"

"I suppose you're right..."

"I am! And remember, It was at the very moment when we were at that pharmacist and you were suffering like the hero you are that I discovered the clue that guided me through the darkness."

"That's true. That was a fortuitous thing after all."

The doors were being locked.

"Take your seats, please. Hurry up, gentlemen."

The porter climbed into the empty compartment and placed the bags in the racks above. Meanwhile, Holmes was helping Watson climb in.

"Hurry up, old friend. Pull yourself together!"

"Sorry, Holmes, but that's very hard to do when you've only got one good hand."

"What? Ah, yes. Well, don't fuss about. You're hardly the only man to have experienced a broken arm. What about the fellows who have actually lost an arm? Are you settled now? Thank goodness!"

The Detective gave the porter a half-franc coin.

"Here, my good man. That's for you."

"Thank you, Mister Holmes."

Sherlock Holmes raised his eyes and recognized Arsène Lupin.

"You! You!" he exclaimed.

And Watson, too, stammered, waving his one hand.

"You! You! But you've been arrested. Holmes told me so. When he left you, Ganimard and 30 of his men held you prisoner."

Lupin crossed his arms and affected an air of indignation.

"And so you thought I'd let you go without coming to see you off? After the excellent friendly relations we've had these last ten days? Why, that would have been unspeakably rude of me! What do you take me for?"

The train engine whistled.

"However, I forgive you! Do you have everything you want? Tobacco? Matches? The evening papers? You'll read all the details about my arrest; your latest exploit, I believe, Mister Holmes. And now, good-bye! I was truly delighted to have made your acquaintance, I mean it! If I can ever do anything for you, please don't hesitate to let me know... I'll only be too pleased..."

He jumped down to the platform and shut the door.

"Good-bye!" he shouted again, waving his handkerchief. "I promise to write. You too. Let me know how your broken arm is, Dr. Watson. I shall expect to hear from both of you. Just a postcard now and then... Address it to 'Arsène Lupin, Paris,' It'll always reach me, it's quite enough. Never mind about putting a stamp on it! Good-bye! See you soon, I hope!"

# Arsène Lupin Arrives Too Late

**by**
**Jean-Marc & Randy Lofficier**

*Excerpt of a letter from Jeanne Darcieux to Paul Daubreuil,
Tuesday, January 12, 1904:*
Dear Paul,
As you have surely heard, the Belgian Police arrested my stepfather, Paul Darcieux, in Brussels. Last week, I received a
communication from a Belgian policeman named Poirot, who
confirmed that he would soon be extradited to France. Oh,
how I shudder when I remember the horrible events that took
place at Maupertuis. I still see my stepfather's evil face as he
prepared to plunge his dagger into my body that terrible night.
I don't think I shall ever be able to banish that image from my
mind... I will never have the right words to thank you for all
that you did for me, my dearest friend. (...) I have followed Dr.
Gueroult's sage advice and come to London to start my life
afresh. Thank you for recommending a good solicitor in Versailles to oversee the management of the Maupertuis estate,
but all that is now a part of the life that I left behind...

*Excerpt of a letter from Jeanne Darcieux to Paul Daubreuil,
Monday, February 1, 1904:*
Dear Paul,
Your letter filled me with joy. Since you were kind enough to
inquire as to my progress here, I shall report news that, I am
sure, will please you greatly. Yesterday, I found a position as a
tutor teaching French to Lord Strongborough's 12-year-old
son, Anthony. Lord Strongborough is a charming widower
who is very much involved with the Jockey Club, of which I
understand he is one of the stewards. I am expected to live in
his beautiful estate in Surrey. My duties will include...

*Excerpt of a letter from Jeanne Darcieux to Paul Daubreuil, Friday, May 6, 1904:*

Dear Paul,

Edward and I are just back from the Riviera, where he has a house near Saint Paul de Vence. We had the grandest time. Upon our return, Edward decided to announce our formal engagement. A wonderful party was held at the Manor. I so wish that you could have been there. The entire Jockey Club attended. Dr. Taylor regaled us with stories of when he and Edward used to race horses in America, in Kentucky, I believe. Major Roland told us of his service in India...

*Announcement published in* The Times *of London, Friday, July 1, 1904:*

The forthcoming marriage is announced between Sir Edward, 31st Lord Strongborough, Baron of Cuthbert, and Mademoiselle Jeanne Darcieux de Maupertuis of Vendôme, France. The ceremony will take place at Strongborough Hall, Surrey, later this month.

*Excerpt of a letter from Jeanne Darcieux to Paul Daubreuil, Thursday, September 8, 1904:*

Dear Paul,

I cannot believe that I am writing this to you, but the nightmare has returned. Death again surrounds me, creeping over me, casting an invisible shroud over my life. As I wrote to you in my last letter, young Anthony passed away of gastric fever two weeks ago. Edward was, understandably, devastated by the death of his only son, who was the light of both our lives. Major Roland, Dr. Taylor and the other stewards of the Jockey Club have all tried to console him and shake him out of his dark mood, but nothing seems to work. He had the most terrible row with Dr. Taylor, and has simply refused to see Major Roland. He now spends most of his time alone, barricaded in his room, just like my stepfather once did. That is a most horrible reminder of the evil days at Maupertuis...

*Excerpt of a letter from Jeanne Darcieux to Paul Daubreuil, Tuesday, September 20, 1904:*

Dear Paul,

My life is now worse than it has ever been, if such a thing is possible. There have been foul words spread about Anthony's death. Hushed whispers about poison. I see the way the staff now looks at me. I am the foreign Jezebel who has taken the place of their beloved mistress...

*Excerpt of a letter from Jeanne Darcieux to Paul Daubreuil, Monday, October 3, 1904:*

Dear Paul,

Last night, Major Roland called to see Edward. They spent some time together in his office. The Major looked quite unhappy when he left. We talked a bit afterwards. He mentioned that Mister Sherlock Holmes himself had agreed to come out of retirement and travel to Paris to tackle the affair of the Blue Diamond and give a sound thrashing to "that wretched braggart, Lupin," as he called you. He does not know what happened between us at Maupertuis, of course. I am so worried about you, my dearest friend. They say that Mister Holmes has no equal. Please, be careful. Here, even Edward, when I do see him, which is not often these days, has started to regard me with suspicion. I do not know to whom to turn. I feel as if an invisible noose is tightening around my neck and I am utterly powerless to stop it...

*Excerpt of a letter from Jeanne Darcieux to Paul Daubreuil, Tuesday, November 1, 1904:*

Dear Paul,

The news is too horrible for words. Edward died last night. He succumbed to the same gastric fever as Anthony. He had been complaining of stomach pains, then fell prey to nausea and much vomiting. He was taken to the hospital yesterday. Dr. Taylor rushed to his side but it was too late.

*Excerpt of a letter from Jeanne Darcieux to Paul Daubreuil, Thursday, November 17, 1904:*

Dear Paul,

There is now talk of an inquest. The Police were here and questioned me and the staff... That man of yours whom you mentioned in your last letter never arrived. I hope nothing befell him. I feel as if I am being watched. In your last letter, you said you were *en route* to Uruguay. I so wish you could be here. I am certain you would untangle the mystery of what happened in no time. I have made a note of the lawyer you recommended, Sir Edward Leithen, should the need arise...

*Article published in* The Times *of London, Tuesday, December 6, 1904:*

Lady Strongborough was arrested today on suspicion of having poisoned her husband. The Home Secretary ordered that the bodies of Lord Strongborough and that of his son, Anthony, deceased August 25 last, be exhumed and checked for poison...

*Excerpt of a letter from Jeanne Darcieux to Paul Daubreuil, Monday, December 12, 1904:*

Dear Paul,

Dr. Taylor does not trust the Police; he insisted on supervising the removal of the organs for analysis. I think he is afraid of the scandal. I am being treated as if I had the plague. No one will see me or talk to me. I have written to Sir Edward to retain his counsel, although I pray every day that his assistance will not be required and I will awaken from this nightmare...

*Article published in* The Times *of London, Thursday, December 15, 1904:*

Traces of a poison called cadmium were found in both bodies. Cadmium is soluble in acid foods and the Police suspect it was administered to the victims in lemonade prepared by Lady Strongborough. Traces of cadmium were also found in medicine being taken by Lord Strongborough...

*Article published in* The Times *of London, Monday, December 19, 1904:*
Today, at the inquest into the death of Lord Strongborough, Constable Barnaby presented evidence that bottles containing cadmium compounds were found in the photographic laboratory set up for Lady Strongborough by her late husband in what used to be the conservatory...

*Article published in* The Times *of London, Wednesday, December 21, 1904:*
Today, at the inquest into the death of Lord Strongborough, the jury recorded a verdict of willful murder against person or persons unknown...

*Excerpt of a letter from Jeanne Darcieux to Paul Daubreuil, Thursday, January 12, 1905:*
Dear Paul,

It has now been two months since your last letter and I am still without news of you. I continue to write to the safe address you gave me in Paris, hoping that my letters are reaching you, wherever you might be. I pray every day for your safe return, for I believe you, and you alone, can put an end to this awful nightmare I am living. I did not poison my husband, Paul, upon my soul, and neither did I poison young Anthony, who was as dear to me as if he had been my own son. The Press has reported that serious irregularities have been discovered in the accounts of the Jockey Club. Apparently, Edward had a secret life about which I knew nothing. They say I killed him because I wanted to get my hands on his fortune before he was irremediably disgraced and ruined, but this is ridiculous, for I am wealthy too in my own right. I have property in France and I could have helped poor Edward had he but asked. They also say that I was the only one who could have poisoned him because I have access to cadmium, even though I was always careful to lock up my laboratory and none of the chemicals were ever missing...

*Article published in* The Times *of London, Wednesday, February 1, 1905:*

Lady Strongborough's trial began today at the Old Bailey. As the prosecuting counsel, Mister Erskine-Brown, laid out his case, everyone present was silent and sombre. Lady Strongborough appeared vulnerable, seemingly on the verge of tears and, at one stage, she shook her head in grief as she heard some of the agonizing details of her husband's last moments. Sir Edward Leithen, counsel for the defense, made a remarkable opening statement in which he urged the jury to look beyond the circumstantial evidence that he called a "web of deceit." Right from the outset, the jury was left in no doubts as to the magnitude of the case. The judge, Mister Justice Wargrave, warned them that a case of this length, lasting possibly up to three months, was physically strenuous and advised them not to be swayed by the oratorical tricks of the defense and to look at "nothing but the facts"...

*Excerpt of a letter from Jeanne Darcieux to Paul Daubreuil, Tuesday, March 14, 1905*

Dear Paul,

I am still without news of you. I fear the worst. Sir Edward Leithen is mounting what I believe they call a "vigorous defense," yet the autopsy results speak against me. No one, certainly not I, can explain the presence of the fatal cadmium in the bodies. The Judge seems prejudiced against me. They call him a "hanging judge." I fear the worst...

*Article published in* The Times *of London, Monday, April 3, 1905:*

Lady Strongborough Found Guilty... Lady Strongborough burst into tears as Mister Justice Wargrave delivered the ritual sentence: "The sentence of the court upon you is that you be taken from this place to a lawful place of execution and that you be hanged by the neck until you are dead. And may God have mercy on your soul."

Dear Paul,

This is my last letter to you and I can only pray that it will find you in good health, even if comes too late to alter my fate, which now seems sealed. I am innocent, but I have reconciled myself to my destiny. Tomorrow, I shall walk to the gallows praying only that nothing evil has befallen you, my dearest friend...

The execution was set for 8 a.m. The night before, Lady Strongborough was visited by her counsel, Sir Edward Leithen. I was told that she had accepted her fate and that, apart from a slight nervous twitch at the corner of her mouth, she was calm. After Sir Edward had left, she was given brandy and water and at 11 p.m. she slept. She was awakened at 5 a.m. to prepare herself for a visit from the Prison Chaplin, Reverend Fergusson. The Reverend stayed with Lady Strongborough until 7 a.m. and tried to get her to confess that she was guilty, but she steadfastly denied that she had poisoned either her husband or his son and categorically maintained her innocence. At 7:30 a.m., Lady Strongborough was given a cup of tea with more brandy and water. At 7:40 a.m., she was joined in the condemned's cell by Under Sheriff Regan and myself. We told her that the time had come to carry out the sentence and she was quietly led to courtyard where the gallows had been erected the day before. Here, we were joined by William Billington, the hangman, who was introduced to Lady Strongborough, who showed no emotion. Mister Billington tied her hands and she asked that he not draw the rope too tight before the drop. She was extremely calm at this point. She was then taken to the chapel where she received the final sacraments. At 7:55 a.m., the prison's death bell tolled, which marked the start of the procession to the gallows. Reverend

165

Fergusson read extracts from the burial service. We were joined by the Head Turnkey, Mister Daley, and two warders, George Bulman and Derek Willis. As we walked across the yard to the gallows, a man was suddenly ushered in by warder Kavanagh. He shouted that the execution be stopped and indicated that he was holding a reprieve signed by Mister Akers-Douglas, the Home Secretary himself. "It's him!" screamed Lady Strongborough. "I knew he would not abandon me. I knew he would not be too late! It's Arsène Lupin!" "Shut up, you little git," said Mister Daley. "Don't you recognize Mister Sherlock Holmes?"

*Excerpt from the Private Notebooks of John H. Watson, M.D., undated, but likely written in late April 1905:*
My friend Mister Sherlock Holmes asked me to pen a few notes on the strange case of Lady Strongborough in which he was so fortunate as to be able to save her from the hangman's noose with but minutes to spare.

For reasons that will become clear to my reader, I seriously doubt that I will ever write, even less publish, a full account of this case, but it is sufficiently worthy for me to record some of the bare facts in this Journal.

As I have recorded in my account entitled "The Reigate Puzzle," Holmes had already crossed the path of, and thwarted Paul Darcieux, Baron Maupertuis, in the Spring of 1887. It was, therefore, the most amazing coincidence that he was called upon to save the life of the man's stepdaughter 18 years later, during his retirement in the South Downs.

On referring to my notes, I see that I made a copy of the cable which Holmes received on March 22, and that started his investigation. It came from some God-forsaken city called Malatya, deep inside the Ottoman Empire, and had been relayed through the British Embassy in Constantinople. It merely read: "STRONGBOROUGH MURDER STOP DEADLY COURT STOP SIGNED AL."

Under normal circumstances, Holmes would have ignored the message, as he receives many such nonsensical correspondences from various benighted souls all around England and even from other parts of the Empire. But there was the signatory: "AL."

At Holmes' request, his brother, Mycroft, called on some of his associates in Turkey and, two days later, we learned that Malatya was deep inside hostile territory held by a mad warlord known locally as the "Red Sultan." As the report went, a single westerner, a man in his thirties, had fought and defeated 40 of the Red Sultan's warriors to invade a telegram office and, there, had held a small army at bay during the time it took to relay that cable via Constantinople. Apparently, no more could be sent. The report labeled the man "clearly insane" while praising his bravery. When he read this, Holmes no longer had any doubts as to the identity of "AL."

Of all the enemies Holmes has fought during his tumultuous career, none, not even the nefarious Professor Moriarty or Charles-Augustus Milverton, have ever been able to get under my friend's skin as much as the Frenchman. "The Frenchman" or *He* or *Him* was, in fact, how he most often referred to *him* when we discussed *him*, which was a rare occurrence at best. Perhaps it was a habit unconsciously borrowed from Chief Inspector Ganimard. All of Holmes' other foes had, in effect, played the game according to the same rules. But with *him*, there were no rules. It was like grappling with quicksilver.

Having ascertained that the cable from Malatya came from *him*, my friend set to work immediately.

In just under a week, he had untangled the mystery. However, it took all of his considerable influence to convince the Home Secretary of Lady Strongborough's innocence and get him to sign the reprieve which, thank God, he was able to deliver just in time to spare the poor woman's life.

I shall now jot down the conversation that ensued later that selfsame day between Sherlock Holmes and Lady Strongborough, which I had the privilege of attending.

"I owe you my life, Mister Holmes," said Lady Strongborough, who was still understandably shaken by her ordeal.

At that point, my friend pulled out the cablegram and showed it to her.

"This is not entirely true, Madam," said Holmes, thoughtfully. "Your guardian angel came through, I believe."

Lady Strongborough read the cable and began crying, silently, without sobs; tears rolled gently down her cheeks as if the weight of the grim fate she had just been spared had suddenly crushed her gentle soul. We gave her time to recover. Then, she said:

"I am most grateful that you showed me this, Mister Holmes. And naturally thrilled that it made sense to you. But I confess that I do not understand. What does 'deadly court' mean? Is it a reference to Judge Wargrave?..."

"It is not 'deadly court,' Lady Strongborough–that was likely an error in the transmission–but 'deadly cort,' also known as deadly galerina or *cortinarius speciosissimus*, one of the deadliest brown-capped fungi, found commonly throughout the American Northwest, and the symptoms of which could easily be mistaken for cadmium poisoning."

"But the autopsy said..."

"This was a most unusual case. The man who strived to engineer your doom had a diabolical mind. Your husband, Lady Strongborough, was in fact murdered after all of you thought he had been poisoned. The evidence was then retroactively tampered with to make the facts fit the theory formulated by the Police."

"So cadmium is not what killed Edward?"

"No. I will tell you the story as I reconstructed it. Your husband, I am sorry to say, Lady Strongborough, had been involved in some unpleasant business while in America 20 years ago. The sins of youth, some would say. A woman died in childbirth and so did the child. Much cause for scandal, if it were revealed publicly. Two years ago, the man whom you knew as Dr. Taylor appeared in London. He had known your husband in America and was well-acquainted with his past. He blackmailed him, first to get a position on the board of the Jockey Club, then to embezzle funds. But after his marriage to you, Lord Strongborough began to rebel; I believe he threatened to report Taylor to the Police.

"I have no doubt that Taylor decided to murder your husband at once, but I believe what gave him the idea on how to do it was young Anthony's death, which was, in fact, completely natural and due to gastric fever, as had been correctly diagnosed at the time.

"Taylor knew of your photographic laboratory and saw how Anthony's death could retroactively be made to look like cadmium poisoning. The criminal carried with him some finely ground deadly cort that, no doubt, he had collected while in America. He merely waited for Lord Strongborough to be afflicted with gastroenteritis, as Anthony had been, and perhaps did as much he could to inflame the condition. When your husband was taken to the hospital, he rushed to his side and there, he administered the poison. Deadly cort is instantly fatal and would mimic the symptoms of cadmium poisoning, which is slower and more painful. Since everyone later assumed that your husband had been poisoned at the Manor, when he was initially taken ill, no one bothered to look at the hospital records.

"Then, the only thing left for Taylor to do was to fool the medical examiners by lacing the samples with carefully measured traces of cadmium. If you recall, he insisted on supervising the autopsies. All the evidence against you was retroactively fabricated to fit the case that he wanted the Police to make against you. As I said, it was one of the most diabolically ingenious murder schemes I have ever come across."

"Have they arrested Dr. Taylor?" asked Lady Strongborough.

"I'm afraid that, as soon as he got wind of my involvement, he fled the country. That was, in fact, how I was able to persuade the Home Secretary that he was the murderer and that he should immediately grant your reprieve. I heard he's fled back to France."

"Fled back to France?"

"My investigation showed that he arrived from Paris in 1902. But I could find no more about him. He obviously is a most remarkable criminal. Perhaps *he*, I mean, your friend, will be able to shed more light on this... But, at least, you no longer have anything to fear, Lady Strongborough."

And thus did my friend Sherlock Holmes solve the murder of Lord Strongborough and save the life of a most gracious Lady. I have recorded this as an appendix to the case of Baron Maupertuis in the event that I ever decide to write it in full. But as Holmes mentioned, the case still contains some loose ends, and besides I know that my friend does not like me to write about *him*, so it is probably best to let it lie for the time being...

The village of Saint Paul de Vence in Provence was a jewel located in the hills above Nice. It was bright and beautiful this sunny afternoon of June. The sky was a deep penetrating blue and the quality of the light made every object stand out in sharp relief.

Lady Strongborough waited at the terrace of the single café that serviced the village, sipping on a *grenadine*. He had told her that he would be there precisely at 5 p.m. and she knew that he would not betray his word.

The village clock in the church tower tolled five.

"I deeply apologize for not being able to make it back in time," said a voice from behind her.

He had appeared as if by magic. She had seen no car, heard no engine, yet there he was, looking very much like the Paul Dubreuil she had met 18 months earlier. He pulled out a chair and sat down. He gestured to the *garçon* to bring him a *pastis*.

"When did you get back?" she asked.

"Two months ago. I lost the lives of a couple of good men trying to reach Constantinople in time, but the Red Sultan barred my way. I knew, however, that if I could send that cable to Sherlock Holmes, he, of all people, would have both the mental abilities and the power to rescue you. I was thrilled to discover upon my return to Marseilles that I hadn't been mistaken. I never would have forgiven myself if..."

She put her hand on his to dispel the ghastly image of the fate that they knew had almost been hers.

"Mister Holmes said that you knew more about this case than he had uncovered," Lady Strongborough said.

"How perceptive of him," he smiled. "His mind is as penetrating as ever. Yes, the trick that the so-called Dr. Taylor used, that bit of misdirection, of sleight of hand, reminded me of another case, one that was much covered in the Press, three years ago. *The Affair of the Glandier. The Mystery of the Yellow Room.* The murderer was exposed as Ballmeyer, an international criminal of the first order. We never met but I like to keep an eye on the competition. I knew that he had been in America, at the same time as your late husband, and that he would have been familiar with poisons found on that Continent. He also had been in London in 1901 and was implicated in a murky business of stolen bonds... But more to the point, when he was finally unmasked by a young reporter from *L'Epoque* at the end of the Yellow Room case, we discovered that Ballmeyer had had the prodigious idea of masquerading as an Inspector of the Sûreté, Frédéric Larsan! What a strike of genius! Ballmeyer, a man wanted by half the police forces of Europe and America, was hiding in plain sight in the French Sûreté! You have to admire that inventiveness! Why, I was almost jealous!"

"So Dr. Taylor was Ballmeyer?"

"Yes. And Ballmeyer was Frédéric Larsan, and I knew that Larsan had been involved in the famous case of the gold bar robbery of the Hôtel de la Monnaie, in which, if you recall, your stepfather, Paul Darcieux, Baron Maupertuis, was one of the suspects."

"Yes, that's true... I remember. He was one of the Trustees, but was cleared of all suspicion."

"By Frédéric Larsan, his accomplice, the man who likely devised the whole scheme and used his position as Inspector of the Sûreté to frame an innocent man. You see, it all ties

171

together. So, I asked myself, what if Ballmeyer-Larsan was up to his old tricks again, seeking to kill two birds with one stone: he murders your husband to cover his tracks with the Jockey Club, and he pins the blame on you to have you hung afterwards. If Lord Strongborough had been the only intended victim, I have no doubt that Ballmeyer could have dispatched him quickly and easily. Why resort to such a complicated scheme? Because he wanted you dead as well. Why? Ask yourself: who would have profited from your death?"

"My stepfather! He's the only family I have."

"Indeed. We're drawn back to the Ballmeyer-Darcieux connection. So, one of the first things I did upon my return to this country was to check your stepfather's fate. And I wasn't surprised to discover that someone had organized his escape soon after his extradition to France."

"Oh my God! He's free?"

"Don't fear, Jeanne. I would have taken steps, but I had no need. They say there's no honor among thieves, you know... They found an unidentified body not far from here, which I know to be Paul Darcieux. There is no doubt in my mind that when Holmes exposed Ballmeyer, and his plans to have you hung failed, Ballmeyer killed your stepfather."

"And Ballmeyer?"

"My inquiries lead me to believe that the same young journalist who exposed him the first time is back on his case. He has a brilliant mind, almost as good as Sherlock Holmes, to tell the truth. And he can be quite ruthless, under his college boy manners. I hope we never cross swords. I have no doubt he'll deal with Ballmeyer–definitively."

"You see, Sainclair, I had only condemned Larsan to life in prison, but he killed himself! It was God's will. May God have mercy on his soul!"
Joseph Rouletabille revealing Ballmeyer's fate to his friend Sainclair at the conclusion of *The Perfume of the Lady in Black*, Summer 1905.

# The Jewish Lamp

*Chapter I*

Sherlock Holmes and Watson were seated on either side of the great fireplace in Holmes' drawing-room, their feet warmed by a comfortable coal fire.

The Detective's pipe, a small briar with a silver ferrule, went out. He knocked the ashes out, refilled it, lit it and gathered the folds of his dressing-gown around his knees. Then, he again began to puff away, sending graceful little rings of smoke floating towards the ceiling.

Watson watched him. He watched like a soldier watches an officer on the eve of battle: with intent, staring eyes, unblinking, waiting only for some kind of signal, ready to spring into action at the least gesture from his fellow soldier. Would Holmes break his silence? Would he share the products of his thoughts, a domain the entrance of which, Watson felt, was often denied to him?

Holmes remained lost in silent contemplation.

"Things are very quiet," Watson ventured. "There's not a single case for us to nibble at."

Holmes remained aggressively silent, but his rings of smoke became more and more perfect and an observer might have guessed that he was drawing from this a sense of profound contentment, the kind of achievement one enjoys when one's mind is otherwise devoid of any important thoughts.

Disheartened, Watson rose and walked to the window.

Baker Street stretched out between the gloomy house fronts beneath a dark sky from which fell an angry downpour. A cab drove by, followed by another. Watson jotted down their numbers. One can never tell.

"Ah!" he said. "The postman."

Minutes later, Mrs. Hudson showed the man into the drawing-room.

"Two registered letters, Mister Holmes... If you'd care to sign here?"

Holmes signed the register and walked the postman back to the door. He then returned, opened the first letter and started to read it.

"You look quite pleased," said Watson after a moment.

"This letter contains a very attractive proposal. You wanted a new case; here it is. Read it..."

Watson read:

> *18, rue Murillo*
> *Paris*
>
> *Sir:*
>
> *I am writing to ask for the benefit of your assistance and experience. I have been the victim of a serious theft and none of the inquiries undertaken so far have produced any results.*
>
> *I am sending, under separate cover, several press articles that will provide you with all the necessary information about the case. After you have reviewed them, should you be inclined to accept my offer and come to Paris, please consider yourself my honored guest. I am enclosing here a pre-signed check, which you may fill in for any amount which you would like to name for your expenses.*
>
> *Please telegraph me to inform me of your decision.*
>
> *I remain, Sir,*
>
> *Yours very truly,*
>
> *Baron Victor d'Imblevalle*

"Well," said Holmes. "This sounds rather enticing... A little trip to Paris, why not? I haven't been back there since our battle with Arsène Lupin, and I wouldn't mind revisiting that beautiful city under more peaceful circumstances."

The Detective tore the check into four pieces. While Watson, whose arm had not fully recovered from the injury received in the course of said battle, was complaining bitterly about Paris and its citizens, he opened the second envelope.

At once, Holmes reacted with an involuntarily angry gesture, which he quickly suppressed. He read the letter attentively, his brow furrowed; then, he crumpled it and irritably threw it on the floor.

"What? What's the matter?" asked Watson, surprised.

He picked up the letter, unfolded it and read with growing stupefaction:

*My Dear Mister Holmes:*

*You know the admiration I have for you and the interest which I take in your reputation. Therefore, please accept my heartfelt advice to not take on the case which you have been asked to solve. Your interference would cause much harm, your efforts would only result in a pitiful result and you might be forced to publicly acknowledge failure.*

*I am exceedingly anxious to spare you such public humiliation and I beg you, in the name of our mutual friendship, to stay comfortably in your Baker Street residence.*

*Please convey my kindest wishes to your colleague Dr. Watson, and accept for yourself the respectful homage of*

*Yours most sincerely,*

*Arsène Lupin*

"Arsène Lupin!" repeated a bewildered Watson.

Holmes banged the table with his fist.

"Oh! I'm getting tired of that... that Frenchman! He treats me as if I were a schoolboy! '*Publicly acknowledge failure,*' eh? Didn't I force him to give up the Blue Diamond?"

"Maybe he's afraid of you?" suggested Watson.

"Don't be ridiculous! That man is afraid of no one. The proof is that he dares challenge me."

"But how did he learn of the Baron d'Imblevalle's letter?"

175

"How can I know that at this stage? You're asking silly questions, my dear fellow!"

"I thought... I imagined..."

"What? That I am a wizard?"

"No, of course not, but I've seen you perform such miracles!"

"No man can perform miracles, Watson. I no more than any other. I reflect, I deduct, I conclude, but I do not guess. Only fools make guesses."

Watson reflected that his friend, who was pacing up and down the room angrily, did not want to be bothered with more questions, and concluded that it was better to let the matter rest for the time being. When he finally heard Holmes ring Mrs. Hudson and ask for his traveling-bag, he further felt justified, based on that inescapable material fact, to deduct and conclude that his friend was going on a journey.

That deductive process enabled him to declare, in the tone of a man who is certain of his conclusions:

"Holmes, you're going to Paris."

"Possibly."

"And you're going in response to Lupin's challenge even more than to accept the Baron's offer."

"Possibly."

"Then, I am going with you."

"My old friend," said Holmes, interrupting his pacing. "Aren't you concerned that your left arm might share the fate of the right?"

"What could happen to me? You will be there."

"Well said! You're a fine fellow! And we will show Lupin that he made a mistake in defying us so boldly. Quick, Watson! Meet me at the first train."

"Shouldn't we wait for the press articles which the Baron mentioned?"

"What for?"

"Should I send a telegram?"

"No. It would only serve to inform Lupin of our arrival. This time, Watson, we must play a very cautious game."

That same afternoon, the two Englishmen stepped on board the ferry at Dover. The Channel crossing was eventless. In the express train from Calais to Paris, Holmes indulged in three hours of the soundest sleep, while Watson kept watch at the door of their compartment, mulling over vague thoughts about the case.

Holmes awoke feeling happy and well. The prospect of a new duel with Arsène Lupin delighted him. He rubbed his hands with the contented air of a man preparing to enjoy a feast.

"I'm glad to see you so excited," remarked Watson, feeling happy for his friend and unconsciously rubbing his hand in imitation.

At the Gare du Nord, the Englishmen hired a porter to carry their bags, handed their tickets to the collector and cheerfully stepped into the street.

"A fine day, Watson. Sunshine! Paris puts on her best to welcome us."

"What a crowd!"

"So much the better, old friend. We stand less chance of being noticed. No one will recognize us in the midst of such a throng."

"Mister Sherlock Holmes, I presume?"

The Detective stopped, somewhat taken aback. Who on Earth could be addressing him by his name?

A young woman stood beside him, a girl whose simple dress accentuated her attractive silhouette and whose pretty face wore a sad and anxious expression.

"You are Mister Sherlock Holmes, are you not?" she repeated.

The Detective remained silent, as much from perplexity as from a lifelong habit of prudence. So, she asked for the third time:

"It is Mister Sherlock Holmes whom I have the honor of addressing?"

"What do you want, girl?" replied the Detective, purposefully rude, to discourage what might be a questionable proposition.

The girl placed herself squarely in front of him.

"Please, listen to me, Mister Holmes," she said. "This is a very serious matter. I know that you are going to the Rue Murillo..."

"What did you say?"

"I know everything... You're going to Baron d'Imblevalle's residence... 18 Rue Murillo... Please, don't go... You mustn't! I assure you, you'll regret it. I'm telling you this not because I have a stake in the matter, but because I know what will happen. It's a question of conscience..."

Holmes tried to push her aside, but she continued, with more insistence.

"Please! I beg you! Don't be stubborn... Ah! If only I knew how to convince you! Look deep into my eyes, into my soul... I'm sincere... I speak the truth."

Desperately, she raised her eyes, beautiful, clear and tragic, that seemed to reflect her very soul. Watson nodded in sympathy.

"The young lady seems quite sincere," he said.

"Yes, yes I am," she implored. "You must trust me."

"I do trust you, Mademoiselle," replied the Doctor.

"Oh, how happy you make me! And your friend trusts me too, doesn't he? I feel he does, I'm sure of it! All will be well! What a good idea I had to come and meet you here! Please, Mister Holmes, there's a train for Calais in 20 minutes. You must take it. Quick, follow me... it's this way and you don't have much time..."

She tried to drag him along, but Holmes grabbed her arm and, in a voice that he strove to make as gentle as possible, said:

"Forgive me, Mademoiselle, if I do not comply with your wishes. But I have never turned away from a case once I've undertaken to solve it."

"Please! Make an exception! I beg you! Ah! If only you knew…"

The Detective walked briskly away. Watson briefly lingered behind.

"Don't feel sad. Be hopeful. My friend is the best of men. He will see that right will prevail in the end. And he has never failed."

Then, he ran after Holmes to catch up to him.

### SHERLOCK HOLMES VS. ARSENE LUPIN

These words, printed in large, black, bold letters, hit them as soon as they set foot on the boulevard. They appeared on sandwich boards being carried by a procession of men moving along the avenue in a single file. They held metal-tipped canes which they tapped in unison on the sidewalk to better attract the eyes of passers-by. On the back of their boards, there was another, similarly large poster, upon which the following notice was printed:

*The Rematch of Sherlock Holmes & Arsène Lupin!*
*The Great English Detective Arrives In Paris!*
*Will He Solve The Rue Murillo Mystery?*
*Read All The News In*
*L'ECHO DE FRANCE*

Watson shook his head.

"I say, Holmes, so much for not letting anyone know that we're here. I wouldn't be surprised to find a squadron of the National Guard waiting for us in the Rue Murillo, along with an official reception, complete with toasts and champagne."

"When you try to be witty, Watson," snarled Holmes, "you fail miserably!"

He stepped towards one of the board-wearing men, looking almost as if he intended to tear off the board and snap it between his powerful hands. Meanwhile, a crowd had begun

179

to gather around and look at the posters. Some were laughing and joking.

Controlling his anger, Holmes asked the man:

"When were you hired?"

"This morning."

"When did your start your rounds?"

"Barely an hour ago."

"But the posters were already printed?"

"Lord, yes! They were already there when we reported to the advertising office this morning."

So Arsène Lupin had foreseen that Sherlock Holmes would accept the challenge. More so, Lupin's own letter proved that he himself wished for it as well, and that it was part of his plan to once again cross swords with his rival. But why? What possible motive could he have to wish for a new confrontation?

Holmes experienced a brief moment of hesitation. Lupin must feel supremely confident of his victory to display such assurance. Was it not playing into his hands to acquiesce to the Baron's request? But then, the Detective summoned all of his prodigious energy. With veins throbbing in his temples and fists clenched as if for a boxing match, Holmes hailed a cab.

"Driver! No. 18, Rue Murillo! Come on, Watson! The game's afoot!"

The Rue Murillo was lined with luxurious private residences, the back of which look out onto the Parc Monceau. No. 18 was one of the handsomest of these houses, and Baron d'Imblevalle, who lived there with his wife and two children, had furnished it in the most lavish style, as befitted the millionaire and patron of the arts that he was. A courtyard stood in front of the house, with the stables and the servants' quarters on either side. At the back, there was a beautiful garden the trees of which mingled their branches with those of the Parc.

After having rung the bell, the two Englishmen crossed the courtyard and were ushered inside by a butler who showed them into a small drawing-room located on the first floor, on the far side of the house.

They sat down and took a rapid inventory of the many valuable objects with which the room was filled.

"Very pretty things," whispered Watson. "Taste and fancy... I'd be inclined to think that the people who had the inclination to gather this collection are persons of a certain age... Fifty perhaps..."

The Doctor did not have time to finish. Baron d'Imblevalle had just entered the room, followed by his wife.

Contrary to Watson's suppositions, they were both young, fashionably dressed, and lively in speech and manner. The two of them profusely thanked Holmes.

"It is really too good of you! To put yourself out like this! We'd almost be thankful for the trouble we're having since it gives us the pleasure..."

*How civilized these French people are!* thought Watson, who was easily charmed by the courtesies of high society.

"... But as you English say, time is money," the Baron continued. "Especially yours, Mister Holmes. So let us come to the point! What do you think of the case? Do you have any hopes of solving it?"

"To solve it, I must first know what it is."

"Don't you know?"

"No. We felt it better to leave immediately, without waiting for your second dispatch. Therefore, I would like you to explain the matter fully, omitting nothing. What is it all about?"

"It is a theft."

"When did it occur?"

"Last Saturday," the Baron replied. "Or rather, during the night of Saturday to Sunday."

"Six days ago, therefore. Please, do go on."

"I first must tell you, Mister Holmes, that my wife and I, while trying to lead the kind of social life that is expected of people in our position, go out very little. The education of our children, a few receptions, the embellishment of our home,

181

these make up our existence. All, or nearly all, of our evenings are spent here, in this room, which is my wife's boudoir and in which we have collected a few pretty things. Last Saturday, then, at about 11 p.m., I turned off the lights and my wife and I retired, as usual, to our bedroom."

"Which is?…"

"The next room. That door over there. On the following morning, that is to say, on Sunday, I got up early. As Suzanne–my wife–was still asleep, I came into this room as silently as possible so as not to wake her. Imagine my surprise at finding the window open, after we had left it closed the night before!"

"A servant?…"

"No. Nobody enters this room in the morning before we ring. Besides, I always take the precaution of bolting the main door that leads to the hallway. The window was, in fact, opened from the outside. The second pane of glass on the right-hand casement–next to the latch–was cut out."

"And that window?…"

"That window, as you can see, opens onto a small balcony enclosed by a stone balustrade. We are on the first floor and from here, you can see the garden at the back of the house and the railing that separates it from the Parc Monceau. I'm certain that the thief came from the Parc, using a ladder to climb over the railings, and from there, gained access to the balcony."

"You're certain, you say?"

"Yes. We found the holes left by the ladder in the soft earth of the garden and the Parc on both sides of the railing. And we found the same two holes just below the balcony. Finally, the balustrade shows two slight scratches, obviously caused by the top of the ladder."

"Isn't the Parc Monceau closed at night?"

"Not really. In any event, there is a house under construction at No. 14. It would have been easy to get in that way."

Sherlock Holmes reflected for a few moments, then resumed his questioning.

"Let's discuss the theft. Was it committed in this very room?"

"Yes. There was a small Jewish lamp just in front of that 12th century Madonna and silver tabernacle. It has disappeared."

"And that is all?"

"Yes. That is all."

"I see. What do you mean by a 'Jewish lamp'?"

"It's one of those lamps they used long ago, consisting of a handle and a recipient for the oil. That recipient had two burners through which one inserted the wicks."

"All in all, not an artifact of great value?"

"Normally, you'd be correct. But that lamp had a secret compartment, which we used as a hiding place. We kept a magnificent, antique jewel in it, a chimera of gold, set with rubies and emeralds, worth a great deal of money."

"Ah-ha. And why did you keep it there?"

"Honestly, I can't say, Mister Holmes. We just thought it was amusing to a have a secret hiding place."

"Did anyone else know of it?"

"No one."

"Except, of course, the thief," remarked Holmes. "Or else, he would not have gone to so much trouble to steal the Jewish lamp."

"Obviously. But how could he have known of the secret compartment? My wife and I only discovered it ourselves by accident..."

"A similar accident may have revealed it to someone else... A servant... A visitor... But let's continue: have you informed the Police?"

"Of course! The Investigating Magistrate looked into it and so did several journalists from the major newspapers, but as I wrote to you in my letter, without discovering any clues. It looks as if the case will remain unsolved."

Holmes got up, went to the window, inspected the casement, the balcony, the balustrade, and carefully looked at the scratches through a magnifying glass; he then asked the Baron to lead him down to the garden.

When they were outside, Holmes merely sat in a wicker chair, staring at the roof of the house with a thoughtful eye. Then, he suddenly walked towards two little wooden cases which had been used to protect the holes left by the ladder. He removed them, got down on his knees and, his nose six inches from the ground, scrutinized the holes and took exact measurements. He then repeated the same operation near the railings, but more quickly.

That was all.

They returned to the boudoir, where Madame d'Imblevalle was waiting for them.

Holmes was silent for a few minutes longer, then began to speak:

"Ever since you told me your story, Monsieur le Baron, I was struck by how simple it all looked–too simple, really. Using a ladder to get over the railing, cutting out a pane of glass, finding the right object, getting away... No, things normally don't happen as easily as that. This was all too easy, all too simple..."

"I don't understand. Do you mean to say?..."

"I mean to say that your Jewish lamp was stolen by none other than Arsène Lupin."

"Arsène Lupin!" exclaimed the Baron.

"Or rather, under his direction, outside of his presence, without anyone entering your house from the outside... Perhaps a servant who slipped down to the balcony from his garret, along one of the rain-spouts I saw from the garden..."

"Do you have any proof?..."

"Arsène Lupin wouldn't have left empty-handed."

"Empty-handed! What about the lamp?"

"Taking the lamp wouldn't have prevented him from taking that diamond-studded snuff-box, or that opal necklace.

It was only a matter of another minute or so. If he didn't take them, it was because he wasn't here."

"What about all the evidence?"

"A sham! Mere tricks to divert our attention."

"The scratches on the balustrade?"

"They were made with sandpaper. I even found some tiny particles from it which I picked up."

"And the holes in the garden?"

"More misdirection. Examine closely the two rectangular holes below the balcony and compare them with the ones by the railing. The shapes are similar, but one pair is parallel, the other one not. Also look at the distance between the two holes: nine inches below the balcony, ten and a half by the railing."

"What do you conclude?"

"I conclude that, since their shapes are identical, that all the holes were made with a single stump of wood."

"Perhaps, but could you prove it?"

"I can, and I do!" said Holmes, pulling something out of his coat pocket. "This is the piece of wood. I found it in your garden, hidden behind a laurel-tree."

The Baron gave in. It had only been 40 minutes since the Detective had crossed his threshold and already, not a vestige remained of all the evidence that had, so far, been carefully gathered in the case. The truth, another, different truth, had come to light, based on something far more unassailable: the deductive powers of Sherlock Holmes.

"It is a very serious accusation to bring against our staff, Mister Holmes," said the Baroness. "They are all old family servants and not one of them is capable to betraying us."

"If one of them did not betray you, Madame, how do you explain that this letter reached me on the same day and by the same post as the one your husband sent me?" said Holmes, handing the Baroness Arsène Lupin's letter.

Madame d'Imblevalle was stupefied.

"Arsène Lupin! How did he know?..."

"You told no one of your letter?"

"No one," said the Baron. "The idea only occurred to us the other evening, at dinner."

"In front of the servants?"

"There were only our two children... No, actually, Sophie and Henriette had already left the table, hadn't they, Suzanne?"

Madame d'Imblevalle frowned, trying to remember the exact circumstances.

"Why, I think you're right. They'd already gone up to see Mademoiselle Alice," she declared.

"Mademoiselle Alice?" asked Holmes.

"Alice Demun. Our governess."

"Doesn't she take her meals with you?"

"No. She likes to retire to her room to eat alone."

Suddenly, Watson ventured an idea:

"The letter written to my friend Sherlock Holmes was mailed at the Post Office..."

"Naturally."

"So someone must have taken it there. Whom?"

"Dominique," answered the Baron. "But he's been my butler for 20 years. I trust him totally. Any inquiries in that direction would be a waste of time, in my opinion."

"It is never a waste of time to make inquiries," corrected Watson.

However, as Holmes asked leave to withdraw, this appeared to conclude the first part of the investigation.

An hour later, at dinner, the two Englishmen met the Imblevalle children, Sophie and Henriette, two pretty little girls of respectively eight and six. The conversation languished. Holmes responded to the Baron and his wife's attempts at making small talk in such a preoccupied fashion that, after a while, they thought it better to stay silent. Eventually, coffee was served. The Detective swallowed the contents of his cup and rose from his chair.

At that moment, a servant entered with a telegram for him. Holmes opened it and read:

*Please accept my enthusiastic admiration. The results obtained by you in so short a time are truly extraordinary. I am amazed.*

*Arsène Lupin*

Holmes could not suppress his irritation as he showed the telegram to the Baron.

"Now, do you believe, Monsieur, that your walls have eyes and ears?"

"I... I don't understand," muttered the Baron d'Imblevalle, dumbfounded.

"Candidly, nor do I. Not yet, anyway. But what I do understand is that not a movement takes place inside this house that *he* doesn't learn about it. Not a word is spoken that *he* doesn't hear about it."

That night, Watson went to bed with the clear conscience of a man who has done his duty, and is now ready to enjoy a good night's rest. He fell asleep quickly and enjoyed peaceful dreams in which he, personally, found the clues that were about to lead to Lupin's arrest. Just as he was about to capture the Frenchman with his own hands, he woke up.

Someone was touching his bed. He seized his gun.

"Another move, Lupin, and I shoot!"

"Steady, old friend! I'm not Lupin."

"Holmes? What time is it? Do you need me?"

"I need your eyes. Get up..."

The Detective led the Doctor to the window.

"Look over there... Beyond the railing..."

"In the Parc?"

"Yes. Do you see anything?"

"No, nothing."

"Look again. To the right."

"By Jove! You're right, Holmes! I see a shadow... Two shadows in fact!"

"I thought so… By the railing… Look! They're moving! Let's not waste a second!"

Groping through the dark and holding on to the banister, the two Englishmen quickly ran downstairs and found a room that opened on to a terrace leading to the garden. Through the French doors, they saw the two figures still in the same place.

"Listen," said Holmes. "Is that a noise coming from inside the house?"

"From inside? Impossible! Everybody's asleep."

"Listen!"

At that moment, a faint whistle sounded from the other side of the railing and they saw a pale light come from the floors above.

"The d'Imblevalles must have turned on their light," whispered Holmes. "Their room is just above us."

"Do you think it's them we heard?" asked Watson. "Maybe they were watching the railing, too?"

They heard a second whistle, even fainter than the first.

"I don't understand, I don't understand," said Holmes, sounding aggrieved.

"Neither do I," admitted Watson.

Holmes quietly unbolted the French doors and gently pushed them open.

He heard a third whistle, a little louder this time, and with a different pitch. Above their heads, the noise grew louder, more hurried.

"It sounds as if it comes from the boudoir balcony," whispered the Detective.

He took a quick look outside, but at once stepped back muttering a curse under his breath. Watson, too, looked outside. He saw a ladder, only a few feet away, leaning against the balustrade of the balcony.

"By Jove!" said Holmes. "There *is* someone in the boudoir! That's what we heard! Quick! Let's remove the ladder!"

But at that moment, a shape slid down the ladder. The man then picked it up and carried it away, running swiftly towards the railing, to the spot where his partners were waiting.

Holmes and Watson immediately ran after him. They caught up with the man just as he had reached the railing and was placing the ladder against the iron bars. Suddenly, two shots rang out from the other side of the fence.

"Are you hurt?" cried Holmes.

"No," replied Watson.

The Doctor grabbed the fugitive and tried to throw him down, but the man turned around, seized him with one hand, and with the other, savagely stabbed him in the chest. Watson let out a deep sigh, staggered and fell to the ground.

"Damnation!" shouted Holmes. "If they've killed him, I swear, they'll pay with their lives!"

The Detective laid his companion on the lawn and rushed at the ladder. But he was too late: the man was already on the other side and he and his accomplices were running off into the trees.

"Watson, Watson! How do you feel? Tell me it's only a scratch!"

The doors of the house opened suddenly. The Baron d'Imblevalle was the first to appear, followed by his servants carrying candles.

"What happened?" asked the Baron. "Is Dr. Watson hurt?"

"Nothing, only a scratch," repeated Holmes forcefully, as if he could make it so by the sheer power of his will.

Yet, Watson was bleeding copiously and his face was deathly pale. A doctor was immediately called in. Twenty minutes later, after he had seen to his English colleague, who was now resting peacefully, he confirmed that Watson had been lucky indeed: the point of his assailant's blade had stopped within a quarter of an inch of his heart!

"A quarter of an inch," said Holmes, shaking his head. "Watson was always lucky…"

"I don't know if I'd use that word," muttered the doctor.

"Why? With his strong constitution, he'll be back on his feet in…"

"After six weeks in bed and two months' convalescence," said the doctor, firmly.

"Hm. That much?"

"More, if there are any complications."

"Why on Earth should there be any complications!"

Now feeling fully reassured about his friend's condition, Holmes returned to see the Baron in the boudoir. The time, the mysterious visitor had not shown the same delicacy. He had shamelessly grabbed the diamond-studded snuff-box and the opal necklace and, more generally, anything that could be stashed in the pockets of any self-respecting burglar.

The window was still open. One of the glass panes had been cut out. At dawn, a quick investigation showed that the ladder came from the construction site at No. 14, which was how the burglars had reached the Parc.

"In short," said the Baron, with a certain irony, "it is the exact repetition of the theft of the Jewish lamp."

"Yes, if you believe in the first version as set forth by the Police," said Holmes.

"Do you still refuse to believe that's what happened? Doesn't this second theft shake your opinion as regards the first?"

"On the contrary, Monsieur le Baron. It confirms it."

"It defies belief! You have irrefutable proof that last night's burglary was committed by outside thieves, yet you persist in believing that the Jewish lamp was stolen by someone from inside this house?"

"Yes, Monsieur le Baron."

"Then, how do you explain…"

"I do not. Yet. I am looking at two separate sets of facts, which only resemble each other on the surface. I must weigh them separately, and try to find the connection between them."

Holmes' conviction was so profound, his actions based upon such powerful logic, that the Baron chose not to argue.

"Very well then. Let us call the Police."

"Please don't," exclaimed Holmes. "On no account! I want them involved only when, and to the extent, that I need them. And that time is not yet here."

"But the shots…"

"Never mind the shots!"

"And Dr. Watson…"

"…Is only wounded. Ask your doctor to hold his tongue. I will take full responsibility as regards the Police."

Two days went by with no further incident, leaving Sherlock Holmes time to carry on his investigation with the most precise care and a feeling of wounded pride caused by the aggression on Dr. Watson, committed under his very nose, without his being able to prevent it. He searched the house and the garden tirelessly, talked to the staff and paid long visits to the kitchen and stables. Though he gathered no clues, he did not lose hope.

*I shall find what I'm looking for here*, he thought. *This is not like the Case of the Blonde Phantom, where I progressed boldly, taking roads unknown to me towards an equally mysterious goal. This time, the battlefield is clear. My foe is not merely the invisible, elusive Lupin, but his flesh and blood accomplice who lives within these very walls. If I find the most insignificant of clues, I will unravel this entire case!*

That insignificant clue, from which Sherlock Holmes was indeed able to extrapolate and solve the mystery of the Jewish lamp, with a skill so prodigious that this case may be looked upon as one of his most remarkable triumphs, was revealed to him in the most accidental manner.

On the afternoon of the third day, as the Detective entered a room located above the boudoir, which was used as a school room for the d'Imblevalle children, he came upon Henriette, the youngest of the two girls. She was looking for her scissors.

"You know, Monsieur," she said to Holmes, "I make papers too, like the one you got the other evening."

"The other evening?"

"Yes, after dinner. You got a paper with strips on it..."
"The telegram?"

"Yes. I make paper strips, too."

She left the room. To anyone else, her words would have been only the innocent musings of a child. Holmes himself, at first, heard them without paying them much attention. But, suddenly, he started running after the child, whose last sentence had, all at once, struck him. He caught up with her at the top of the stairs.

"So, you cut and paste strips of paper, do you?" he asked.

"Yes! I cut out words and stick them on," replied Henriette, proudly.

"Who taught you that pretty game?"

"Mademoiselle Alice... Our governess... I saw her do it. She cuts words out of newspapers and sticks them on..."

"And what does she do with them?"

"She makes letters and telegrams which she sends somewhere."

Sherlock Holmes returned to the school room, singularly puzzled by this revelation, trying to extract some useful information from it.

There was a bundle of newspapers on the fireplace. He opened them and saw that groups of words, or lines, had indeed been cut out. But he had only to read the words that came before or after them to realize that the missing words had been removed randomly, in all likelihood by Henriette herself. It was possible that, in the pile of newspapers, there was one which Mademoiselle Demun had cut herself, but how to make sure?

Mechanically, Holmes leafed through the pages of the schoolbooks on the desk, then through other books on a shelf in a closet. Suddenly, he cried out in joy. In a corner of the closet, under a pile of old notebooks, he had found a children's alphabet picture book, and on one of the pages, a word was missing.

It was a book naming the days of the week: Sunday, Monday, Tuesday, etc. The missing word was "Saturday." And the Detective knew that the Jewish lamp had been stolen on a Saturday night.

Holmes felt that little tug at the heart which always told him, in the clearest manner possible, that he had hit upon a vital clue. That blinding flash of truth, that feeling of certainty, had never deceived him.

He hastened to turn the pages of the picture book, eager and confident that he would soon find other clues. Indeed, a little further on, he made another discovery.

It was a page consisting of rows of block letters and figures. Nine of these letters, and three of the figures, had been carefully cut out.

Holmes wrote down the missing letters and digits in his notebook, in the order in which they were printed, and came up with the following list:

CDEHNOPRZ – 237

"By Jove!" he muttered. "Not much to go on at first glance."

The Detective asked himself if it was possible to rearrange these letters in order to make one or several words?

He began trying various permutations, until finally, he arrived at the only combination that made sense. Not only did it employ all of the letters that had been cut out, but it also seemed to fit in with the logic of the case.

To the extent that the page of the picture book contained each of the letters of the alphabet only once, it was likely that some letters might be missing, and had been cut out of other, similar books. Given these facts, and allowing for the possibility of errors, the puzzle now read:

REPOND.Z – CH 237

The first word was clear: "*repondez*," "reply," with an "e" missing, because having been once used, it was no longer available.

As to the second word, it, and the figures that followed it, was obviously an address which the sender gave to the intended recipient of the letter. The date of Saturday had been suggested, and one expected a reply sent to "CH 237."

Was "CH 237" the number of a post office box? Or was it part of an incomplete word? Holmes looked through the picture book again, but could find no other missing letters or figures. He had, therefore, to be content with this until; new facts emerged.

"Wasn't it fun?"

Henriette had returned.

"Yes, great fun," replied the Detective. "Only, don't you have other books... With words already cut out that I might use?"

"No. Besides, Mademoiselle Alice wouldn't like it."

"Wouldn't like it?"

"Yes. She's scolded me already."

"Why?"

"Because I told you things... She said one must never tell things about people you're fond of."

"She's absolutely right."

Henriette was so delighted with the Detective's approval, that from a small canvas bag pinned to her dress, she pulled out three buttons, two cubes of sugar, a few pieces of fabric and a square piece of paper, and proudly displayed her entire treasure to Holmes.

"There! I'll show you all my things!"

Holmes looked at the paper. It was a cab receipt and the number of the cab was No. 8279.

"What is this?" he asked.

"It fell from Mademoiselle Alice's wallet."

"When?"

"Sunday, during Mass, when she took some coins out for the collection."

"Interesting... Now I'll tell you how to not get into trouble again... Just don't tell Mademoiselle Alice that you saw me."

Holmes then went off in search of the Baron d'Imblevalle and asked him straightforwardly about Alice Demun.

"Alice?" said the Baron with a start. "Do you suspect her of...? Impossible!"

"How long has she been in your service?"

"Only a year, but I know no one quieter whom I'd trust more."

"How is it that I haven't yet met her?"

"She went away for two days."

"Ah. And is she back?"

"Yes. Immediately on her return, she insisted on taking care of Dr. Watson. She is a first-rate nurse... gentle... attentive... Your friend seems delighted with her."

"I'm sure he is," said Holmes, with a slight smile. He reproached himself for not yet having had time to visit Watson that day. "And on the Sunday morning after the robbery, did she go out?" he added, returning to the subject at hand.

"Yes... I think she might have done so..." The Baron called his wife and put the question to her.

"Alice took the children to the 11 a.m. Mass as usual," confirmed Suzanne.

"But before that?"

"Before? No. Or rather... But I was so upset by the theft... Still, I remember that, the evening before, she'd asked me for leave to go out on Sunday morning... To see a cousin who was passing through Paris, I think. But surely, you don't think that...?"

"I don't know yet, but I should like to see her."

Holmes went up to Watson's room. A woman dressed as a nurse, in a long, grey gown, was bent over the recovering doctor, helping him to drink. When she turned around, the

195

Detective recognized the girl who had spoken to him outside the Gare du Nord.

There was no need for any explanations. No words were exchanged. Alice Demun smiled gently, with her grave and charming eyes, exhibiting no trace of embarrassment. Holmes tried to utter a few words, but finally chose not to. Then, she returned to her task, moving about gracefully before the Detective's piercing eyes. She shifted Watson's body, unrolled some linen bandages and prepared to redress his wound. All the while, she gave the Englishman her brightest smile.

Holmes finally turned on his heels and returned downstairs. In the courtyard, he saw the Baron's motorcar. Struck by an idea, he got into it and asked the driver to take him to the dispatch station at Levallois, the address of which had been printed on the back of the cab receipt Henriette had showed him. Once there, he asked to speak to the man who had been driving cab No. 8279 that Sunday morning. The driver, Duprêt, had not come in yet. Holmes sent back the Baron's car and decided to wait.

An hour later, Duprêt showed up. He told the Detective that he had indeed picked up a lady near the Parc Monceau, a young woman dressed all in black, wearing a long veil, who seemed quite upset.

"Was she carrying a parcel?" inquired Holmes.

"Yes. Something rather long."

"Where did you take her?"

"Avenue des Ternes, at the corner of Place Saint-Ferdinand. She asked me to wait for her. She stayed for ten minutes or so, then returned to the Parc Monceau."

"Would you know the house which she visited at the Avenue des Ternes?"

"Absolutely! Would you like me to take you there now?"

"Not right now. First, take me to No. 36, Quai des Orfèvres."

At the Prefecture de Police, Holmes had the good fortune to be quickly ushered into the office of Chef Inspector Ganimard.

"Are you presently busy, Chief Inspector?" asked the Englishman.

"If it's about Lupin, yes, I am."

"It is about Lupin."

"Then I'm booked solid until the end of the year."

"Come now! You're not going to pass up such an opportunity…"

"…An opportunity to be ridiculed again? No, thank you, Mister Holmes. It may be cowardly, it may be ridiculous, but I don't care. Lupin is the Devil, he's stronger than I. There's nothing else for me to do than to give up."

"I haven't given up."

"You will, eventually, like the rest of us."

"Well, then, you'd want to be there to watch me admit defeat, wouldn't you?"

"True, true," said Ganimard, rather candidly. "I'm buying, Mister Holmes. Tell me what's brought you here."

After the Detective had rapidly briefed his French colleague, they stepped into the cab. Holmes told the driver to now take them to the Avenue des Ternes, but to stop a little before reaching the house visited by Mademoiselle Demun. The cab obligingly stopped on the other side of the street in front of a small café. The two detectives sat down outside, between tubs of laurels and spindle trees. It was getting late.

"Garçon," said Holmes, "would you bring me a pen and some paper?"

The Englishman then wrote a short note, and called the waiter again.

"Please take this note to the concierge of the house across the street. I would surmise it's the man wearing a cap and smoking a pipe in the doorway."

Eventually, the concierge, having read the note, hurried across. Ganimard showed the man his Police credentials.

Holmes asked him if a young lady in black had called at the house on the previous Sunday morning.

"A lady in black?" answered the concierge. "Yes, around 9 a.m. She goes up to the second floor."

"Does she come often?"

"No, but she's been back more regularly, lately…Almost every day for the past two weeks."

"And since Sunday?"

"Only once… Not counting today."

"What? She came today?"

"Yes. She's there now."

"Now?"

"She arrived about ten minutes ago. Her cab is waiting on the Place Saint-Ferdinand, as usual. I passed her in the doorway."

"Who is the tenant of the second floor?"

"There's two of them: Mademoiselle Langeais, a dress-maker, and a gentleman who rented two furnished rooms a month ago under the name of Bresson."

"Why do you say 'under the name of Bresson'?"

"I have an idea that it's an assumed name. My wife does his rooms, and she told me he hasn't got two shirts with the same initials!"

"I see. How does he live?"

"Oh, he's almost always out. Sometimes, he doesn't come home for three days."

"Was he home during the night of Saturday to Sunday?"

"The night of Saturday to Sunday? Let me think about it… Yes! He came back on Saturday night and hasn't left since."

"What sort of man is he?"

"It's hard to tell. I couldn't properly say! Sometimes he's tall and other times he's short, he's fat, he's thin… dark and fair… I don't always recognize him."

Ganimard and Holmes exchanged knowing glances.

"It's *him*," muttered the Chief Inspector. "It's really *him*!"

The old Policeman felt a sense of trepidation; his jaw tightened, his breath become more rapid, his hands clenched into fists. Holmes, too, though more in control, could not help but feel a certain electricity.

"Look!" exclaimed the concierge suddenly. "There's the young lady!"

Indeed, Alice Demun had just appeared in the doorway and was about to cross the street towards the Place Saint-Ferdinand.

"And there's Mister Bresson!"

"Bresson? Where?"

"The man carrying a parcel under his arm."

"He's not going with the girl. He's going to her cab alone."

"To be honest, I've never seen them together," noted the concierge.

The two Policemen rose hurriedly. By the light of the street lamps, they saw the figure of the man whom they suspected of being Lupin walk off in the direction opposite to the Place Saint-Ferdinand.

"Which one will you follow?" asked Ganimard.

"*Him*, of course!" replied Holmes. "He's the biggest fish."

"Then, I'll tail the girl," said the Chief Inspector.

"I'd rather you didn't. I know where to find her, if I need her. Let's follow Lupin together."

Staying at a safe distance behind their target, taking advantage of passers-by and newsstands for cover, Sherlock Holmes and Ganimard set off in pursuit of Lupin. It was an easy enough task, for he did not turn around and walked quickly with a limp in his right leg, so slight that it took a trained eye to notice it.

"He's faking a limp," said Ganimard. "Ah! If only I could find two or three policemen to pounce on him! We might lose him!"

But no policeman appeared as they reached the Porte des Ternes; if they crossed the old Ramparts, they knew they would be on their own. But instead, Lupin took the Boulevard Victor Hugo.

"Let's split up," said Holmes. "The streets are empty."

Each chose a different sidewalk and hid behind the trees that lined the Boulevard as further cover.

They walked like this for 20 minutes. Then, Lupin made a left and walked down to the Seine. They saw him go to the edge of the river. He remained there for a few seconds, during which time they were unable to see what he was doing. Then, he walked back up the street and retraced his steps. The two Policemen quickly hid behind the pillars of a gate in order to not be spotted. Lupin walked right past them. He no longer carried a parcel.

But as he moved away, another figure appeared from the shadows, behind a corner, slipping in and out between the trees.

"That man seems to be following him, too," whispered Holmes.

"Yes. I thought I'd noticed him before."

The chase went on, now made more complicated by the presence of this third man. Lupin backtracked his steps, passing the Porte des Ternes and finally returning to the house on Place Saint-Ferdinand.

The concierge was locking up for the night when Ganimard showed up.

"You saw him, I suppose?"

"Yes. I was turning off the gas upstairs. He went in and locked his door behind him."

"There's no one else inside?"

"Not that I know of. He hasn't got a servant. He never takes his meals here."

"Does the building have a service stairs?"

"No."

"The best thing would be for me to stand guard outside his door," said Ganimard to Holmes, "while you go to the Police Station on the Rue Demours and bring back some help. I'll write you a note."

"What if he tries to escape?" Holmes objected.

"I'll be here!"

"Alone against *him*? It would be far too unequal."

"I can't very well break into his apartment. It's against the law. Especially at night."

"If you arrest Arsène Lupin," shrugged Holmes, "I doubt anyone will question your methods. Besides, why don't we just ring the bell? Then we'll see what happens."

Ganimard agreed. They went up the stairs. There was a double-door on the left of the landing. The Chief Inspector rang the bell.

No one answered. He rang again. Nothing.

"Let's go in," whispered Holmes.

"Yes… let's…"

Yet, they stood there, motionless, irresolute. These two strong men who had, between them, arrested thousands of hardened criminals were, at the last minute, afraid to take the last, decisive step. It suddenly seemed impossible that Arsène Lupin should be there, so near, behind that fragile barrier which they could smash with a single blow of their fists. They both knew the Gentleman Burglar too well; they knew that Lupin would never allow himself to be cornered so easily. No, a thousand times no, he could not be inside that apartment; he had to have escaped, somehow. Through the adjoining house, over the rooftop, by some suitably-arranged secret passage. Once again, the shadow of Arsène Lupin would be all that they could hope to grasp.

They shuddered. They heard an almost imperceptible sound come from the other side of the door. And suddenly, they had the feeling, the certainty even, that *he* was there, separated from them only by that thin wooden partition, listening to them as they listened for him.

What were they to do? The situation was becoming un-bearable. Despite their professional cool, they were almost overcome by emotion; they heard their own hearts beat wildly inside their chests.

Ganimard glanced at Holmes, who nodded silently. The Chief Inspector then banged loudly on the door.

They heard footsteps, no longer trying to hide.

Ganimard shook the door. Holmes, with a mighty thrust of his shoulder, forced it open. The two men rushed inside.

Then, they stopped dead in their tracks. They heard a gunshot come from the next room, then another, followed by the thud of a falling body.

When they entered, they saw the body of a man, his face lying against the marble of the fireplace. He made a final convulsion, then a revolver slipped from his hand.

Ganimard leaned over the dead man and turned his head to look at his face. It was covered in blood which seeped from two large wounds, one in the cheek, the other at the temple.

"He'll be hard to identify," he said.

"But one thing is certain," said Holmes. "It's not *him*."

"Are you certain? You didn't even look at him."

"Do you think Arsène Lupin is the type of man who kills himself?" sneered the Englishman.

"Still, we thought it was him, outside."

"We thought so because we *wanted* to think so. We're obsessed with *him*."

"Then, it must be one of his men."

"No. Lupin's men don't kill themselves either."

"Then who is he?"

They searched the body. In one pocket, Holmes found an empty wallet. In another, Ganimard found a few *louis*. There were no marks anywhere on his clothing.

The luggage–a large trunk and two suitcases–contained only personal effects. There was a pile of newspapers on the mantelpiece. Ganimard looked at them. They all reported the theft of the Jewish lamp.

An hour later, when Holmes and Ganimard left the house, they still knew no more about the mystery man whom their intervention had driven to commit suicide.

Who was he? Why had he taken his own life? What was the connection between him and the theft of the Jewish lamp? Who else had followed him during his nocturnal errand? What was inside the mysterious parcel he had been carrying? So many complex questions... So many mysteries...

Sherlock Holmes went to bed late and in a bad mood. When he woke up the next morning, he found a telegram waiting for him:

*Arsène Lupin is saddened to inform you of his recent passing under the identity of Monsieur R. Bresson and respectfully invites you to attend his funeral, which will be held at public expense on Thursday, June 25.*

## Chapter II

"You see, old friend," said Sherlock Holmes, waving Arsène Lupin's telegram, "what exasperates me in this case is that I feel that infernal Frenchman's eyes constantly upon me! Not one of my thoughts, not even the most secret, escapes him. I am like an actor whose every step is being carefully choreographed by an invisible director, who moves here or there, says this or that, because a superior entity demands it. Do you understand, Watson?"

Watson would have certainly understood, and sympathized, with his colleague had he not been asleep, suffering from a mild fever. Whether or not he heard made no difference to Holmes, who continued:

"I have to summon all my energy and marshal all my resources simply to not feel discouraged. Fortunately, his little gibes are like pin-pricks that only serve to stimulate my interest. Once the sting is gone and my pride salvaged, I always finish by telling myself, 'Have your fun while you can, my lad, for in the end, it is you who will make a mistake and I who will prevail.' For, when all is said and done, Watson, wasn't it Lupin himself who, with his earliest telegram, and the remark it prompted little Henriette to make, gave us the first clue that led to Alice Demun? I haven't forgotten that detail, old friend!"

He walked up and down the room, taking great strides, oblivious of the fact that Watson slept on.

"Still, things are progressing rather well. Even if the end is still obscure, I'm starting to see my way through this thing. Tomorrow, I'll learn more about that mysterious Bresson fellow. Ganimard and I are meeting on the banks of the Seine at the very spot where he threw in his parcel and we'll find out what exact role he played. For the rest, it's a game between Mademoiselle Demun and I. She shouldn't prove too difficult an opponent, should she, Watson? Soon, I'll know what the mysterious sequence of letters and figures cut out from that picture book mean. I'm convinced that C H holds the key to the entire mystery, Watson..."

At that moment, Mademoiselle Demun walked into the room. Seeing Holmes pacing back and forth, she berated him.

"Mister Holmes, I'll be very angry with you if you wake my patient. It's not nice of you to disturb him so. Doctor Watson needs much rest."

He looked at her wordlessly, astonished by her remarkable composure.

"Why are you looking at me like that, Mister Holmes? Do you have something on your mind? Please, tell me."

She asked the question with guileless eyes, smiling with her clear, honest, face. Her entire attitude, hands joined together, body slightly leaning forward, spoke of such candor that the detective suddenly felt inexplicably angry. He confronted her.

"Bresson killed himself last night," he growled.

"Bresson killed himself last night?" she repeated, without appearing to understand. Her features showed no changes, nothing in it revealed the effort of a lie.

"Someone told you," Holmes said, irritably. "Otherwise, you would show some kind of reaction. Ah! You're cleverer than I thought. But why play games?..."

He grabbed the picture book that he had placed on a nearby table and opened it to the page where the letters and figures had been cut out.

"Can you tell me in what order I am supposed to arrange the letters that you cut out of this book so that I may understand the contents of the note which you sent to Bresson four days before the theft of the Jewish lamp?"

"In what order?... Bresson?... The theft of the Jewish lamp?..." She repeated his words slowly, as if trying to figure out their meaning.

"Yes!" he insisted. "Here are the letters you used. On this scrap of paper. What were you conveying to Bresson?"

"The letters I used?... What was I conveying?..." Suddenly, she burst out laughing. "I see now! I understand! You think I'm an accomplice in the burglary. There is a Monsieur Bresson who stole the Jewish lamp and who killed himself afterwards. And I'm supposed to have been his accomplice, is that it? Oh, how amusing!"

"Then whom did you visit last night on the second floor of a house in the Avenue des Ternes?"

"Whom? Why, my dressmaker, Mademoiselle Langeais. Are you implying that my dressmaker and my alleged accomplice, Monsieur Bresson, might be one and the same?"

Holmes began to doubt, despite his conviction. It is possible to fake fear, happiness, concern, virtually every sort of emotion, except her indifference and her happy and carefree laughter.

"One last thing," he nevertheless felt compelled to ask. "Why did you stop me at the Gare du Nord the other day? Why did you beg me to go home and not take up the Baron's case?"

"Oh, you're much too curious, Mister Holmes," she replied, still laughing gaily. "To punish you, I will tell you nothing, and further, you will watch Doctor Watson while I go to the pharmacist... An urgent prescription... I must hurry..."

She left the room.

"She tricked me again," muttered Holmes. "Not only didn't I get anything out of her, but I've showed my hand."

He remembered the Affair of the Blue Diamond and the interrogation which he had inflicted upon Clotilde Destange. Hadn't the Blonde Phantom shown him the same serenity as Alice Demun? Was he again face-to-face with one of Arsène Lupin's protégées who, being under the Gentleman Burglar's influence, managed to retain the most amazing calm even in the midst of the gravest of dangers.

"Holmes... Holmes..."

The Detective went to the bed and leaned over his friend, who was calling him.

"What is it, old friend? You're not in pain, are you?"

Watson moved his lips, but at first, was unable to speak. Finally, after much effort, he managed to stammer out a few words:

"No, Holmes... It wasn't her... Can't be..."

"What nonsense are you talking now? It's got to be her, I tell you. It's only when I'm in the presence of a creature such as she, trained and drilled by Lupin, that I lose my head and behave so foolishly. Now, she knows that I've found the picture book. I bet you that Lupin will know in less than an hour. Less than an hour? What am I saying! Right now, most likely! The pharmacist, an urgent prescription, likely excuse!"

Seized by a sudden inspiration, Holmes ran down the stairs and out of the Baron's house. He went down the Avenue de Messine, where earlier he had noticed the presence of a pharmacy. He arrived just in time to see Alice Demun enter the shop. Ten minutes later, she came out, carrying some medicine bottles in a white paper bag. As she walked back to the Baron's house, she was accosted by a man who ran after her, cap in hand, behaving obsequiously, as if soliciting some money.

She stopped, gave him a few coins and continued on her way.

"She spoke to that man," said Holmes to himself.

Following his intuition, the Detective decided to follow the phony beggar.

This way, one behind the other, they arrived at the Place Saint-Ferdinand. For a while, the man hovered around the house where Bresson had died, occasionally raising his eyes to the second floor windows and watching the people who entered the property.

After an hour, he climbed aboard a bus to Neuilly. Holmes managed to hop aboard and sat a few seats behind the man, in front of a gentleman whose features were concealed behind the newspaper he was reading. As they reached the Ramparts, he lowered the newspaper and Holmes recognized Ganimard.

The Chief Inspector discreetly pointed at the man the detective had been chasing.

"It's the same fellow that followed Bresson last night," he whispered. "He's been hanging around the area all day."

"Any news on Bresson?" inquired Holmes.

"A letter arrived for him at his address this morning."

"This morning? Then, it must have been posted yesterday, before its sender learned of his death."

"That's right. It's in the hands of the Investigating Magistrate, but I memorized its contents. It says: '*He refuses any compromise. He wants it all. The first object, as well as those of the second business. Otherwise, he is prepared to act.*' No signature," added Ganimard. "As you can see, those few lines won't be of much use to us."

"I don't agree with you at all, Chief Inspector. On the contrary, I find them very interesting."

"Why on Earth?"

"Personal reasons," replied Holmes, with the casual indifference that he often displayed towards the feelings of police officers.

The bus stopped at its terminus, Rue du Château. The man got off and walked away quietly.

Holmes followed him so closely that Ganimard expressed some concern.

"If he turns around, we're done for."

"He won't, not now."

"How do you know?"

"The man obviously belongs to Lupin's gang. The fact that he walks away like that, with his hands in his pockets, proves first that he knows he's being followed, and second, that he isn't afraid of us."

"Still, we're awfully close to him."

"Barely enough to stop him if he tries to give us the slip. He's too sure of himself."

"Come on, Mister Holmes! There are two policemen on bicycles at that café over there. If I call them and order them to grab our friend, what is he going to do about it?"

208

"Yet, he doesn't seem too worried by that eventuality, does he? Look! He's calling to them himself!"

"Sacrebleu!" exclaimed Ganimard. "What impudence!"

The man had indeed walked up to the two policemen just as they were preparing to ride away on their bicycles. He spoke a few words to them, then, suddenly, jumped on a third bicycle that had been leaning against the wall of the café and pedaled away furiously with the two policemen.

Holmes burst out with laughter.

"Ha! Ha! There! Didn't I tell you? Off before we could lift a finger! And with two of your colleagues, no less, Chief Inspector! Didn't I tell you that that fellow was much too relaxed to be worried?"

"Well, what do you think we should do now?" said Ganimard, angrily. "Laughing doesn't help matters."

"Come, come, Chief Inspector, don't be cross. We'll have our revenge yet. For now, we need reinforcements."

"Folenfant is waiting for me at the end of the Avenue de Neuilly..."

"All right! Pick him up and join me, both of you."

Ganimard left while Holmes started to follow the bicycle's trail, easily visible in the dust of the road thanks to the groove of its tires. He soon realized that the trail was taking him to the bank of the Seine, and that the three men had turned in the same direction as Bresson the night before. He eventually walked past the gate behind which he and Ganimard had hidden. A little further on, he noticed a tangle of lines in the dust that indicated that the men had stopped there. Just opposite, a small bit of land jutted into the river and an old boat was moored there.

This was the place where Bresson had dropped his mysterious parcel. Holmes walked down to the river and noticed that the bank sloped gently and the water was very low; he thought that they would easily find the parcel, unless the three men had already grabbed it.

"No," he said to himself, "they didn't have enough time. It's been 15 minutes at most. Yet, why did they come here, and where are they?"

An angler was sitting in the boat, fishing.

"Did you see three men on bicycles" Holmes asked him.

The man shook his head.

"Yes, three men," the Englishman insisted. "They stopped just over there."

The fisherman pulled his rod from the water, put it under his arm, took a notebook from his pocket and wrote a few words on one of its pages. Then, he tore out the page and handed it to the Detective.

When he read it, Holmes experienced a sudden thrill. At a glance, he recognized, in the middle of the page, the same combination of letters and figures that had been cut out from Henriette's picture book:

CDEHNOPRZEO – 237

The Sun hung heavily over the Seine. The fisherman had resumed his work, sheltered under the brim of a large, straw hat. His jacket and waistcoat lay folded by his side. He fished attentively while the float of his line bobbed idly on the water.

A minute went on, a long, solemn and terrible minute of silence.

*Is it* him? wondered Holmes, with almost painful anxiety. *It must be* him! *Only* he *can sit like that, without a tremor of apprehension, without any fear of what will happen... And who else could know about the picture book? Alice used that messenger to warn him...*

Holmes felt his own hand, almost involuntarily, grabbing the gun he kept inside his jacket. He stared at the stranger's back, the nape of his neck. A single gesture and it would all be over; the prodigious life of the Gentleman Burglar who had defied the Police of Europe would end miserably here, on the banks of the Seine...

The angler did not stir.

Holmes clutched his weapon nervously, experiencing both the desire to fire and be done with it, and the horror of a deed against which his very nature revolted.

*If only he got up and would fight back*, he thought. *I would shoot him... He'd have only himself to blame... I'll wait another second and...*

Unexpectedly, he heard footsteps; he turned around and saw Ganimard running towards him, accompanied by Folenfant and several policemen.

Moved by a sudden impulse, the Englishman leapt onto the boat, causing its painter to come untied and the embarkation to start drifting away on the river; he grappled the man and they both rolled to the bottom of the boat.

"So what if you win?" said Arsène Lupin. "What will you do with me if you succeed in capturing me? What are you trying to accomplish, Holmes? You can no more defeat me than I can defeat you! We're going to be stuck here with each other like a couple of fools!"

The oars slipped into the water. The boat was now drifting towards the middle of the river. A jumble of exclamations were heard from the bank.

"Come on, Holmes, I expected better of you than this schoolboy's tumble! Have you lost your mind?"

Lupin finally managed to break free of the Englishman's hold. Holmes, grimly determined, put his hand into his jacket, looking for his gun–but it was gone! He swore under his breath as he caught hold of one of the oars and desperately tried to steer the boat back towards the riverbank, but Lupin grabbed the other oar and successfully fought off Holmes' efforts, managing to keep the boat in mid-stream.

"You're wasting your time, Holmes," jeered Lupin. "For each stroke you make, I can make an equal counterstroke. Aren't we a beautiful allegory of our struggle: the Law pushing in one direction, Crime in another... And in the end, it's all according to the whims of fate... Today, fate favors me. Look! The currents are taking us away."

211

Indeed, the boat had started to drift further away from the shore.

"Watch out!" cried Lupin suddenly.

A policeman on the bank was pointing a gun. A shot rang out. They heard the bullet whiz by, then splash harmlessly into the water.

"Heaven help us!" laughed Lupin. "Ganimard has called in the artillery!" He then shouted at the Police: "What you're doing is very naughty, Ganimard! You have no right to shoot, except in self-defense! Are you that mad at me? Ah-ah, they're about to do it again... Watch out, Holmes! They're capable of hitting you instead!"

Lupin stood up and shielded Holmes with his body, while continuing to taunt the Police.

"Come on, Ganimard! I don't mind! Tell your men to aim straight for the heart!" A shot rang out. "Higher and to the left!" Another shot. "Missed again! What clumsy oafs!" And another. "I can't believe it! Their hands are shaking! Where is the legendary sang-froid of the French Police? Three, two, one... Fire!" A volley of shots. "And they miss again! Sacrebleu! Does the Government issue toys for guns now?"

Lupin produced a long, massive, flat revolver and casually fired it, without bothering to take aim. On the riverbank, a policeman threw himself to the ground. The Gentleman-Burglar's bullet had made a hole through his hat.

"What do you say to that, Ganimard? That's what I call a gun. Hats off, gentlemen! It's the very revolver of my trusted friend, Mister Sherlock Holmes!"

And, with a prodigious toss, he threw the weapon onto the bank, right at Ganimard's feet.

Holmes could not help smiling in admiration. What superhuman zest for life! What fantastic energy! And how Lupin seemed to enjoy himself! It was as if the sense of danger gave him a physical thrill, as if life for that extraordinary man had no other purpose than to seek some new, extravagant perils from which to extricate himself.

Meantime, crowds had gathered on both sides of the Seine. Ganimard and his men followed the boat, still drifting downstream. Lupin's capture must have seemed inevitable, a mathematical certainty.

"You must admit, my dear Mister Holmes," said Lupin, "that right now, you wouldn't trade your place for all the gold in the Transvaal. You've got a front-row seat. But first and foremost, the prologue, after which we'll cut straight to the fifth act, the capture or escape of Arsène Lupin. I have a question to ask of you, and I beg you to answer it with only a 'yes' or a 'no' to avoid any ambiguities. Will you stop your investigation? There's still time, and I can still repair the harm you might have caused. Later, I won't be able to. So what is your answer?"

"No."

Lupin's features contracted; visibly, the Detective's answer upset him.

"Yet I must insist that you do. More for your sake than my own. I give you my word that you'll be the first to regret your intervention. One last time: yes or no?"

"No."

Lupin bent down and did something to the bottom of the boat that Holmes could not see. Then, he straightened and sat down, facing the Englishman.

"I believe, Mister Holmes, that you and I came to this river bank with the same purpose," he said. "To find the object that Bresson tossed in. For my part, I had made an appointment to meet a few friends and, as my inexpensive attire shows, I was about to explore the depths of the Seine. Then, my friends alerted me of your approach. I'll gladly admit that it didn't surprise me, since I'd been kept informed hourly–I can admit that, too–of the progress of your investigation. As soon as the least thing which could be of interest to me occurs Rue Murillo, a telephone rings and I find out about it! You'll understand that, under such circumstances…"

He stopped. The plank at the bottom of the boat that he had unbolted was now letting in rivulets of water.

"How unforgivable of me!" jeered Lupin. "I seem to have accidentally dislodged something and we're now taking on water. We might even sink. Aren't you concerned, Detective?"

Holmes shrugged.

"As I was saying," Lupin continued, "under such circumstances, and knowing beforehand that you sought a confrontation which I, myself, was desperately trying to avoid, it was still relatively easy for me to plan for a battle, the result of which was assured since I held all of the trump cards. That is why I sought to give our final meeting the greatest publicity, so that your defeat will be widely acknowledged and that, in the future, no new Comtesse de Crozon or Baron d'Imblevalle is ever again tempted to solicit your aid against me. Please don't see anything else here but..."

He interrupted himself again. Using his half-closed hands as he would a pair of binoculars, he watched the banks.

"Amazing! They've managed to find a real boat, why, it's almost a frigate! They're rowing like devils. They'll be boarding us in five minutes, and I'll be captured. You can still try to grab me, tie me up and deliver me to French justice, Detective. Would you like that? On the other hand, we might sink before they reach us, in which case, the undercurrents being treacherous on this part of the river, perhaps instead we should worry about writing our wills... What do you think?"

Their eyes met. Holmes knew that Lupin had purposefully made a hole in the boat and that the water was rising rapidly. It had already reached the soles of his boots. He made no move and said nothing.

The water rose to cover their feet, then went above their ankles. The Englishman took his tobacco pouch and his pipe, stuffed it and lit it. It was now Lupin's turn to smile with admiration.

"Please don't see here anything but the humble admission of my own sense of powerlessness before you," he continued, as if nothing had happened. "It is tantamount to yielding to you to accept only those battles which I'm certain of winning, and avoiding those where I have not chosen the battlefield beforehand. It is the recognition that you, Sherlock Holmes, are the only enemy whom I fear. It is trumpeting to the world my dread of crossing swords with you. This, Mister Holmes, is what I wished to tell you in person, on this occasion when fate has granted me the honor of a conversation with you. I regret only one thing: that this conversation is taking place in a sinking boat, for we are sinking... Somehow, it lacks dignity..."

The water had reached the benches upon which they sat, and the boat was sinking lower and lower in the water.

Holmes sat unperturbed, puffing on his pipe, seemingly lost in his thoughts. Nothing in the world could have made him display the least sign of fear in front of that man, surrounded by the Police, cornered, virtually caught, or worse, and yet who managed to retain both his good humor and civility.

They both seemed to be saying: Are men like us to be moved by such trifles? Don't people drown in rivers everyday? Is it worthy of any attention? One chattered and the other thought, after their own tastes, but the same mask of indifference concealed the formidable clash of their iron wills.

Another minute and they would be submerged.

"The important thing," said Lupin, "is to estimate if we'll sink before or after the arrival of those champions of the Law. All depends upon that! In doubt, it might be wise for me to start on my will. What if I leave you all my personal goods and belongings, Mister Holmes? No? My God, how fast they're rowing! They're better rowers than shooters. It's a delight to see them do something so well for once. Look at the precision of that stroke! Why, that's Sergeant Folenfant in the lead! Well done, Folenfant! Bravo! Finding that boat was a stroke of genius. I'll write you a letter of recommendation for your superiors. I hope you get a medal. In fact, I'll see to it! And where is your fellow Sergeant, Dieuzy? On the other bank, I bet? Amongst the crowd. So that if I escape death by drowning, I'll be captured on the left by Dieuzy, or on the right by the worthy Ganimard and the rest of his troops, is that it? A good plan, even if I do say so myself!"

Suddenly, the boat threatened to tip over. Holmes was forced to cling to the oarlocks.

"Please, take off your jacket," said Lupin. "You'll be more comfortable for swimming... You won't? Then I'll put mine back on again."

He slipped on his jacket and buttoned it tightly, like Holmes'.

"What a fine fellow you are, Detective," he signed. "A pity that you're so stubborn, in a case where I have no doubt that you'll triumph, but at what price... You're wasting your talent, you know?"

"Monsieur Lupin," said Sherlock Holmes, finally breaking his silence, "you talk too much, and you often err through an excess of confidence and frivolity."

"That is a serious reproach."

"It was in this way that you unknowingly supplied me a moment ago with the information that I sought."

"What? You sought some information and didn't think of asking me?"

"I wouldn't dream of asking you what I can find by myself. In three hours' time, I shall reveal the solution of the mystery to Monsieur and Madame d'Imblevalle. That is the only course I'll..."

He did not finish his sentence. The boat had suddenly foundered, threatening to drag them both down. She then rose to the surface again, overturned, her keel in the air. On the two banks, people were screaming. Then, there was a silence fraught with anxiety. Finally, one man emerged from the water.

It was Sherlock Holmes.

The Detective was an excellent swimmer and struck out boldly towards Sergeant Folenfant's boat.

"Come on, Mister Holmes, sir!" shouted the Policeman. "You're almost there... Don't worry about him, we'll take care of him afterwards... We've got him now! One last effort! We've got you! Grab the rope! Hold on tight! Pull, men! Pull!"

The Englishman seized the rope that the Policemen threw to him. But while they were pulling him on board, a voice behind him called out:

"The solution to the mystery? Of course, you've found it. I never doubted you would. But so what? It's at that very moment that you will lose the battle..."

Seated comfortably astride the keel of the boat, which he had scaled while the Police had rescued the Detective, Lupin continued his argument with Sherlock Holmes. It was as if he was making a last, desperate attempt to convince his enemy.

"Please, believe me, Mister Holmes. There's nothing you can do, absolutely nothing... You'll only find yourself in the situation of a man who..."

"Shut up, Lupin! Give yourself up!" Folenfant was pointing his gun straight at the Gentleman Burglar.

"You're very rude, Sergeant. You've interrupted me in the middle of a sentence. I was saying..."

"Surrender! In the name of the Law!"

"For God's sake, Folenfant, one surrenders only if one's life is in danger. Surely you don't think I'm in the least danger..."

"For the last time, surrender of I'll shoot."

"Come on, Folenfant, you're not going to kill me; at most, you'll try to wound me so afraid are you that I'll slip through your grasp. But what if, by accident, that wound turns deadly, eh? Think of the remorse you'll feel when you're old and decrepit..."

The shot went off.

Lupin staggered, clung for a brief moment to the boat, then let go and sank like a stone in the water.

It was exactly 3 p.m. when the above events took place. At 6 p.m. precisely, Sherlock Holmes, as he had declared, walked into the boudoir of the Rue Murillo, after sending word to Monsieur and Madame d'Imblevalle that he wished to speak to them.

The Detective was clad in ill-fitting clothes borrowed from a Neuilly innkeeper. The Baron and his wife almost laughed when they first saw his accoutrement, but the air of utmost gravity on the Detective's face stifled any desire for hilarity. Holmes paced back and forth, like an automaton, from the door to the window and back, each time taking the same number of steps and turning on the very same spot.

He stopped, picked up a knick-knack, looked at it distractedly, then put it back before resuming his agitated walk.

"Is Mademoiselle Demun here?" he finally asked.

"Yes, in the garden with the children," said Suzanne.

"Monsieur le Baron, as this will likely be our final conversation, I would like her to be present."

"So you think she…?"

"Have a little patience, Monsieur. The truth will emerge plainly from the facts I will lay before you with the utmost precision."

"As you wish. Suzanne, will you…?"

Madame d'Imblevalle rose and returned almost at once, accompanied by Alice Demun. She looked a little paler than usual. She stood, leaning against the mantelpiece, without asking the reason why she had been summoned.

Holmes took no notice of her. Turning abruptly towards the Baron, he began to speak in a tone that brooked no argument.

"After several days spent investigating your theft, Monsieur le Baron, and even though certain events somewhat modified my view of things, I will reaffirm what I told you the first night: the Jewish lamp was stolen by someone living under your roof."

"Do you know who is it?"

"I do."

"Do you have any evidence?"

"Ample evidence."

"It's not enough to catch the thief, we must also re-cover…"

"The Jewish lamp? I have it."

"The opal necklace? The snuff-box?…"

"The necklace, the snuff-box, everything that was stolen during the second burglary is also in my possession."

Holmes liked this dry, yet somewhat theatrical way of announcing his triumphs. It was effective for the Baron and his wife looked at him with a silent, almost reverential awe that was, in itself, the highest praise.

The Detective then narrated in detail what he had done during the last three days. He told them about the discovery of the picture book, then wrote on a piece of paper the mysterious combination of letters and figures:

CDEHNOPRZ – 237

He described Bresson's expedition to the Seine, the man's subsequent suicide and, finally, the clash that had pitted him against Lupin, culminating with the sinking of their boat and the shooting of the Gentleman Burglar by Sergeant Folenfant.

When he had finished, the Baron spoke in a hushed voice.

"Nothing remains but for you tell us who the thief was," he said. "Whom do you accuse?"

"The person who cut up the picture book and used that means to communicate with Lupin."

"How do you know that the intended recipient of these messages was Lupin?"

"Because he told me so himself."

Holmes held out a scrap of wet paper.

It was the page that Lupin had torn out of his notebook and upon which he had written the very same combination of letters and figures that had puzzled Holmes before.

"Please note," said the Englishman, with some satisfaction, "that Lupin had no need to write this and give it to me, and consequently to expose himself. This was an act of pure bravado, which provided me with the final clue I sought."

"The final clue you sought?" said the Baron. "I don't understand."

Holmes again drew their attention to Lupin's cryptogram:

CDEHNOPRZEO – 237

"Well?" said Monsieur d'Imblevalle. "It's the same formula that you've just shown us."

"No, it isn't," said Holmes. "Lupin's cryptogram, written in haste and without knowing exactly what I had found, contained two additional letters–an E and an O after the Z."

"You're right! I hadn't noticed it!"

"Now if you try incorporating these two letters into my earlier decyphering of that cryptogram, REPOND.Z – CH 237, you will realize that there is only one version that makes sense: REPOND.Z ECHO 237!"

"Meaning?"

"Meaning *L'Echo de France*, Lupin's own newspaper, or so they say, which in any event, he uses to communicate with the public. The cryptogram's meaning becomes clear: Reply to Echo de France, Classifieds, Box No. 237! That was the final clue I needed, and that Lupin unwittingly gave me. I have just come from the offices of that newspaper..."

"And what have you found?"

"I found the detailed story of the relationship between Lupin and his... accomplice."

Holmes then spread out seven newspapers, opened at the fourth page, and picked out the following advertisements:

1. *ARS.LUP. Woman needs help. 540.*
2. *540. Please explain.*
3. *A.L. Helpless before enemy. Urgent.*
4. *540. Send address. Will investigate.*
5. *A.L. 18 Rue Murillo.*
6. *540. Parc 3 p.m. Bring violets.*
7. *A.L. Sat. Repondz Echo 237.*
8. *237. Sat. OK. Come Parc Sun. Morn.*

"And you call that a detailed story?" exclaimed the Baron.

"Why, of course. And if you read it carefully, you'd agree with me. First line: a woman who uses Box No. 540 needs help; she seeks Lupin's assistance. Lupin then responds, asking for more details. 540 replies that she is helpless before an enemy and that she is lost if Lupin does not come to her rescue at once. One might deduce that she may be the victim of a blackmailer, someone like Bresson for instance... Lupin, who still does not trust the mystery woman, asks for her address, offering to more fully investigate the matter. The lady hesitates for four days–look at the newspapers' dates–then, finally, gives in, probably feeling the heat of Bresson's threats. She gives Lupin your address. The next day, Lupin tells her to meet him at the Parc Monceau at 3 p.m., carrying a bunch of violets so that he can recognize her. After that, there is an eight day interruption in the correspondence. I suppose that Lupin and the lady no longer need to use *L'Echo* as an intermediary since they now know each other; presumably, they talk and see each other during that time. A plan is set up: to satisfy Bresson's demands, the lady will steal the Jewish lamp. The only thing left to decide is the day. The lady, who uses cut out letters in order to protect her identity, decides on Saturday, and adds '*Reply Echo 237*' to her message. Lupin then confirms that he received the message, and adds that he'll also be in the Parc on Sunday Morning, if need be. And on that morning, the Jewish lamp was gone."

"Yes. Everything fits," said the Baron approvingly. "The story is complete."

"The lady goes out that Sunday morning, informs Lupin of what she did, and takes the Jewish lamp to Bresson. Things then happen as Lupin had arranged, and predicted. You and the Police are misled by the clues left purposefully to make everyone believe that the thief came from outside: the broken window, the holes in the ground, the scratches on the balustrade... The lady can rest; no one will suspect her."

"I accept that your theory is perfectly logical so far," said the Baron. "But what about the second burglary?"

"The second burglary was the direct consequence of the first. The newspapers having 'explained' how the Jewish lamp was stolen, someone had the idea of organizing a real burglary this time, and taking everything else. The second burglary was not a pretend theft, like the first, but a real crime, with real ladders, real break-in, etc."

"Lupin, of course!"

"No, not Lupin," said Holmes, slightly aggravated. "Lupin doesn't act like an idiot. Lupin doesn't fire at people for no good reason."

"So who was it then?"

"Bresson, of course! Without telling the lady whom he had been blackmailing. It was Bresson who broke in here, whom we chased, and who stabbed my friend, Doctor Watson."

"Are you certain?"

"Yes. One of his partners in crime sent him a letter yesterday, which was intercepted by Chief Inspector Ganimard. That letter indicated that negotiations had begun between the real thieves and Lupin regarding the restitution of all your property. That letter said: '*He* Lupin *refuses any compromise. He wants it all. The first object,* the Jewish lamp, of course, *as well as those of the second business.* The second burglary. *Otherwise, he is prepared to act.*' Needless to say, Lupin's intervention struck fear in the hearts of these bandits. They knew they were being watched. In fact, when Bresson went to the Seine, Ganimard and I caught one of Lupin's men tailing him."

"What was he doing there?"

"Bresson knew the circle was closing around him. He'd been warned about my own investigation..."

"By whom?"

"By the same lady who feared that, if I found the Jewish lamp, I'd find Bresson, and if I found him, her misadventure, whatever she was being blackmailed for, would become public knowledge. Bresson, therefore, felt it more prudent to gather all the loot into a single package and hide it in a place where he knew it could be safely recovered later, perhaps by one of his accomplices after he'd fled the country. Unfortunately, after he returned to his apartment Avenue des Ternes, he found Ganimard and me knocking at his door. He probably had many other crimes on his conscience. He panicked and killed himself."

"So the package contained...?"

"Yes, the Jewish lamp and all the other things that were stolen from you."

"You said you had them in your possession?"

"Indeed. After Lupin had vanished, I had the Police take me to the very spot where Bresson had thrown his package, and I recovered your property, carefully wrapped inside a blanket and some waterproof sheets..."

Holmes went to the door and returned with what looked like a wet bundle of rags, tied together with a string. He put it on a table.

The Baron carefully cut the string, tore through the wet fabric, and took out the Jewish lamp. Then, he turned a hidden screw under its base and pushed with both thumbs against a sculpted motif. A spring was released and a small, hidden compartment slid open, revealing the beautiful golden chimera studded with rubies and emeralds.

It had not been touched.

There was something terribly tragic in that scene that otherwise seemed so natural and which, on the surface, had merely consisted of a recital of indisputable facts. Every fact Holmes had laid out, every word he had uttered, directly, irrefutably and mercilessly accused Alice Demun. And that accusation seemed to be borne out by the governess' obstinate silence.

During that long, even cruel, accumulation of facts, not a muscle of her face had moved, not a gleam of fear or revolt had crossed her eyes, which had remained serene and undisturbed. What could she be thinking? What would she answer when the time came for her to defend herself, to break the iron circle of evidence in which the great detective had so cleverly trapped her?

That time had come, and yet, she remained silent.

"Alice, say something! Speak!" cried Monsieur d'Imblevalle.

She did not speak.

"A word, one single word of protest from you and I will believe you."

She did not utter that word.

The Baron paced back and forth across the room a few times. Finally, he returned to confront Holmes.

"No, sir! I can't believe you! I just can't! There are some crimes that are simply not believable. What you said contradicts everything I've known or seen of Alice for a year." He put his hand on the Englishman's shoulder. "I beg you, Mister Holmes, are you certain, absolutely certain of not being mistaken?"

Holmes showed a moment of hesitation, as a man attacked by surprise and not yet ready to defend himself. He hemmed and hawed for a minute, then said:

"The person whom I'm accusing would have had to know of the secret of the Jewish lamp, hence she would have been close to you…"

"Confound it! I still can't believe it!"

"Why don't you ask Mademoiselle Demun?"

It was, in fact, the only thing the Baron had not tried, so great was his confidence in the young governess' honesty. But now, it was no longer possible to deny the evidence.

Monsieur d'Imblevalle went up to Alice and looked her straight in the eyes.

"Was it you, Mademoiselle? Did you take the Jewish lamp? Did you secretly communicate with Arsène Lupin and fake the theft?"

"Yes, it was I, Monsieur," she replied. She did not lower her head; her face expressed neither shame nor embarrassment.

"How can that be?" muttered the Baron. "I never would have believed it possible... You were the last person whom I'd have suspected... What did you do, you miserable girl?"

"I did just as Mister Holmes said," she answered. "During the night of Saturday to Sunday, I came down here and took the lamp. And the next morning, I took it to... that man, Bresson."

"No!" said the Baron. "What you're saying can't be true."

"Why?"

"Because on Sunday morning, when I got up, the door to this boudoir was still locked!"

Alice blushed, lost some of her poise and looked at Holmes as if asking for his advice.

The Englishman seemed as embarrassed as Alice, even more so by her reaction than by the Baron's objection. And yet, wasn't the girl's confession a full vindication of the explanations he had given to the Baron? Why was the Detective not eager to bolster the governess' version of events?

Without waiting for Holmes to say anything, the Baron continued:

"That door was locked, I repeat! I found it bolted in the morning just as I had left it the night before when going to bed! If you'd come through the door, as you claim, then someone would have had to let you in from inside, that is to

225

say, from the boudoir or our bedroom. But there was no one else in here except my wife and myself..."

Holmes covered his face with his hands. He had suddenly flushed scarlet. He felt dazed and ill at ease. What he feared most had happened. The truth, like a powerful light that cannot be blinded, had burst out. It stood for all to see, like a stark, dim landscape from which darkness was suddenly lifted.

Alice Demun was innocent.

The Detective now saw clearly why, since the very first day of the case, he had felt uncomfortable targeting the young woman. His instincts had not lied. Alice Demun was, indeed, innocent. He now saw clearly why Lupin had tried so hard to stop him from revealing the truth, the whole truth. He now only had but a single gesture to make, a single word to say, and the case would truly and conclusively be solved.

He did not say that word, but after a few seconds, he could not keep his eyes from turning slowly towards Suzanne d'Imblevalle.

Her face was deathly pale, that pallor which overcomes a human being when he knows that death is truly near. Her hands, which she tried to hide, trembled.

*Another second*, thought Holmes, *and she is going to confess.*

He interposed himself between her and her husband, moved by the powerful urge to protect the woman from the danger that, *through his own actions*, now threatened her. But watching the face of Monsieur d'Imblevalle, he realized with a sinking heart that he was too late. The Baron, too, had just been struck by the same revelation; he had followed the same, merciless path of logic to its inescapable conclusion. He knew! He saw!

Desperately, Alice Demun made a brave, last attempt to block out the truth.

"You're right, Monsieur," she stumbled, "I didn't come in this way. I went through the hall and the garden, and I used a ladder..."

Her supreme effort of devotion to her mistress was, by now, entirely useless. Her words no longer rang true. Her voice had lost all its assurance. The poor girl's eyes no longer looked truthful and sincere. She realized it and hung her head, defeated.

The silence that ensued was dreadful.

Madame d'Imblevalle waited, livid, trembling with anguish and fear. The Baron was still struggling with himself, as if he refused to believe in the end of all that he held dear.

"Speak! Explain yourself!" he finally stammered.

"I have little to add, my love," Suzanne said, softly, her features wracked with despair.

"Then Mademoiselle Demun...?"

"Alice tried to protect me... Through devotion, through affection... She accused herself in my stead..."

"To protect you? From whom?"

"From that man."

"Bresson?"

"Yes. I was the one being blackmailed. I met him through a mutual friend, and I was mad enough to listen to his honeyed words... Oh! I didn't do anything that you couldn't forgive, but I was careless enough to write him... Two letters, that might have been misconstrued... You'll read them. I got them back... You now know how... Oh, have pity on me! I've been so miserable! I cried so much!"

"You! You, Suzanne!"

He raised his clenched fists in anger, as if he was going to hit her, even kill her. But his arms fell to his side, and his face became soft again.

"You, Suzanne, you... How could you?..." he muttered.

In short, fractured sentences, interrupted by her tears, she told him her sad and banal tale, her terrified realization of the situation into which she had put herself, her panic faced with Bresson's merciless demands, her remorse, her desperation... She also told him of Alice's admirable behavior... Sensing her mistress' predicament, she had extracted her confession, had

had the idea of seeking Lupin's help, had written to him and organized the fake burglary to save Suzanne from Bresson's clutches.

"You, Suzanne, you," repeated Monsieur d'Imblevalle, hunched over, overwhelmed. "How could you…?"

That same evening, the steamer *Ville-de-Londres*, from Calais to Dover, was gliding slowly across the peaceful waters of the Channel. The night was dark and calm. A few wispy clouds floated leisurely above the ship and, all around it, a misty, white veil was the only thing that seemed to separate it from infinite space where the Moon and the stars shone.

Most of the passengers had returned to their cabins, or gone into the salons. A few, however, bolder than the rest, walked up and down the deck, or dozed under thick blankets in the fold-out chairs. Here and there, one saw the gleam of a cigar, or mingling with the gentle caress of the wind, a few hushed voices that dared not disturb the great silence of the sea.

One of the passengers who had been walking back and forth with even strides stopped beside a person stretched out on a bench. He looked at her and, as he saw her move slightly, he spoke to her.

"I thought you were asleep, Mademoiselle Demun?"

"No, Mister Holmes. I don't feel sleepy. I was thinking."

"What about, if I may be so bold as to ask?"

"I was think of Madame d'Imblevalle. How sad she must be! Her life is ruined."

"Not at all, not at all," the Detective said, a little too quickly. "Her mistake is not of the kind that cannot be forgiven. The Baron is a kind, loving man. He will forgive her that lapse. Already, when I left, he was looking at her less harshly…"

"Perhaps… But it will take time… And she has already suffered much."

"You… loved her?"

"Very much. That's what gave me the strength to smile when inside, I was quivering with fear, to look you in the eyes when I wanted to avoid your glance."

"And you're sad at leaving her?"

"Very. I'm all alone. I have no family, no friends. I had only her."

"You shall have friends," said Holmes, who felt saddened by her confession. "I promise you that. I have connections, much influence... I assure you that you will not regret your position..."

"Perhaps, but Madame d'Imblevalle will not be there..."

They exchanged no more words.

Holmes took two or three more turns around the deck, then came back and settled down next to the young woman.

The misty veil slowly lifted and the clouds began to dissipate. The stars shone brightly in the firmament.

Holmes took his pipe from the pocket of his coat, filled it and struck four matches, one after the other, without managing to light it. As he had run out of matches, he got up and approached a gentleman seated a few chairs away.

"Could you oblige me with a light, please?" he asked.

"Certainly."

The man pulled out a lighter and, at once, struck a flame. By its light, Sherlock Holmes recognized Arsène Lupin.

If the Englishman had not made a tiny gesture, a nearly imperceptible movement of recoil, the Gentleman Burglar might have believed that the Detective had been aware of his presence on board all along, so great was Holmes' self-control and so natural was the ease with which he held out his hand to his adversary.

"Keeping well, Monsieur Lupin?" he inquired.

"Bravo!" exclaimed Lupin, from whom this self-control drew a cry of admiration.

"Bravo? What for?"

"What for? You see me reappear before you like a ghost, after witnessing my being shot and sinking into the Seine, and through pride and self-control–qualities that, if you don't mind, I would label as very British–you utter not a word of surprise, you make no startled gestures? Upon my word, I repeat, bravo! It's admirable!"

"Pah! It's nothing of the sort. From the way you fell off that boat, I could tell that you hadn't been hit by the Sergeant's shot. You fell of your own accord."

"And you left without knowing what became of me?"

"As far as I was concerned, there were hundreds of men looking for you on each bank of the river for three-quarters of a mile in every direction. If you managed not to drown, your capture was certain."

"Yet, here I am."

"Monsieur Lupin, there are two men in the world of whom nothing can surprise me: the first is myself, and the other is you."

Peace was concluded.

If Sherlock Holmes had not succeeded in his undertakings against Arsène Lupin, if the Gentleman Burglar remained his one and only enemy whom he was unable to take prisoner, it nevertheless was true that, thanks to his genius and perseverance, the Detective had recovered the Jewish lamp, as he had recovered the Blue Diamond. Perhaps, this time, the results were less than satisfactory, at least from a public standpoint, since Holmes had understandably not revealed the name of the true culprit and kept the exact circumstances of the recovery hidden. But between Arsène Lupin and Sherlock Holmes, between Burglar and Detective, man and man, there was, in all fairness, neither winner nor loser. Each could lay claim to equal victory.

They talked, therefore, like courteous adversaries who have laid down their arms and who esteem each other at their true worth.

At Holmes' request, Lupin described his escape:

"If indeed you can call it an escape!" he said. "It was so simple! My friends were on watch, too, since we had arranged to meet there in order to fish out Bresson's package. After spending a good half-hour under the overturned keel of the boat, I took advantage of a moment when Ganimard and his men were looking for my body along the banks to climb back on top of it. My friends then picked me up in a high-speed motorboat, and we all dashed off before the amazed eyes of 500 good citizens, not including the Chief Inspector and his cohorts."

"Well done!" said Holmes. "Most successful! And now you have business in England?"

"Yes. A few accounts to settle... But, I forgot, what about Monsieur d'Imblevalle...?"

"He knows everything."

"Ah, what did I tell you, Mister Holmes? The harm's done now, beyond repair! Wouldn't it have been better to let me work according to my own methods? Another couple of days and I would have recovered the Jewish lamp and the rest of the loot from Bresson. I'd have sent them back to the d'Imblevalles and those two good people who could have gone on living their peaceful lives... Instead of which..."

"Instead of which," said Holmes, "I muddled everything up and brought discord into a family under your protection?"

"Under my protection, yes! Do you think I spend all my time stealing, cheating and hurting others?"

"So you do good too..."

"When I have time. It amuses me. I think it's rather ironic that, in the Affair of the Jewish Lamp, Arsène Lupin was the good genius who tried to rescue the hapless maiden, while Sherlock Holmes was the one who brought despair and tears."

"Tears, tears..." protested the Englishman.

"Yes, tears! The d'Imblevalle home is broken and Mademoiselle Demun is weeping."

"She couldn't stay in France… Ganimard would have eventually discovered her role… and through her, Madame d'Imblevalle's."

"I agree, Mister Holmes, but whose fault is that?"

Two men passed in front of them.

"Do you know who those two gentlemen are?" said Holmes, in a tone of voice that seemed a little altered.

"I thought I recognized our Captain."

"And the other?"

"I don't know who he is."

"It's Mister Austin Gilett who, in England, occupies a position roughly similar to that of Monsieur Dudouis, your Head of the Sûreté."

"How lucky! Would you be kind enough to introduce us? Monsieur Dudouis is a great friend of mine and I should like to be able to say as much of Mister Gilett."

The two men reappeared.

"And suppose I were to take you at your word, Lupin?" said Holmes, getting up.

He had grabbed the Gentleman Burglar's wrist and held it in a grip of steel.

"No need to grip so hard, Holmes. I'm quite ready to go with you."

Indeed, he allowed himself to be dragged along, offering no resistance. The two men were walking away from them.

Holmes increased his pace. His nails dug into Lupin's very flesh.

"Come on, come on," he said under his breath, in a sort of fevered haste to finish as quickly as possible. "Come along! Faster!"

But suddenly, he stopped short: Alice Demun had followed them.

"What are you doing, Mademoiselle? Don't come nearer! We don't need you…"

But it was Lupin who replied:

"I beg you to observe, Mister Holmes, that Mademoiselle Demun is not coming entirely of her own free will. I'm holding her wrist as energetically as you're holding mine."

"Why?"

"Because I want to introduce her to Mister Gilett too. Her part in the Affair of the Jewish Lamp is, truth to tell, far more important than mine. As an accomplice of Arsène Lupin, and Bresson, too, think of all that she will have to confess... Not to mention revealing the true role played by Madame d'Imblevalle... All of it will be of great interest to the Police, I'm sure! And in this way, you'll have reached the utmost limits of your benevolent meddling, O generous Detective!"

Holmes let go of Lupin's wrist, and the Gentleman Burglar released Alice.

They stood there, for a few minutes, without moving or talking to each other. Then, the Englishman walked back to his bench and sat down. Lupin and the girl returned to their places.

Then, Lupin broke the silence.

"You see, Mister Holmes, do what we may, you and I shall never belong in the same camp. You will always be on one side of the fence, and I on the other. We may talk, shake hands, nod to each other, but the fence remains. You will always be Sherlock Holmes, the Detective, and I, Arsène Lupin, the Burglar. And you will always follow, more or less spontaneously, your instincts as a detective, which is to try to arrest the burglar, and I will always follow my own instincts, which is to evade capture and thumb my nose at the Law. As I just did. Ha! Ha!"

His laugh was taunting, cruel, even hateful. Then, suddenly becoming serious again, he turned towards Alice.

"Be sure, Mademoiselle, that even in the last extremity, I would never betray you. Arsène Lupin would never betray anyone, especially not one whom he respects and admires. And you must permit me to say that I respect and admire the brave and valiant woman that you are..."

He took a business card from his pocket, tore it in two and gave Alice one half.

"If Mister Holmes does not succeed in his efforts on your behalf, Mademoiselle," he added in an emotional and respectful voice, "please call on Lady Strongborough. You will easily find her address. Give her this half-card and say 'faithful memories.' She will be like a sister to you."

"Thank you, Monsieur Lupin," said Alice. "I will go to see her tomorrow."

"And now, my dear Mister Holmes," said Lupin, in the satisfied tone of a man who has done his duty, "let me bid you good night. We still have some time before we land. I'll take this opportunity to catch up on some sleep."

He stretched himself out and crossed his hands behind his head.

The sky had opened in front of the Moon. She shed her radiance around the stars and over the sea. Her image reflected upon the waters and the Heavens, where the last clouds were drifting away, belonged to her.

The coastline stood out against the dark horizon. Some passengers came up on deck, which was soon covered with people. Mister Gilett walked by with two gentlemen whom Holmes recognized as members of Scotland Yard.

On his bench, Lupin slept...

# The Unkindest Cut

**by**
**Jean-Marc & Randy Lofficier**

It is only with deep reluctance that I take up my pen to explain
the prodigious well of anger and extraordinary circumstances
that drove my friend, Sherlock Holmes, to accidentally take
the life of Raymonde de Saint-Veran, who almost became
Arsène Lupin's second wife, on that tragic night in the Pays de
Caux in December 1909.

After I was wounded during that wretched business of
the Jewish Lamp in June of the preceding year, I spent three
weeks in Paris recovering. I was often visited by my fellow
biographer, Monsieur Maurice Leblanc, and we enjoyed exchanging notes and confidences about our respective illustri-
ous companions. We have since kept up a secret correspondence, and it is only at his behest and to satisfy his curiosity
that I am writing this account.

As those who have read Monsieur Leblanc's account of
the remarkable case of the Jewish Lamp know, Holmes and
Lupin had separated on courteous, if not friendly, terms
aboard the ferry that was taking them both to London.

In Paris, Lupin was king. In London, things were much
different. Holmes, of course, could not let an opportunity to
arrest his rival pass. Immediately upon his return to Baker
Street, he devoted all his efforts to discovering why Lupin had
come to England.

Perhaps, some day, Monsieur Leblanc and I will get together, gather our notes and try to piece together the formidable adventure of the Silver Knight that occupied both our
friends during the fall of 1908. Lupin was after a young mad-
man named Flax, who had just killed Sonia Krichnoff, one of
his paramours. Holmes was after Lupin. In the end, the mon-

ster managed to slip through the net, but much bloodshed was averted. Indeed, the death toll of the Great War might have been even more horrendous had Flax successfully accomplished his evil plan.

When I returned from France, fully recovered, I found Holmes in an exultant mood. He had finally managed to trap Lupin, and a new female accomplice of his who had also been pursuing Flax across the Balkans, at the Bertram's, where they were staying under assumed identities. This time, my friend left nothing to chance and even enlisted the assistance of Lestrade and his men.

The following day, however, I saw Holmes return in the darkest mood in which I have ever seen him. He locked himself in his rooms and I heard incessant violin music for the following day and night. He refused all of Mrs. Hudson's entreaties to eat something, anything.

When I asked him what had happened, he muttered something about that "infernal Frenchman" and almost slammed the door in my face. I never got a straight answer. I finally went to Monsieur Leblanc to learn the truth. It turned out that Lupin had pulled another of his amazing escapes. He had used the corpse of a recently deceased guest to fool the police, while at the same time impersonating the crippled brother of Grafin Von Schwarzburg, a Prussian aristocrat who, of course, turned out to be his new paramour. Still, Lupin had escaped from Holmes' clutches before and I could not see why this time was so different as to send my friend into virtual seclusion.

It was only by accident that I learned the secret that drove my friend to such a degree of hatred towards Lupin that he was driven to do what he did on that night of December 1909 near that deserted farmhouse at Neuvillette. It was a hatred that I am confident he never felt towards any of his adversaries before. Not even Professor Moriarty could invoke such cold-blooded fury as Holmes felt that winter when the name of "that infernal Frenchman" was mentioned in his presence.

As do all great discoveries, this one occurred virtually by happenstance. I was invited to the Christmas Ball at the Spanish Embassy. There, I was introduced to the notorious explorer Hubert d'Andresy who had just returned from Tibet. Not being gifted with Holmes' prodigious powers of observation, I naturally did not recognize Lupin. At least, not at once. But during the evening, he let something slip that echoed a confidence that Monsieur Leblanc had shared with me. No one else could have known, of course. I thought d'Andresy was Lupin, but to be frank, I wasn't sure. I then pondered what to do next. Should I call Holmes? Should I summon Lestrade and his men, at the risk of being wrong and causing a major diplomatic incident?

Then, when I saw who Lupin's companion was, I finally understood the real cause of Holmes' rage. She was older, but as beautiful as ever. Together, they made a dashing couple as they danced to the admiring whispers of all the guests. To my friend, she had always been *The* Woman. Irene Adler.

I went home that night. I never mentioned this encounter to Holmes, nor do I know if he ever learned of it. I simply never said a word about it.

It would truly have been the unkindest cut of all.

# Afterword
## The Lupin-Holmes Chronology

The stories written by Maurice Leblanc pitting his Gentleman Burglar, Arsène Lupin, against Sir Arthur Conan Doyle's Great Detective, Sherlock Holmes, number four in total: one short story, two novellas and one full-blown novel. They are respectively:

- *Sherlock Holmes arrive trop tard,* (*Sherlock Holmes Arrives Too Late*), originally published in *Je Sais Tout* No. 17 (June 1906). It was printed in our first volume, *The Hollow Needle.* [8]

- *La Dame Blonde* (*The Blonde Phantom*), originally serialized in *Je Sais Tout* Nos. 22-27 from November 1905 to April 1907.)

- *La Lampe Juive* (*The Jewish Lamp*), originally serialized in *Je Sais Tout* Nos. 32-33 from July-August 1907.) (Both comprise the substance of this volume.)

- *L'Aiguille Creuse* (*The Hollow Needle*), originally serialized in *Je Sais Tout* Nos. 44-52 from November 1908 to May 1909, translated in our first volume, *The Hollow Needle.*

To this list must be added a brief mention of Holmes in another Leblanc novel, *813* (1910).

The first original Lupin-Holmes story penned by another writer was a four-act play, *Arsène Lupin contre Herlock Sholmes,* first performed on October 28, 1910 at the Theâtre du Châtelet in Paris, written by Victor Darlay and Henry de Gorsse. This play, translated by Frank J. Morlock, as well as

---

[8] ISBN 0-9740711-9-6.

another original Lupin-Holmes play by Morlock, will comprise our third and final volume of crossovers: *Arsène Lupin vs. Sherlock Holmes: The Stage Play*, to be published later this year by Black Coat Press.[9]

Unfortunately, the Darlay-de Gorsse play, like most of today's film adaptations of a literary property, does not fit within the established Arsène Lupin continuity, nor does it match that of Sherlock Homes, burdening the Great Detective with a French-raised son, Fred, nicknamed "Little Sherlock." Hypothetically, it would take place in 1909, but we have chosen to leave it out of this timeline.

Both Holmes and Lupin next appeared as members of the Society of Infallible Detectives in Carolyn Wells' *The Adventure of the Clothes-Line* (1915).[10] Lupin and Dr. Watson also shared the same ward during World War I in Thomas Narcejac's *Confidences dans ma Nuit* (1946).[11] However, the canonicity of these amusing literary pastiches can legitimately be questioned and they, too, are not included in the timeline below.

John Hall's *Sherlock Holmes and the Boulevard Assassin* (1998)[12] raises an interesting issue. The novel is usually deemed to take place in 1894 when Holmes, while investigating the assassination of a French politician, likely President Sadi Carnot, crosses paths with a mysterious gentleman-burglar named "Arsène Jupin." Jupin only appears in the last 25 pages of the novel, but when he reveals himself, Watson recognizes him. At one point, Holmes tells Watson that Professor Moriarty was trying to expand his nefarious operations into Europe, and that, if successful, would have possibly appointed Jupin as his second-in-command.

Many scholars have assumed that "Jupin" was a transparent alias for Lupin–as "Herlock Sholmes" was for Sherlock

---

9 ISBN 1-932983-16-3.

[10] *The Century*, 1915.

[11] Athénée, Paris, 1946, reprinted as *Usurpation d'Identité*.

[12] Breese Books, 1998.

Holmes. But there are several problems with that theory. The first, probably the most insurmountable, is that Lupin was born in 1874 (Holmes was born in 1854) and that, in 1894, he would have been only 20 and had not yet become the notorious Gentleman-Burglar, a career he fully embraced only after his wife Clarisse was murdered by Josephine Balsamo later that year, as revealed by Maurice Leblanc in *La Comtesse de Cagliostro* (1924). [13] Further, one cannot imagine Lupin, who acknowledges no master, working as a second-in-command to Moriarty. So we are forced to the conclusion that "Arsène Jupin" was not Arsène Lupin. Who, then, might have he been?

There is an obvious choice: Victor "Toto" Chupin from Emile Gaboriau's novels *Monsieur Lecoq* (1869), *Les Esclaves de Paris* (1867),[14] *La Vie Infernale* (1870) [15] and *L'Argent des Autres* (1874). Victor Chupin, whose name, when said aloud, sounds very much like Jupin (in French, Chupin is pronounced with a soft c, not a tch-, like in shoppin') was born c. 1850, and so was only a little older than Holmes. Victor was introduced as a small boy, the product of a family of criminals, in *Monsieur Lecoq*; he returned as a "young rascal," a teen-aged criminal in *Les Esclaves de Paris*. Then, he allegedly reformed and became a private investigator in *La Vie Infernale* and played a small part in the investigation of *L'Argent des Autres*, which took place in 1872. Like the notorious Vidocq, Chupin likely used his private investigator status to cover other, shadier dealings.

There seems to be no problems, therefore, in assuming that Victor Chupin was the 44-year-old master-burglar

---

[13] Translated as *Memoirs of Arsène Lupin* or *The Candlestick with Seven Branches*.

[14] *The Slaves of Paris,* also published as two separate volumes with different titles: *Caught in the Net* and *The Champdoce Mystery.*

[15] *The Count's Secret*, also published as two separate volumes with different titles: *The Count's Millions* and *Baron Trigault's Vengeance.*

"Arsène Jupin" that Sherlock Holmes met in Paris in 1894. Or maybe Victor had a younger brother named Arsène after all?

Finally, there are the three short stories contributed by the undersigned:

- "*Arsène Lupin Arrives Too Late*" and "*The Unkindest Cut*" in this volume and
- "*Escape Not The Thunderbolt*" in *The Hollow Needle*.

These attempt respectively to bridge the continuity between *The Blonde Phantom* and *The Jewish Lamp*, *The Jewish Lamp* and *The Hollow Needle*, and finally to bring a satisfactory conclusion to the saga of these two immortal characters, Arsène Lupin and Sherlock Holmes.

For the reader who would like to be able to read the stories, not necessarily in the order in which they were written, but in their internal chronological order, we have assembled below a timeline of the Lupin and Holmes encounters.[16]

### 1902

*July*–Lupin burglarizes Thibermesnil Castle. He crosses swords with Sherlock Holmes for the first time ["*Sherlock Holmes Arrives Too Late*" in *The Hollow Needle*].

### 1903

*December*–Using the alias of "Paul Daubreuil," Lupin saves Jeanne Darcieux from her stepfather's diabolical scheme ["*La Mort Qui Rôde*" in *Les Confidences d'Arsène Lupin* [17]]. He also steals Professor Gerbois' valuable desk ["*Ticket No. 514-23*" in *The Blonde Phantom*].

---

[16] There is a full chronology of Arsène Lupin's life in our book *Shadowmen: Heroes and Villains of French Pulp Fiction*, ISBN 0-9740711-3-7, Black Coat Press, 2003.

[17] Translated as *The Confessions of Arsène Lupin*.

## 1904

*February*–Lupin and a mysterious female accomplice, the so-called 'Blonde Phantom,' deal with the matter of the winning lottery ticket found in Professor Gerbois' stolen desk [*"Ticket No. 514-23"* in *The Blonde Phantom*].

*March*–The Blonde Phantom is accused of the murder of Baron d'Hautrec [*"The Blue Diamond"* in *The Blonde Phantom*].

*July*–Jeanne Darcieux marries Lord Strongborough [*"Arsène Lupin Arrives too Late"* in *The Blonde Phantom*].

*August-September*–The case of the murder of Baron d'Hautrec resurfaces: the Baron's Blue Diamond is stolen at the chateau de Crozon. Ganimard investigates fruitlessly; Sherlock Holmes is summoned to find the Blue Diamond [*"The Blue Diamond"* in *The Blonde Phantom*].

*October*–Sherlock Holmes and Doctor Watson, have a chance meeting with Lupin and Leblanc in a Paris restaurant. Holmes eventually discovers Lupin's use of secret passages in houses he designed as "Maxime Bermont." Holmes delivers Lupin into the hands of Ganimard, but the Gentleman Burglar makes a daring escape and is at the station to say good-bye to the Great Detective [*"Enter Sherlock Holmes," "The Light at the End of the Tunnel," "Kidnapped"* and *"The Second Arrest of Arsène Lupin"* in *The Blonde Phantom*].

*November*–Lupin leaves France and travels successively to Uruguay, Antarctica and Saigon. Murder of Lord Strongborough [*"Arsène Lupin Arrives Too Late"* in *The Blonde Phantom*].

*December*–Lady Strongborough is arrested [*"Arsène Lupin Arrives Too Late"* in *The Blonde Phantom*].

## 1905

*March*–Lupin is in Armenia and in Turkey, where he fights the Red Sultan.

*April*–Lady Strongborough is sentenced to death [*"Arsène Lupin Arrives too Late"* in *The Blonde Phantom*]. Delayed by his battle with the Red Sultan, Lupin arrives in Marseilles.

*June*–Lupin meets with Lady Strongborough in Saint Paul de Vence [*"Arsène Lupin Arrives too Late"* in *The Blonde Phantom*].

## 1908

*June*–Lupin challenges Holmes again in the case of the Imblevalle Robbery. Holmes lets go of Lupin on the *Ville-de-Londres*. Lupin advises Alice Demun to contact Lady Strongborough [*"The Jewish Lamp"* in *The Blonde Phantom*].

*July-December*–In London, Lupin (unbeknownst to Holmes at first) teams up with Irene Adler to fight Professor Flax in the Case of the Silver Knight. Lupin escapes one of Holmes' traps, but is later recognized by Watson [*"The Unkindest Cut"* in *The Blonde Phantom*].

## 1909

*April-June*–Lupin's latest round of burglaries catches the attention of Isidore Beautrelet, who becomes fascinated by the mystery of the Hollow Needle. Soon, Lupin faces not only Beautrelet and Ganimard, but also Sherlock Holmes. Lupin falls in love with the beautiful Raymonde de Saint-Veran, initially believed to be his victim [*The Hollow Needle*].

*June-October*–Lupin has Holmes and Ganimard kidnapped. He fakes his own death and that of Raymonde. As "Louis Valmeras," he marries Raymonde in October, then decides to go straight and live a peaceful life [*The Hollow Needle*].

*November-December*–Beautrelet, Ganimard and Holmes are not so easily thwarted. Separately, both Beautrelet and Holmes solve the mystery of the Needle. During the final battle, Raymonde is killed when she throws herself in front of Lupin to save him from a bullet fired by Holmes. Lupin, wracked with grief, manages to escape [*The Hollow Needle*].

## 1912

*July*–In jail, Lupin learns that the Kaiser has called upon Holmes to solve the mystery of 813, but the Great Detective fails to solve the riddle [*813*].

### 1922

*December*–Lupin visits Holmes in retirement in his cottage in the South Downs. They talk about their respective destinies and make their peace over the death of Raymonde ["*Escape Not The Thunderbolt*" in *The Hollow Needle*].